The Ghost Mare

Cover and Interior Illustrations by Victoria Auberon

My Grandfather's Horses is dedicated to all the gracious Baja California cattle ranchers who so wonderfully enriched my appreciation of range ponies, burros and mules

My Grandfather's Horses

A Tale of Pearls, Promises and Legendary Horses

Victoria Auberon

Library of Congress Control Number: 2019912893

PAPERBACK: 978-1-951461-00-3
EBOOK: 978-1-951461-01-0

Ordering Information:

For orders and inquiries, please contact:
1-888-404-1388
www.goldtouchpress.com
book.orders@goldtouchpress.com

Printed in the United States of America

AUTHOR'S NOTE

I first became acquainted with the aristocratic Old-World cattle ranchers of Baja California as a child in the late 1950's, 1960's and early 1970's. This book's sometimes-archaic language reflects this culture. My British father, son of colonial missionaries in Uganda Africa, took me to Baja when I was four to start what became a cult-like school for mal-adjusted American teenagers. At an early age, I accompanied him on trips by horseback to treat local patients in isolated cattle ranches. All of the horses and mules and most of the people in My Grandfather's Horses are based on animals and people I have known.

ACKNOWLEDGEMENTS

Many thanks are due to the following:

To a very conscientious researcher of the Cerralvo Island (Isla Jacques Cousteau) area, Thomas Spradley, for reading my book and reconnecting me with Cerralvo Island friends of the past. In addition, to Robert Allen Fisher and Jerry Becker for helping me with periodic earlier rewrites of the book along the way.

In memoriam, special tribute is due to my mother, Virginia Tower, for sharing her own experiences in Baja, and for helping me with some of the original drama and writing of My Grandfather's Horses. Special thanks go to Gary Milton, editor, director, and Emmy Award winning cinematographer, for his help in modernizing some of the original language. Exclusive thanks go to John Forsblad for writing dramatic inserts pertinent to the times. Also, to Topaz Jan Abbott for her 2009 song titled, "The Ballad of the Azulejo." This inspired composition is her own individual achievement and separate literary property.

Readers who offered helpful suggestions: Tom and Patrice Drew, Terry Hess, Joseph Paul, Iris Steinlein, Melody Vandewater, and Vincent Orsini.

ABOUT THE BOOK

The voice I adopted in writing <u>My Grandfather's Horses</u> was originally intended to echo the formal, Old World Spanish spoken by the upper class ranch owners of early Baja Sur. Schools were nonexistent in rural areas in those days, so these families doubtless continued the same conservative traditions that had been passed down by their forefathers from the time of the Conquistadores.

Both the homeliest and most beautiful horses I have ever seen were natives of Southern Baja California. The most spectacular was an Azulejo.

Horses from the coastal regions south of the city of La Paz were generally very small, poorly conformed specimens compared with those from herds owned by some of the larger inland ranchers. This may have been because the fishermen looked to the sea and their little *canoas* for long-distance transportation rather than becoming horsemen.

My father was an eccentric British explorer who originally intended to become a medical missionary. He first took me to Mexico when I was four. He forged some of the original dirt roads to isolated outlying regions. These include the road connecting El Camino Real with the property that later developed into the Punta Pescadero resort, the village of Cardonal, and the small coastal ranch settlement called, Boca de Alamo. My father also administered simple doctoring and extracted teeth among the poor people. It was during long horseback rides to visit remote ranches that I garnered some of the experiences that later became memories for this book.

From late fall of 1966 when I was thirteen and a half, to winter of 1969, I spent long periods camping on the eighteen-mile long uninhabited island of Cerralvo (Isla Jacques Cousteau), located in the Sea of Cortez, just south of La Paz. For the first nine months my only companion was my very temperamental, ailing mother who spent most of her time writing or meditating. Later, after wasps and the rigorous conditions drove her off the island, for around two years my nearly constant companion became a young "student" who my father sent to join me when the boy was nine. Visiting staff and students who attended my parent's International Pioneering School joined us for short periods. During my stay on the island, I handled the horses, burros and imported Nubian goats my family brought over from the Baja Peninsula. The burro, *Pancho Villa*, is based on a vicious wild jack that I trained at great risk to life and limb when I was fifteen. He liked to eat cardboard boxes as well as his lead rope, so as described in my book, I did tie him up with an anchor chain.

From 1969 to 1972, my parents relocated their undertaking to Rancho San Juan de La Costa. In those days, this isolated stretch of property was described as a dry mainland delta situated south of the ill-famed point named, *Punta el Mechudo*. No mining operations had begun, and five pristine oases graced the inland regions. It was here that my burro, *Pancho Villa*, acquired fame among the local ranchers.

Horsemen and muleteers sometimes dropped by my corrals to visit with me on their way to La Paz. Many of them had already traveled miles of arduous trails all the way from their ranches, yet they usually finished the fatiguing trip in a day.

One of my visitors was an old gentleman who routinely traveled from Ensenada to La Paz with his band of pinto burros, selling cartons of cigarettes to the inhabitants of the ranches and fishing settlements he visited along the way.

Unlike some of the city folk, many of the rural horsemen and muleteers lived by a chivalrous old-world ethic and treated both people and their fine animals with the utmost respect. I based the account of Don Tomas on the true-life story of the son of a French immigrant. *Alazán*, the burro *Pancho Villa*, the giant mule *Machismo*, and the Azulejo type of horse all existed as I described them in these pages. The Azulejo sported a silvery-white mane and tail and a sleek metallic coat. As with most good-looking colts in Baja, the animal I knew was eventually gelded and made into a saddle horse.

Similar to the blue-black roan Azulejos with white manes and tails in my story, there is a reference to black horses with white manes and tails in the 1969 publication of the Time Life book, *The Kingdom of the Horse*, by H.—H. Isenbart & E. M.Bührer. However, this coloring is so rare that I have talked to only one other person who claimed to have seen it. That was John Derek, the actor and director, who described an Azulejo he had seen in mainland Mexico. Also, like the blue-eyed black-bay standardbreds that showed up among the On to Glory bloodline, strange genetic exceptions do apparently sometimes occur.

Tales I heard from fishermen inspired my accounts of pearls and buried treasure. The descriptions of various mysterious "light sightings" described in this story, combine elements of my own unexplained reports with experiences shared with me by locals originating from isolated parts of Mexico and Guatemala.

ILLUSTRATIONS

ANIMAL CHARACTER NAMES

Azulejo 1 *Azulina* – The ghost mare of legend

Azulejo 2 *Carbonera* – Descendent of *Azulina,* and mother to *Espíritu* and *La Perla*

Azulejo 3 *Espíritu* – Wild Azulejo stallion

Azulejo 4 *La Perla* – *Espíritu's* twin

Azulejo 5 *Azulita* – Azulejo foal

Alazán – Donato's chestnut stallion

Carbona – Rancho La Primavera pacing mare

Cenizas – Don Tomas' white mare

Chispa – Local racehorse, brother to *Alazán*

Cometa – Rancho La Primavera *burra*

Machismo – Señor Bartolo's *fenómeno* mount

Mala Cara – Rancho La Primavera mule

Pancho Villa – Rancho La Primavera Somali-Wild-Ass type of *burro*

Pavo – Rancho La Primavera white burro

Pico Blanco – Don Tomas' exceptional breeding stallion

Pronto – Local racehorse from Rancho La Primavera

Rosillo – Strawberry roan gelding belonging to Ramón

Volador – Don Paco, magistrate of San Antonio's imported part quarter horse racehorse

PUNTA PRIETA and SURROUNDING REGION
in
DON TOMAS' TIME

HUMAN CHARACTER NAMES BY ASSOCIATION

MEXICO CITY

Uncle Mario – Donato's uncle from Mexico City
Aunt Consuela – Donato's aunt
Donato Perry – Mario's orphaned Caucasian-Latino nephew
Luisa – Mexico City matron
Marta – Mexico City matron

RANCHO LA PRIMAVERA

Don Tomas Rienza – Owner of Rancho La Primavera, and Donato's
    great-great-grandfather
Doña Blanca – Don Tomas' third wife
Maria Elena – Doña Blanca's daughter, Don Tomas' stepdaughter
Pedro Valenzuela – Doña Blanca's nephew
Doña Josephina – Don Tomas' senior housekeeper
Doña Lupe – Don Tomas' housekeeper
Julio – Don Tomas' gardener from San Antonio
Ramón – Julio's son and later Donato's ranch foreman
Bruno – Don Tomas' ranch foreman
Chevalo – Rancho La Primavera ranch hand
Luis – Rancho La Primavera ranch hand

RANCHO LOS SANTOS

Señor Aliseo Bartolo – Owner of Rancho Los Santos
Don Aliseo – Señor Bartolo's title after he became sheriff of El Santo
Señora Margarita Bartolo – Señor Bartolo's wife
Doña Margarita Bartolo – Señora Bartolo
Carmen – Señor Bartolo's stepdaughter
Telmo – Señor and Margarita Bartolo's son from La Paz
Prieto Bartolo – Señor Bartolo's great-great-grandfather
Seino Bartolo – Señor Bartolo's father
Chico Martinez – Midget in Señor Bartolo's employ
Raul – Muleteer in Señor Bartolo's employ

RANCHO SALVATIERRA

Señor Manuel Lucero – Owner of Rancho Salvatierra
Señora Lucero – Señor Lucero's wife
Pepe Lucero – Señor Lucero's son

OTHERS

Don Diego Montenegro – *Azulina's* ghost rider
Señor Alejandro Gomez – Businessman from La Paz
Señor Fidel Martinez – Mining engineer from La Paz
Celestino – Opal mine worker
Don Paco – Friendly magistrate of San Antonio
Zenen – Señor Bartolo's, and later Don Paco's, horse boy
Elyse Sutton – Student from Dallas, Texas
Señor Cuevas – One-eyed muleteer
Señor and Señora Hernandez – Punta Gorda storekeepers
Don Chepe – Old sheriff of El Santo
Uncle Stanley – Donato's uncle in Texas

TABLE OF CONTENTS

CHAPTER 1

Natural Miracles: A Safe Place to Foal

THE beautiful black mare, *Carbonera*, stood on the rim of La Mesa Alta, the southeast wind ruffling her flowing mane and tail. She surveyed the stark Punta Prieta coastline facing the blue waters of the Sea of Cortez, scenting the wind for news of a refuge where she might safely foal her twins. Instinct told her she must reach this place before she became too heavy with foal to scale the slopes of the rugged Southern Baja Mountains.

Three hours later, the mare stood snatching at the clumps of dried grasses dotting El Rey, a mountaintop which towered over the low volcanic coastal range of Punta Prieta like an immense white anthill. Here, the same southeast winds that howled and whined around the summit like a flock of furies also ushered in the tropical storm clouds overhead.

One misstep might have sent *Carbonera* toppling to her death had not the inner conviction that supported her, urged her ever upward. When she reached the crater valley at the mountain's summit, the clouds released their rain, and she quenched her thirst from the pools of rainwater left in the natural granite basins lining the crater's perimeter. As evidenced by the tall, dried, amaranth stalks left from the previous rainy season, the fertile soil had retained enough moisture to support a green ecosystem for several months into the Baja dry season.

Carbonera gave birth on a full moon night after a fresh crop of amaranth had grown up in El Rey's sunken crater valley. Moreover, as though to usher in the miracle, the celebrated ghost mare of Punta Prieta, *Azulina*, appeared among the greenery. Within the mutable depths of her enigmatic blue eyes, a timeless quintessence resided. Like a fantastic nocturnal mirage, her flowing white mane and tail streamed away like vapor in the moonlight. *Carbonera's* twin foals were throwbacks to the old grand dam of legend, whose phantom spirit she was.

Providentially, during the youngsters' first year of life, unusually heavy storms showered the coastal mountains with enough rain to plump out even the shriveled cacti and tubers that dotted the inner banks of their mountain refuge. These succulents swelled with so much moisture *Carbonera* and her foals quenched their thirst on them well into the dry season. Once they had eaten up all of the succulent cacti, *Carbonera* lead her foals down El Rey's dangerously precipitous slopes in search of water in the desert foothills below. Portions of the mountain's steep sides were comprised of compacted coral gravel pushed up from beneath the ancient ocean floor. When a heavy animal's weight dislodged it, quantities ran off in landslides.

Tragically, *Carbonera* allowed her twins to suckle until she became too feeble to maintain her balance on El Rey's treacherous slopes. She scrabbled to keep her footing, but doing so only made her skid further down the mountain until she reached the edge of a precipice, teetered on its brink, and then fell to her death in one of the many canyons traversing the low-lying hills below.

Had it not been for the airless whinny of the ghost mare encouraging the youngsters down the mountainside, they would surely have returned to their familiar crater valley to perish of thirst. Instead, sinking their slender legs knee-deep into the chafing coral gravel, the twins followed their guardian spirit in a spiraling path around the mountain and beyond to a three-palm-tree oasis hidden in the belly of a ravine. There, the youngsters instinctively dug the sand up with their hooves and sipped the brackish water seeping into the excavation.

In the years that followed, as a result of the ghost mare's unearthly fostering, the twin colt and filly kept to themselves—never visiting the same water hole twice in succession. This was because any good-looking, unbranded, wild horse or burro the native Mexican *muleros* spotted in the foothills was in danger of being captured for use as a riding or pack animal.

So long as no enemies appeared, the horse twins ran together. However, when these shy but canny animals sensed human beings nearby, they carried out a cunning stratagem. The colt ran out into the open to divert potential pursuers while the filly quietly slipped away deeper into the *campo*. Since observers never sighted the nearly identical *azulejos* side by side, the animals further confounded pursuers by leaving similar hoofprints behind. As a result, the twins continually fooled animal trackers into believing they hunted a single, phenomenal quarry. Some even testified the creature was gifted with invisible wings and the miraculous powers to appear in two places at once! Thus, because of his mysterious ways and ghostly coloring, they called him *el caballo espíritu*, "The Spirit Horse."

In 1961, the year the colt grew into a four-year-old stallion, *Espíritu* occasionally ran with the mares and geldings of nearby Rancho La Primavera. This was the same year a sixteen-year-old boy newly arrived at the ranch began his quest to win the wild horse's trust.

BALLAD OF THE AZULEJO

Long time ago on Mexico's wildest shore
There lived a horse that had never been seen before.
Dark was his coat like the feather of crow,
Throughout the land everyone came to know,
Azulejo - hear his song!

I am the Azulejo watch me fly,
On whispering hooves across the desert plain.
My eyes are blue, bluer than the sky,
Listen, you will hear the wind calling my name,
I am the spirit horse of this desert land.

Old men tell of me keeping their voices low,
Ghostly tales told by the firelight glow.
Young men speak of me in boastful pride,
Dreaming of the day that they might ride,
The Azulejo, hear my song!

I am the Azulejo watch me fly,
On whispering hooves across the desert plain.
My eyes are blue, bluer than the sky,
Rays of light shine in my mane,
I am the spirit horse of this desert land.

An eerie silence settles all around,
A cloud of dust rises from the ground.
Swift as an eagle in flight,
Vanishing from sight!

Some say I am not beast of flesh and bone,
Hoofbeats echoing across the ancient stone.
A shadow in the moonlight, a ghostly mystery,
You can ride me only if your heart is free,
Azulejo, hear my song!

I am the Azulejo watch me fly,
On whispering hooves across the desert plane.
My eyes are blue, bluer than the sky,
And nothing can quench my heart of flame.
I am the spirit horse of this desert land.

Copyright © 2009 Topaz Jan Abbott

CHAPTER 2

A New Land: Time of Change

ONE...two...three...proclaimed the sonorous bells of the Catedral Metropolitana. Even on the noisiest, busiest days citizens lifted their heads and paused to listen when they rang the hour. The venerable building seemed to cast its blessing over all the wayfarers throughout Central Mexico City and the adjacent Plaza Zocalo like a Holy Father casting a benediction.

It was autumn of 1961. Two women passing in front of the cathedral stopped to point out a sixteen-year-old boy feeding the pigeons in the plaza.

"What an attractive young man! See his liquid brown eyes peeking out from under his curly, brown bangs?" the plump one, Marta, remarked.

"*Ay*," her companion replied. "His name is Donato; he inherited his good looks from his parents, the beautiful Señora Maria Esperanza and handsome Señor Roger Perry, the blond *gringo* archeologist who worked for the Museo National de Antropología. A terrible auto accident took Señor Perry's life and the lives of his wife and two daughters. By the grace of the Lord, the boy remained home with the *gripa* and was spared."

"You don't say!"

The news breaker adjusted her shawl with an air of importance. "I am surprised you didn't hear of this, Marta. It was in all the newspapers and on the television last November!"

Marta sighed with deep satisfaction as the spectacle of the tragic drama filled her fantasies. "Ah, well, I am lazy and read nothing but *novelas*. But, tell me more, Luisa."

Luisa warmed to the gossip. "The Perry family was on their way to the theater when a petrol truck lost its brakes at the corner of the plaza and ran into their car, killing all the passengers. The traffic is a horror these days and everyone is in a hurry. Such a waste!"

"*Qué lástima!* What a sad story!" Marta exclaimed. She shifted her basket of fresh cheese and bread from the crook of her right arm to her left and crossed herself.

"They say Donato's *gringo* father was a peculiar man and seldom socialized. It is said he never even visited his wife's family or attended Mass. The Señora did, though, poor thing. She went for both of them. I used to see her in the chapel during the week. Who knows what troubles she may have had? Now the boy is all alone. *Pobrecito!*"

"You are right, Marta. He looks sad."

"I hear good Father Alfredo has advised his uncle, Señor Moreno, to send Donato to the country to recover his spirits. It is a wise plan, for he is a simple boy. They say he has a great love for animals and wants to become a veterinarian. See how the birds hover about him! *Ay!* This wretched city is no place for such as he. Nothing but silly pigeons to comfort him." The two women walked off down the sidewalk, joining the medley of sights and sounds of the city streets.

* * *

Donato had named the friendly gray pigeon strutting about his feet, "Mario," after his uncle. The perky little bird seemed oblivious to the problems of the world around it. No plumage was out of place. A shimmering purple iridescence on its chest and neck rippled as its head bobbed. And its gray and white pinion and tail feathers looked crisp and neatly arranged as though it were wearing a starched white shirt and gray business suit.

Thinking of how his uncle might react if told he resembled a pigeon, the beginning of a chuckle escaped Donato. The sound startled him, for he had nearly forgotten how to laugh. He tossed Mario the last of the crumbs from his lunch box.

Donato knelt down and held out his finger. "Come here, *pajarito*, perch on my hand!" However, motivated by some unknown impulse, instead of responding, the pigeon flew away to perch on the arch above the cathedral's main entrance. Donato admired the intricate artwork adorning the facade. He knew the building cloistered wise men, but though the padres invited him to come inside for counsel, he preferred to stay outdoors. There he could gaze at the sky on a clear, windy day with the clouds scampering for the horizon.

Remembering his circumstances, Donato's wandering thoughts soon fell to Earth. Seen in a more serious light, the image of his uncle Mario was no longer comical. He guessed it must be an inconvenience to Mario to have his sister's child foisted upon him unexpectedly. His firstborn was still in diapers, and his wife, Consuela, was again pregnant.

Donato had heard that his mother and Uncle Mario drifted apart after she married an American. He remembered his mother only inviting Mario and Aunt Consuela over to their house during the holidays. Of course, his father never participated. He was always working or studying books of some kind, so Donato's mother had to make excuses for him.

Now that he was living at his uncle's house, Donato always tried his best to stay out of the man's way. He overheard him say to his aunt Consuela that Donato was like his father, *un hombre solitario*, a solitary man. Donato did not know exactly what was wrong with keeping to oneself, but he supposed his uncle thought it wasn't good or he would not have mentioned it.

Mario seemed to expect him to act bright and cheerful, and to have a good time in school. He acted as though Donato ought to ignore the grief that lay in his gut, large and fibered like the seed of a mango. How could one digest such a thing?

To Donato, Uncle Mario expressed no interest in livestock except in the final form on his dinner plate. When Donato told him he wanted to become a veterinarian, his uncle was disapproving. "Veterinarians earn low wages and have no social standing! Who would be so foolish as to want to attend sick pigs, cows, and horses, working among the flies in the hot sun under the dictates of some peevish ranch owner? The legal profession is much cleaner and much more profitable!"

Mario pointed out that if Donato were to enter the business world, he could one day own his own ranch and hire his own veterinarian; then he would see.

In the end, however, Mario grumbled his grudging consent to the plan proposed by Padre Alfredo, and agreed to escort Donato to Baja California to live on his great-great-grandfather's ranch.

"Alright, go live on a ranch and get the country out of your system, then. Spending a year or two in the isolation of remote Baja California might teach you to appreciate the advantages of civilization."

"May I ask you just one question?" Donato asked timidly.

Mario motioned impatiently with his hand. "Speak up!"

Donato cleared his throat. "How is Don Tomas my great-great-grandfather?"

Mario raised his eyebrows. "It's complicated, son. Your mother's and my grandmother, Sonya Balboa, who you never met because she died before you were born, is the child of old Don Tomas Rienza and his first wife Consuela Mendoza—your great-great-grandmother. Sonya's first child, Mercedes Esperanza, who you knew before she passed away, is therefore your direct grandmother. Don Tomas has even outlived his own grandchildren!"

"How old is he?"

"I don't know. But no matter how old the *anciano*, I recently heard that he still rides horses and manages his ranch. Ask around when you get there, maybe you can learn his age!"

"I will," Donato replied, nodding his enthusiasm.

Donato tried to imagine the primitive land of Baja. Even his classmates teased him that nothing survived on the peninsula except rattlesnakes and thorn bushes. "Probably," they said, "a sun-bleached cow's skull stuck on a cactus will mark the spot where a toothless old man lives in an adobe hut. Most likely, he needs a goat herder to tend a few scrawny nanny goats. Even more probably, you will find the old man has passed away in the time it takes to complete such a long and dangerous journey!"

* * *

January 20th, 1962 found Donato sleeping late into the morning on a handmade cowhide cot laced with rawhide. Clean muslin sheets covered the cotton mattress. Nothing had ever felt so comfortable.

At first, flashing images of his difficult passage over the Gulf from the mainland filled his dreams. The water roiled around this small fishing boat converted to carry passengers in cramped quarters. He tumbled about in a dirty bunk with one sheet, while Mario retched into an enamel pitcher, his face a green shade of algae.

Next, in the city of La Paz, the sons of fishermen stared at Donato as he walked the *malecón*, a pleasant walkway overlooking the bay lined with palm trees. A showy display of fine yachts dominated the collage of small working boats with their multicolored layers of peeling paint and decks strewn with debris.

Later, Donato was bumping along on his way to the village of El Santo in a rickety bus with worn tires and a coughing engine that had to be doctored frequently. He felt small and insignificant stuffed in among the country people burdened with small babies, tired children, chickens, turkeys, and a bleating nanny goat. He felt so cramped he could scarcely breathe, and his uncle grumbled and cursed the whole way.

Donato scarcely remembered the long, exhausting horseback ride from Rancho Salvatierra, a ranch located on the outskirts of the town of El Santo. It was here his Uncle Mario took leave of him and entrusted his care to two weatherworn *vaqueros*. Donato noticed the strong, persistent odors of a Baja ranch mingled with the smell of wood smoke and tortillas cooking. He smelled the steaming rennet, aging cheeses, and the heavy sweet scent of the sugar mill where workers pressed the sugarcane and boiled the juice down into small, dark, conical lumps.

The men had set Donato on a slow mule, whose monotonous plodding lulled him into a doze; yet the difficult trail caused him to hold the saddle horn tightly to keep from falling off. The ride lasted most of the afternoon and late into the night. When he awoke late the next morning to the sound of a horse neighing, the comfort of his rawhide cot gave way to curiosity about his new home.

CHAPTER 3

Azulejo: The Legend

LA Primavera," Donato whispered, gazing across the expansive green vista from the shady veranda of his great-great-grandfather, Don Tomas', hacienda. His eyes were clear and bright with excitement after his long rest. The ranch name meant "springtime." For Donato, it would also signify rebirth and renewal. The potential for this was in the essence of this enchanting land. It was in the buzzing of the bees gathering pollen, and the large and small butterflies floating from flower to flower. It was in the twittering of a hundred different songbirds and the cooing of the doves. It was also in the ringing sound of silence that stretched across the *campo*. This silence seemed as though it had always been here, and it always would be.

The sandaled footfall of an aristocratic country matron dressed in fine handsewn clothes signaled mystery and wonderment as she walked up beside him. She put a strong, weathered hand on his shoulder. "*Pobrecito, mi hijito! Cómo te amanecistes?* My poor little son, how have you awakened?" she said in the rural dialect of the local people.

"*Bien, gracias, Doña*, I am fine, thank you," Donato muttered, ducking his head.

The Doña continued, "My name is Doña Blanca. I am your *abuelo*, Don Tomas' fouth wife," she explained. "I can see him riding down the hillside yonder with the *muchachos*." She pointed toward the southern skyline, but Donato had not yet developed the trained

13

eyes and observational skill of the natives and could not immediately see the small group.

"Since in the rainy season the *campo* turns lush and the fresh water springs overflow, the horses stray far from the ranch. Don Tomas says it is *Alazán* who leads them away."

Donato was feeling less timid and very curious about the horses. "Who is *Alazán*?"

"*Alazán* is a horse of a rare color; fiery red like the setting sun. *Tan hermoso!* What a beauty! They say his dam fell in love with a chestnut stallion born on the Pacific Coast west of here, so, *Alazán*, he is a love child, no?"

While Donato and his gracious hostess were talking, they heard a distant sound like thunder rolling down the nearby arroyo bed. In a few minutes, a herd of horses, mostly bays and grays, galloped up the path leading to the watering trough in the big corral. No dust rose from their hooves as they pounded the resilient, red adobe clay that still held moisture from the last rain. Donato counted their heads as they raced by, "...*cuarenta y nueve, cinquenta, cincuenta y uno, cincuenta y dos!*" There were fifty-two head!

Smooth, polished contours formed the gleaming surfaces on those undulating bodies. The red bays' gold and flame-orange tones contrasted with their black manes and tails. Dark roans and grays shone with muted highlights while honey buckskins, duns, and dark bays glistened in the sunlight. There were no chestnuts.

The sight of the galloping herd caused Donato to think of his younger sister, Ana, who had loved horses. "Ana," he whispered, "I wonder if the horses in Heaven look like these?"

The last animal to follow the herd was the most beautiful creature Donato had ever seen or, surely, was ever likely to see again. The myriad of fine silvery hairs interspersed throughout his black, glossy coat glistened with a varnished liquid sheen as though the tips had been dipped in egg white, and the silvery white strands of his luxurious mane and tail sparkled like spun crystal. A perfectly round, white spot gleamed from the stallion's forehead, accentuating his bright expression.

The marking reminded Donato of the moon shining through storm clouds, encircled as it was by the dark hide of the animal.

When the horse stopped in front of the veranda to inspect the newcomer to the ranch, Donato noticed his eyes were as dark blue as deep water. His velvety muzzle was silvery and the horn of his hooves soft gray, not shiny black like the hooves of the dark-pigmented bays.

Doña Blanca put her finger to her lips. "Shh, it is *Espíritu*, the wild azulejo stallion with the unusual eyes!"

Donato shivered. He felt honored that this splendid animal should notice him. He was not sure whether the unique color of the eyes produced the effect, but he thought the horse was trying to study him and look into his soul. Finally, his curiosity satisfied, the creature ambled after the other horses who were drinking from the watering trough and rolling on the cool, clay floor of the big corral. After taking his turn to drink water and then lying down for a roll, he got up and wandered off on his own into the green *campo*.

"It is an omen the Azulejo stallion comes here today," Doña Blanca whispered. "According to legend, his grand dam and her owner lie buried in an unmarked grave overlooking our coast. Their ghosts still haunt our land—the land of Punta Prieta."

"Tell me the legend, Doña!" Donato entreated, his dark eyes looking huge in his pale face.

"You should wait to hear it from Don Tomas. He tells it best." The old lady paused when she noted Donato's disappointment and then patted his shoulder. "Alright then, let us sit awhile under the shade trees and finish our story."

"Oh, please do, Doña!" Donato exclaimed, his eyes shining with excitement. He took her arm and walked with her to one of the spreading jacaranda trees shading the beautifully landscaped garden slope in front of Don Tomas' veranda. There, they seated themselves in two comfortable wicker chairs with bright cushions. Donato listened eagerly while Doña Blanca narrated her surprising tale, her voice low and reverential, and her Spanish formal in keeping with her old-world traditions and natural dignity.

THE LEGEND OF THE AZULEJO

Four generations ago, a fateful storm blew a great Spanish ship bound for La Paz aground on our coast. On board were a Spanish lord and his fiery mare with blue eyes and a gleaming metallic Azulejo coat. Near the end of the long voyage from Spain, the nobleman ordered his groom to reserve the best grain and water for this mare and her filly.

Intuitively sensing the hungry crew's resentment of her, she pawed the air with her hooves whenever any of them approached. This behavior begot the rumor that an evil spirit possessed this animal with the spooky eyes.

As a result, Prieto Bartolo, one of the officers, conspired with some of the crewmembers to rid themselves of the mare and her master once and for all. When the storm marooned the ship on a rocky point off our coast, Prieto seized the opportunity to lead a revolt. With the advantage of surprise, the mutineers proceeded to hang the nobleman from a yardarm propped at an angle among the wreckage. But before he drew his last breath, the condemned man screamed out a curse.

"Damn you rabble, one and all! None of you shall wake to see tomorrow, except Prieto Bartolo." He glared pointedly at the first mate. "May your descendants perish of mysterious causes through the generations!"

Knowing that rescuing all the horses on board would aid in their survival, the mutineers managed to swim the small herd safely to shore. On the beach that night, Prieto spared the azulejo filly but ordered the slaughter of her dam, the hated blue-eyed mare. The seamen prepared the carcass by skewering the finest cuts onto spars positioned over the coals left from a great bonfire. They were sitting around drinking rum and periodically turning the meat, when to their horror, a ghostly horse and rider continually took shape in the smoke and effluvium rising from the sizzling meat and then galloped away on the wind with a dolorous moan.

When Prieto Bartolo awoke the next morning, he found his comrades lying dead all about him. Looking frantically around, he spotted the nobleman's corpse hanging from the wreckage—his eyes vacantly staring and mouth agape, as though still pronouncing the curse.

Spurred on by fear of the spell, Prieto climbed the tall cliff overlooking the beach, and on top dug a deep grave out of reach of the stormy surf. He used a halyard to hoist the mare and her master's grisly remains up to the gravesite along with a chest of valuables the sailors recovered from the ship, and buried everything in the pit.

Still in mortal fear of retribution from beyond the grave, Prieto freed the remaining horses and left the dreadful place on foot, swearing never to return or speak of it again.

Some hours later, Prieto wandered south along the beach until he reached the coastal village of Punta Gorda. There the local fishermen offered him hospitality. After a few days recuperation, he determined to settle there and live a simple life reminiscent of the days when he grew up off the coast of Spain.

Before many months had passed, Prieto married and built a small ranchito in a secluded spot with an oasis nearby. All went well until a pirate ship appeared on the horizon, sailed in, and anchored offshore. A local elder of Punta Gorda had warned Prieto that pirates sometimes showed up looking to barter for pearls. But instead, soon after the ship's arrival, a party of drunken buccaneers seeking, "The Spaniard," arrived at Prieto's door to ask him what had become of the valuables on board the wrecked merchant ship.

The rum the pirates offered Prieto to soften him up, soon loosened his tongue. Before long he ignored his vow of silence and informed them of the treasure hidden in the nobleman's grave.

While their spirits were high, the treasure seekers bravely set off to search for the gravesite. When the party arrived at the Punta Prieta headland however, they found that the strong offshore winds had erased all trace of the burial mound. Now, once again, Prieto's fortunes took a downward turn. He and the pirates searched and searched for the grave but encountered only the nobleman's curse.

Believers hold that buried treasure gives off a faint glow in the dark. It is said that this glow lured Prieto and his pirate friends to the edge of the *cliff where they fell to their deaths on the treacherous rocks below. Some also say their spirits then arose as luminous orbs condemned to live suspended between Heaven and Hell forever.*

To this day, the sightings of strange ghostly lights seen floating over Don Tomas' land are thought to be the spirits of Prieto and the pirates searching for the treasure. Some travelers through our region also claim to have seen a ghost ship, while others see a shimmering horseman patrolling the countryside, as though keeping careful watch over the descendants of the fine horses he brought so long ago as cargo on board his Spanish ship.

"What became of Prieto's family after he died?" Donato asked, staring at Doña Blanca again with fascination in his dark eyes. "Did he have any children?"

"Yes, it is as though our history was shaped by the family's ill luck. Prieto's wife and only son, Tito Bartolo, both survived him. When Tito grew up, fear of the curse so dominated his life that he decided to donate the haunted property to the Bishop in La Paz, Monseigneur Escalante. He even suggested to Monseigneur Escalante that the spot by the cliffs, where subsequent to the curse, wayfarers had lost their lives in mysterious ways over the years, would be an ideal place to erect a shrine to the virgin.

"However, Tito had no sooner presented the bishop with the family deed to Punta Prieta, than to the holy minister's horror, Tito fell dead as stone, as though the curse against his father, Prieto Bartolo, had struck again.

"When, many years later, your great-great-grandfather, Don Tomas, showed interest in raising horses and mules for service in the San Antonio goldmines, the bishop joined Punta Prieta and the two more hospitable adjoining deltas together under the title, Los Terrenos de Punta Prieta, and then signed the deed over to Don Tomas, free and clear. Eighty years have now passed since Monseigneur Escalante signed the haunted properties over to Don Tomas. Don Tomas christened this fertile oasis delta, Rancho La

Primavera, because it becomes so beautiful after the rains. He has experienced nothing but good fortune here ever since!"

Donato looked worried. "Wasn't Don Tomas also afraid of the nobleman's curse?" he asked.

The *viejita* peered fondly into the boy's anxious eyes, her face breaking into many lines like tiny arroyos. "No. Like the remarkable Azulejo horse, the good Lord endowed Don Tomas with singular spiritual strength. He feared neither the curse nor the ghost whose hostility was never against his family."

The old lady laid her hand on the boy's shoulder. "Come, you must be hungry. Doña Josephina and my daughter, Maria Elena, are setting the lunch table on the veranda for the *vaqueros* who drove the horses down to the corral today. They follow down the arroyo at a slower pace so as not to tire their mounts. However, now that the Azulejo has once more left the company of the other animals to tend to his mysterious concerns in the wild *campo*, let us first go down to the corral and close the gate so none of the other horses leave."

"How did the men know the horses would all run into the corral?" Donato asked, glad to change the topic of conversation from spooks and whammies back to horses.

"It is simple, *joven*. The *vaqueros* know the horses will want to drink from the watering trough because they become thirsty after their long gallop down the arroyo from La Mesa Alta."

Doña Blanca had finished shutting the corral gate when Donato heard a tinkling sound coming from the direction of the arroyo. He remembered a similar sound on a recording of Christmas music his father had brought from the United States called "Jingle Bells." It was about a sleigh ride in the snow. But sleigh bells in the desert?

Out from behind the low-lying trees obscuring the southern trail leading from the arroyo, there emerged three light-stepping horses ridden by dapper cowboys wearing canvas cowboy hats and calfskin chaps. Every detail of the eye-catching trappings complemented the stately riders and their magnificent mounts. The tinkling melody came from the cowboy's spurs and the short chains and little iron bangles attached to their mount's ornate, old-style California bits. The horses' colorful headstalls were of fine woven deerskin, accented with black, white, and chestnut-mane-hair cord finished in abundant, dangling tassels that bobbed up and down as the animals pranced toward the hacienda.

The saddles were of the type designed by the old Spanish settlers, which envelop the front, back and sides of the horse's body in three layers of heavy leather armor. This leather casing protected an animal's coat from the spiny thorn bushes and cacti growing out in the *campo*. Attached to the outer layer were four saddlebags tooled in flowing designs—two bags in front, and two in the rear. Leather *tapaderos* with long thongs for decoration hooded the stirrups.

The horsemen tipped their hats as they rode up to the veranda where Donato and Doña Blanca stood, awaiting their arrival. "*Buenos días, Doña*, Good morning, Ma'am," said each in turn. Then they dismounted and tied their mounts to the strong upright *horcones* that supported the thatched roof of the veranda.

"*Buenos días, Señores*, Good morning, sirs," Doña Blanca replied, greeting them in return. "I present to you young Donato, Don Tomas' great-great-grandson from Mexico City. Donato wishes to become a *vaquero!*" The old lady turned to Donato. "Donato, this is Bruno, Chevalo, and Luis. Bruno is our foreman, originally from the mainland of Mexico. Chevalo and Luis have worked for Don Tomas many years. They are from Rancho Salvatierra where you first began your journey to La Primavera."

Donato noted Luis was a tall, thin man, with a hairless face and a stoic expression, whereas Chevalo was short and heavy, with a full mustache and twinkling eyes. Bruno wore a thin mustache and was slim like Luis, but not so tall. "Bruno, would you please be so kind as to show Donato around our property?" Doña Blanca spoke politely, but the *vaquero* took the question as a command.

"*Con mucho gusto*, it will be my pleasure," Bruno replied with a bow. "Chevalo will be happy to let you ride his fine horse, *sí*, Chevalo?"

Chevalo grinned wryly, "*Cómo no*, why not!"

Donato bit his lip. He was still saddle sore after the long ride over the mountains from Rancho Salvatierra, but would never rudely refuse the kind offer.

"*Muchas gracias, Señores*, thank you, sirs," he replied shyly. As Donato mounted Chevalo's horse, he eased himself slowly into the saddle, supporting most of his weight in the left stirrup to save his backside. Bruno shared a knowing glance with Chevalo and chuckled, but Bruno cut his little joke short when he noticed the Doña watching him.

Bruno began their tour of the ranch by leading the horse and rider around the perimeter of the hacienda. The veranda on the east side had a magnificent view of the broad, lower arroyo delta and the Sea of Cortez a mile away. Under its shade stood two dining tables hewn of álamo—a hardwood distasteful to termites. Doña Josephina had draped them with embroidered, white tablecloths, painted enamel plates, and the white, gold rimmed china that came inside the imported cartons of oatmeal as promotional gifts.

Donato's appetite heightened almost unbearably as the fragrance of the freshly ground toasted corn filled the air. In Mexico City, the women had used packaged *masa* to make their tortilla dough, but at Rancho La Primavera, they still parched and ground the kernels of corn and rolled them on a stone *metate* into a fine meal. Was there anything in the world that kept its promise as faithfully as the taste of fresh cornmeal properly prepared from the golden kernels and presented warm to the palette? There were also baskets of fruit, bread, cheese, and *dulces*. The main dish was goat stew. This was served with vegetables and rice.

Since Donato's soft backside was not looking forward to any more horseback riding, he was happy to hear a jingling sound approaching again. Everyone knew it was his great-great-grandfather.

wash, contrasted the colorful, fringed gold and white blanket draped over Don Tomas' cot. Beside it on a rustic, wooden nightstand, an old-fashioned lamp stood alongside a bright, red mineral paperweight. (Later, Donato would learn that this beautiful gemstone was called fire opal.) The freshly swept clay floor and everything in its proper place complemented the picture.

Don Tomas made a little smacking sound with his lips after tasting the tea. "*Buen provecho!* A beneficial thing this Brasil tea. It keeps the heart strong and therefore prolongs life. Most people don't concern themselves with eating what is good for them until they are already sick." Don Tomas smiled and leaned closer to whisper confidentially, "I have been drinking this tea since I was only a little older than you are, *hijo*, and I have never been ill. Go ahead, taste it!"

Donato tasted the dark red fluid. "I like it. It looks like dark pomegranate juice and tastes like fresh carrots." Donato then glanced up at the painting that covered a large portion of the wall and dominated the room. He knew it must be the one Maria Elena had spoken of. The bishop had a kindly expression, and the hands folded over his stomach looked like those of a hardworking man.

Don Tomas was still discussing the virtues of folk medicine. "Nowadays, people prefer to learn about progress. They see no reason to remember the secrets of nature. Even my own children have moved away and adopted city ways.

"When your uncle wrote me about your coming here, he mentioned you are interested in studying to become a veterinarian. It is good to want to care for God's creatures. If we observe them with an open mind, plants and animals have much to teach us. Perhaps you will be interested to learn the wisdom of the *campo*, which held little attraction for my children."

Those eyes peering from bony caverns held such a penetrating expression that Donato had difficulty meeting the old man's glance, yet he knew he must. Don Tomas would expect him to. "I would be honored to learn the ways of the *campo*, sir," Donato replied, with as much dignity as he could.

31

Don Tomas smiled with satisfaction. "Perhaps, given time, you will become the son my loins were too ignorant to produce."

Maria Elena arrived at the door carrying a wooden tray. She set the dishes down on the table, then catching Donato's eye on her way out, she gestured toward the painting. "Monsignor Escalante," she whispered, "ask Don Tomas!"

"How do I approach what might be a private matter with Don Tomas?" Donato wondered. "The painting," he said tentatively, "one notices it. It was Padre Alfredo from the Catedral Metropolitana in Mexico City, who advised my uncle Mario to send me to live with you. I am grateful to the padre for taking interest in my future. Indeed, I am very glad to be here, sir."

The old man nodded as though he expected no less. Then his eyes moved to the painting and he sighed. "That is Monsignor Escalante, a great and dynamic man. He was father to one and all, and the guiding icon of the church. The erection of the small cathedral in La Paz remains one of his many achievements."

Don Tomas pushed his chair back from the table and wiped his chin carefully with a cloth napkin. Donato was impressed with the fine manners of this old gentleman from the *campo*. These habits seemed to have been born in him.

Don Tomas began to talk again in his raspy, yet commanding voice. "We will speak of another thing. Doña Blanca told me *Espíritu*, the blue-eyed Azulejo stallion, came here today behind the other horses. This is unusual behavior for him; he is a shy, wild creature who usually comes to drink at night when no one is around."

"I've never seen such a magnificent animal in all my life!" Donato exclaimed with shining eyes. "Doña Blanca told me a little about him and also about the legend behind the creature's appearance. It was spooky the way the animal stood and looked at us. One sounds foolish trying to put the experience into words."

"Yes, all the young men who see *Espíritu* dream of catching and riding him one day."

32

Donato nodded. "First, I would want to win the wild horse's trust. That way, perhaps, he might decide he wanted me to ride him."

"An admirable ambition, lad! As I said before, you appear to be a boy after my own heart. You see, I believe the animal to be like no other. He is a unique genetic exception—a perfect throwback to a magnificent ancestor. It is a mischievous prank of nature's that none of my mares running out in the *campo* has produced foals like him. This is very disheartening to me from the viewpoint of a horse breeder, for any look-alike offspring *Espíritu* sired would bring high prices.

"I have reason to hope, though, that a wild Azulejo mare may also exist, who chooses to live out her life camouflaged under cover of the wilderness. The first time I saw *Espíritu*, he was crossing in front of a sheer, red adobe arroyo bank alongside a youngster who looked just like his twin. As soon as they noticed me, she bolted for the cover of the grayish underbrush in the way of a skittish filly. *Espíritu* remained standing guard in the attitude of a stallion on the lookout. Considering the filly was never spotted again, my men are all convinced it was not a real horse I saw, but the ghost mare of legend."

"Could she have been *Espíritu's* mother?"

"It is astute of you to bring up that possibility, Son, but no, both animals looked like slender, tight-lipped two year olds. No matter how I try to figure the question, there is no way to explain how two identically marked living horses that looked to be the same age came to be running together. It is a stretch of the imagination to think that horse twins could have matured into adults out in the *campo*. Twins are not only invariably weaklings, but the one that is slower to stand and nurse is sure to die or be taken by mountain lions or coyotes, or..."

The old man's whispery voice trailed off into silence, as he sat in contemplation. Then, as though making up his mind, he renewed the conversation with an unexpected energy.

"I have always lived with an unhurried sense of the passing of the years. Here in the *campo*, life has a natural flow and events pass in their own time. If it were that way everywhere, everyone would be happier. No? Nevertheless, with so many years upon me, I will not live forever, Brasil tea notwithstanding!"

Don Tomas' eyes twinkled over his teacup as he lifted it to his lips and took several swallows. "Now, I shall share a story with you I have kept to myself since I was a boy."

"You honor me, sir," Donato said, wondering what sort of strange tale a one-hundred-year-old man would wish to share with a boy of sixteen, especially one whom he hardly knew.

CHAPTER 5

The Pearls: A Trust

WITH mounting excitement, Donato watched Don Tomas draw a long burnished knife from its case that measured approximately thirty-six *centimeters. Seascapes inlaid with seashell and coral adorned the bone handle, and a smooth, brass cap decorated the end.

Don Tomas rotated the cap to expose a hollow chamber inside the handle and then pulled out a piece of musty marine caulking permeated with a greasy substance. As Donato watched in wonder, he tipped two opalescent black balls into the palm of his hand.

Don Tomas polished the spheres on his napkin until they gleamed in the candlelight. "These are gem-quality black pearls. I coated them with a smear of turtle grease so they wouldn't dry out and turn to dust. Hold them carefully," he said, tipping them out of his hand into Donato's palm.

While Donato was admiring the treasure, Don Tomas extracted three progressively larger gems, all of different hues. The first was a pale-yellow pearl followed by a round, smoky-pink one. The last was an enormous silvery-blue gem pearl.

"These, my Son, are mementos from the summers when I used to dive among the island coves and rocky shallows. My father was a notorious French pearl merchant, driven by an obsession to accumulate wealth. He shamed us by looking into our mouths and prodding us when we came up from a dive, to ensure we never kept any pearls for ourselves. This kind of treatment can make an intelligent boy very sly.

35

"My best friend, an orphan named Juliano, was gifted with the ability to hold his breath for a long time, and brought up many of the most valuable pearls. One evening, while Juliano and I were back at the orphanage, we secretly conspired to try and hold onto some of the finest gem pearls we found. He and I saw no sin in outwitting such a heartless man as my father. So, while diving, we were always on the lookout for the exceptionally fine ones. The two black pearls you hold in your hand came from the waters off Mechudo Point north of La Paz. And as far as I know, the yellow and pink pearls were the two finest my father's divers ever brought up from the Espíritu Santo Island oyster beds.

"Juliano gave me the yellow pearl as a token of fellowship the day we became best friends. The pink one signifies good luck, for it was his greatest find. But the blue pearl is the rarest, for it is a perfectly round abalone pearl. The day I found it, we were diving off the southern tip of Cerralvo Island. To me, that one signifies courage, for I was swept up in the strong, cold current that comes in from the Pacific, and nearly met my Maker. Only through praying to God did I summon the strength to swim out of the stream, which would have carried me out to sea to become food for the sharks."

Donato's wide eyes looked bright in his pale face. "How did you conceal your pearls from your father?"

A gratified smile lit up Don Tomas' face. "That is another astute question, *joven*. Your earnest desire to understand the details of my story demonstrates your keen interest!"

Don Tomas leaned closer to Donato, and as though still fearful the ghosts of his past might overhear, lowered his voice. "Sometimes we wedged one under the gunnels of an old rowboat or pushed them under the steel strip that covered the keel. Once we got back to La Paz, we waited until no one else was around, then concealed them in a jar that we hid in a small hideaway I had excavated beneath a pile of boulders known to be visited by rattlesnakes.

"The worst day of my childhood was the day my father caught Juliano concealing a pearl between the webs of his large fingers, a trick that, in the end, led to his death. I am sure my father did not intend to do Juliano any lasting harm, but his temper got the better of him. As a lesson to the rest of us, he beat my friend with the club used to kill fish until he was too badly injured to stand. Juliano summoned barely enough strength to open his eyes and whisper one last request in my ear. *'Amigo mío*, never part with our pearls for the sake of another man's greed, or I will have died in vain.' After I solemnly promised my friend to do as he asked, he drew his last breath.

"My father tossed Juliano's body into the sea to become shark food. He then told us to tell anyone who questioned us about Juliano's death that he never came up from his last dive.

"I wanted to offer one of our pearls to the priests in exchange for having a eulogy said in my friend's memory. The problem was that they might have interrogated me about the details of Juliano's death and asked where I obtained my pearl.

"Forced to keep my father's secret, I never shared Juliano's story with anyone. Our five pearls were doubly precious to me now; my friend had sacrificed his life for them. And as it turned out, these small treasures later brought me greater wealth in the form of optimism and self-assurance than if I had parted with them for material gain."

Don Tomas reflected upon the blue pearl with a look of sorrow and regret. "It is unlikely a gem as fine as this round abalone pearl will ever be found again. Usually, these pearls come too curiously shaped to fit conventional jewelry settings. Some merchants believe the Japanese fishermen poisoned the oyster and abalone beds to eliminate competition with their own commerce."

After placing the gems back in the knife handle, Don Tomas closed the cap. "No one has ever questioned why I kept such a serviceable tool close to me and never lent it to anyone. Even Padre Paseo who taught me to forge knives never realized that I had designed mine with a hollow handle. I have replaced the blade several times, but the pearls have remained safe for eighty-five years.

"To keep them from falling into the wrong hands upon my death, in the end, I resolved to drop the pearls back into the sea whence they came. However," and Don Tomas emphasized his next words with a meaningful look. "Now that you and I have met, I have a hunch that Juliano's and my keepsake pearls may yet have an important role to play."

"What do you mean?" Donato asked.

"Ah! That is for you to discover, my Son," Don Tomas explained philosophically, holding the knife out for Donato to take.

"Why do me this tremendous honor, Sir?" Donato asked, accepting the knife. "I only hope..."

Don Tomas stopped Donato with a gesture. With his left hand, Don Tomas drew his grandson's right hand toward him, and enclosed it under his own. This was the way of his people when sealing a bargain. The gesture meant the subject was closed.

"For now, don't worry yourself about what the future has in store, Son. Simply view this knife and its contents as heirlooms handed down to you by your venerable *abuelo*," Don Tomas counseled, smiling. "I have no doubt you will act with good judgment when the time comes. Until then, simply handle the knife the way you would a small machete, and always keep it with you."

Donato passed a hand over his damp brow. His shadowy recollections of faraway Mexico City now seemed like a dream. He somehow felt older and different. A shiver ran down his spine as he imagined a gathering of spirits following close behind him to ensure he acted wisely regarding this solemn trust: Juliano's ghost, the phantoms of Punta Prieta, and perhaps even the specter of the mean old Frenchman.

Don Tomas interrupted Donato's thoughts with a question. "Tell me, what do you know of horsemanship? Can you saddle a horse and throw a lariat?"

"My father sometimes took me for pony rides in the park, but there were no ranches near where I lived, only the military riding academy."

Don Tomas nodded. "Ramón, the gardener's son, is a talented young *vaquero* and can teach you horsemanship. Since you must have studied both the Spanish and English languages in school, in turn, tell Ramón I suggested you help him increase his Spanish vocabulary and teach him some English. His Spanish has improved some since I took him under my wing, but he still needs tutoring."

"It would be a pleasure!" Donato replied agreeably; then he switched the subject of conversation back to his favorite topic of horses.

"Do you ever race your horses, Grandfather?" he inquired eagerly.

"Not in the short, weekend races. I only see sport in tests of stamina," Don Tomas replied.

"Might I be able to ride one of your horses in a race someday?" Donato asked excitedly. "Once I know how to ride, that is," he added sheepishly, startled by his own enthusiasm.

"I am sure that can be arranged," Don Tomas replied, laughing. "You might like to participate in the challenging day-long Puesta del Sol race where the winner selects his prize from among the other contestants' outstanding horses!"

"What if I lost the race and forfeited one of your magnificent mounts?"

"Don't worry. I would make certain yours is the fastest entrant when the time comes. In any event, like the tension in a Spanish bullfight, the element of risk is what makes this type of competition so exciting!

"Alas," the old man continued, "indiscriminate interbreeding with degenerate stock has degraded the quality of the horses in Baja California. Like the pearls, good animals have become very scarce.

"Even I no longer oversee the breeding of my horses the way I used to. *Alazán* is an example of a well-bred horse, but he is a wanderer and leads my good mares away from home. This is why I

usually stand quietly when you saddle them for the first time. Of course, they go to pieces when you lift the blindfold and let them go, but this is only a temporary setback."

Ramón bridled *Alazán* with a soft bosal attached by a beautifully braided deerskin headstall complete with white tassels, and a light brass curb designed with a low port and copper roller that lubricated the young horse's mouth by encouraging salivation and kept his tongue from sticking to the dry metal. Next, he saddled him with a lightweight saddletree fitted with a breast collar and rear breeching like a packsaddle.

When he was done adjusting *Alazán*'s tack, Ramón gave Donato instructions. "Please open the inside gate to the adjoining corral for me. Then, for your own safety, I recommend you leave via the side gate, so you can watch from outside the corrals."

Once Donato completed his tasks, Ramón lifted *Alazán*'s blindfold. For a moment, the colt stood as though rooted to the spot, blinking his eyes in the glare of the morning sun. However, as soon as he could see well enough, as though thinking he might be able to jump straight out of his saddle—he sprang up into the air. He came down on the other side of the open, inside gate to land splay-legged in the middle of the main corral beyond.

"*Qué caballo!*" Ramón exclaimed in awe. "That is the farthest distance I've ever seen a horse cover in a single bound!"

For a few moments the colt continued to stand splay legged with his belly low to the ground as though the unaccustomed tack were weighing him down. Then, without warning, he humped his back and exploded into a bucking spree. After a spirited effort he alighted alongside the far side of the corral with his back still rounded and his splayed legs stiff.

"What will he do next?" Donato asked.

Ramón laughed, "This is what we will leave him to decide! He's probably thinking, 'All this stuff that's sticking to me looks scary, but when I try bucking it off, I yank my nose. I think I'll just stand and blow through my nostrils awhile and think my situation over!'"

Ramón looked toward the hacienda. "Hoping to improve my horsemanship, Don Tomas gave me *Rosillo* and the mule that stands tied to the veranda when they were only lasso-trained. It took me three months to gentle *Rosillo*. As you saw when we passed him on our way down from the orchard, he is a plain horse with a prominent Roman nose and large ears that have little space between them. Nevertheless, as with many horses of his type not gifted with much imagination, he is now one of the most dependable riding horses on the ranch.

"Now do me the favor of fetching the mule from the veranda that has the scar across her face. We call her *Mala Cara*, or Bad Face. She, too, is very gentle. I'll go get *Rosillo*."

Working with Ramón's placid animals helped to build Donato's confidence. Grooming them reminded him of the days when he helped his sisters shine his mother's furniture; but the animals held more interest for him and moved over when prompted.

Ramón showed Donato how to saddle *Rosillo* with a packsaddle, and the mule, *Mala Cara*, with a *vaquero* saddle complete with leather armor coverings. Donato tried to pretend his sore backside had recovered overnight, and did his best to keep from wincing when Ramón helped him to mount. As he rode *Mala Cara* around the corral, Ramón gave him pointers on horsemanship. When Ramón decided Donato had learned enough to ride her down the Southern Coastal Trail while ponying *Rosillo*, he fetched and mounted *Alazán* who was now more accustomed to his tack. As soon as Ramón was ready, he asked Donato to open the corral gate wide and lead the way down the path.

"The mule has traveled the Southern Coastal Trail many times and knows it well. She will follow it to Punta Prieta and beyond to the village of Punta Gorda where we will end our journey. I will follow you, sometimes riding and sometimes walking *Alazán* as I continue his training."

* * *

To Donato, the terrain surrounding Punta Prieta seemed haunted and forbidding. The *vientos* howled and whistled through the fissures in the cliffs like ghostly voices, and he thought some of the volcanic formations resembled grotesque faces staring vacantly out across the gulf with empty eye sockets. Looking down at the shoreline from high peaks in the trail, Donato could easily picture the sailors all sitting on the inhospitable rocky beach, roasting the Azulejo's carcass around the campfire so many years ago. He looked over his shoulder at Ramón following so quietly behind him on *Alazán*, and wondered whether he was troubled by the legend.

"Ramón, do you believe in the legend of the Azulejo?"

Ramón put his finger to his lips, "Shh."

Donato took this as an affirmation. Trying to still his imagination, he looked out upon the white-capped waves dotting the gulf. He was just thinking how they reminded him of galloping Azulejo horses with their white manes streaming in the breeze, when a spot of light sailing out over the water caught his attention. At first, he thought it might be the setting sun reflecting off the hull of a distant fisherman's *canoa*, but it seemed to hang just above the waves like a hovering gull. After he and Ramón rounded the point, Donato lost sight of the phenomenon and thought no more about it. When the trail finally dropped down onto the sandy beach that lay beyond the headland, Ramón rode *Alazán* up alongside Donato.

"These days, wayfarers choose to pass this way without mentioning the legend. However, from time to time, fishermen still report seeing strange lights floating over the submerged reefs that surround the rocky point. I was only a small child when my father and I saw proof of a ghost ship. It was the time we brought my mother from our home in San Antonio to visit Rancho La Primavera. I remember the trip clearly. To escape the July heat, we traveled at night. The air was still, the sea dead calm, and the full moon lighted our way. We could distinctly hear howling coyotes, hooting owls, and the splash of fish jumping out in the sea. My mother, who came last on the trail, said she could also hear the cadenced hoofbeats of a horse and rider following us. However, when my father and I stopped to listen, we could hear nothing and teased her that her imagination must be playing tricks on her. She said nothing more until we reached Punta Prieta. After we rounded the point, she claimed the horseman had turned onto the path leading up to the cliffs overlooking the shore. Out of curiosity, my father decided to ride up to the precipice and take a look down at the beaches. This was when, to our surprise, about a hundred meters offshore by his reckoning, we saw shimmering vapor hanging above the glassy water that was formed like a ship's sails. The spectacle looked the same both above and below, for the still water was like a mirror. We stared in wonder as misty human shapes wafted in and out of the sea without a ripple. Although the manifestation began to fade with the light of dawn, this spooky experience left us with an enduring respect for the legend."

* * *

The rhythmic plodding of the horse's footfalls had begun lulling Donato to sleep. That was until *Rosillo* left the trail to snack on the far side of a leafy cat's claw bush while *Mala Cara* continued down the main path, thus gulleting the roan around the bush by his lead rope.

Ramón cursed at *Rosillo*. "He follows well but is stubborn and has a mind of his own," he told Donato. After Ramón's tongue-lashing, the roan seemed to pay better attention to the trail, and all continued well until they approached the last steep hill before Punta Gorda.

Donato was so tired he absentmindedly wrapped *Rosillo's* lead around his saddle horn and began to doze. Thus, when *Mala Cara* took a leap up the hill, *Rosillo* felt his lead rope yank him forward and stubbornly planted his feet. The mule's only remedy now was to struggle out of her saddle and drop Donato in the bottom of the sandy gulch behind her, still clutching the saddle horn.

Ramón laughed until his sides ached. "I told you never to wrap an animal's lead around your saddle horn! Are you alright?"

Donato grumbled sourly as he beat the dust from his clothing.

"We don't have far to go now," Ramón continued. "You shouldn't mind walking for a stretch. Your backside can probably use the rest!"

*   *   *

More stars appeared in the night sky than Donato had ever seen. Compared with the hazy orb that traveled across the night skies of Mexico City, the Baja moon glowed with paranormal brilliance, lighting their way as they entered the town of Punta Gorda.

Ramón was a friend of Señor Hernandez, the storekeeper, and put the animals away in his corral without having to wake him to ask permission. He then removed *Alazán*'s bridle but left the colt's saddle on. He explained. "The young horse's muscles will be sore after carrying a rider out on the trail for the first time; he might object to having his saddle put back on in the morning. I padded his saddletree with a thick, soft, sheepskin when I saddled him so he wouldn't develop hot spots. I suggest we leave his saddle on until we get back to La Primavera."

"Agreed," acknowledged a weary and sore Donato. "What are hot spots?"

"These are areas on an animal's back where the hair turns white after wearing an ill-fitting or poorly padded saddle."

After giving the colt some grain and bunches of dried grasses to eat, Ramón and Donato each lay down on the wooden benches situated outside the village store and fell soundly asleep.

At sunrise, Punta Gorda came to life with the sounds of bellowing bulls, crowing roosters, gobbling turkeys, screaming peacocks, clanging dishes, and all the activity of a rural Mexican village. Only when a friendly pig rooting for grub put its bristly snout in Donato's face did he awaken with a shriek.

This started Ramón laughing so hard he came down with a fit of the hiccups. Donato was annoyed. His buttocks were too sore to sit on and his leg muscles were so stiff he could hardly stand.

Once Ramón realized how miserable Donato felt, he became sympathetic. "I'll ask Señora Hernandez for some herbal tea that will help soothe your pain."

Ramón soon reappeared with the storekeeper's wife. She made motherly noises while handing Donato a cup of dark, mysterious liquid. "A cultivated young man from faraway Mexico City—of course he will feel stiff after riding for long hours in a hard saddle!"

The tea's strange flavor contributed to the tranquil mood it brought on, and eased Donato's discomfort. After the soreness in his muscles subsided, he found himself able to focus his attention on the colorful articles Ramón pointed out in the store, admiring the workmanship of the handcrafted items in particular.

Ramón appeared pleased when Donato expressed an interest in learning some of the crafts. "I know how to weave straw hats, baskets, palm manikins, horsehair ropes, and all types of leather goods. As soon as we get back to the ranch, if you like, I can begin teaching you how to weave straw dolls and hats. Now we must have our breakfast. When we are done, we will return to the *tienda* and look for suitable clothes to buy you."

After training *Alazán* the previous day followed by the long journey, the boys were so hungry they ate Señora Hernandez' hot tortillas off the comal as fast as she could pat them out. When they were done with their meal, they returned to the store where Donato picked out a white canvas hat similar to Ramón's. A black and flaxen band woven of horsehair adorned the crown, and a red tassel dangled from the back.

"The colors accent *Alazán*'s chestnut coloring," Ramón observed. "Also, as encouragement to become an accomplished horseman, we need to buy you a pair of riding boots and a set of tinkling spurs to buckle on the heels!"

When the boys finished making their purchases, they packed up all their supplies, along with thirty kilos of corn, ten kilos of bran, and a sack of groceries for Doña Blanca. Nearly incapacitated by another fit of the giggles, Ramón did his best to balance and secure the huge load on *Rosillo*'s packsaddle so nothing would fall off along the trail back to Rancho La Primavera.

"We've heaped *Rosillo*'s pack so high he looks like one of the *camellos* from the Camel cigarette ads!" he exclaimed, giving the roan's well-anchored load a last slap.

Before leaving, Ramón gave Donato another cup of dark tea to drink. Donato now not only felt sleepy, but also he was still too saddle sore to ride. "If you walk holding onto *Mala Cara*'s tail, she will pull you along the trail," Ramón instructed.

By the time the boys reached Punta Prieta, Donato had worked the stiffness out of his muscles but he was too weary to walk any further. "Now is the time for you to ride *Alazán*," Ramón announced. "I'll lead him for you until you two become used to one another. I have put a soft fleece across his saddle to cushion your backside."

Unlike the mule's undulating amble, *Alazán*'s animated gait was smooth and fluid. He bobbed his head spiritedly up and down, and his small pointed ears swiveled back and forth amidst a rich tangle of mane, alert for unexpected sounds. Soon, despite Donato's exhaustion, a growing sense of well-being and excitement filled his soul as he experienced the kind of pride one feels sitting astride so noble an animal.

CHAPTER 7

An Unwelcome Visitor:
Señor Aliseo Bartolo

RAMÓN gave Donato a few days to rest up after their trip to Punta Gorda, and then went to check on him. He found Donato on the east veranda of the hacienda, helping Maria Elena clear the breakfast table.

When he arrived, Ramón was smiling good-naturedly. "Good morning *Patrón*. When Don Tomas returns, he will complain I have allowed the cooks to spoil you and that you've grown fat and lazy! It is time you learned how to do some of the ranch chores. Follow me, and I'll teach you how we drain and clean the *pila*."

As Donato walked with Ramón toward the horse corrals, Ramón explained about the *pila*. "Because of the recent rains, the water isn't used much and breeds waterweeds, mosquitoes, and tadpoles, all of which deplete the water's oxygen. This makes it stagnant and unwholesome for the animals. The *pila* drains through a small, plugged opening into the irrigation canal that waters the trees shading the corrals. When the flow slows to a trickle, this means the *pila* is nearing empty, and you can climb inside to begin cleaning it. You may scrape it out using the trowel I left on top of the wall.

"For the time being, I must leave you to tend the *pila* while I go with my father to harvest sugarcane. I set a galvanized tub of water out for the livestock. After an animal drinks from it, please fill it up again from the well. I'll bring you some fresh sugarcane stalks to slice and enjoy on in the meantime."

Donato noticed that *Alazán* was standing alone in one of the nearby corrals, so after Ramón left, he plucked *Alazán* a handful of *quelite* sprigs growing just inside the fence encircling the well. He hoped the colt would remember him this time and accept the greenery out of his hand. But reminiscent of the time Donato had tried offering him the bundle of grass from Don Tomas' orchard, *Alazán* backed up, eying him warily, while blowing through wide, velvety nostrils.

True to his word, Ramón soon returned carrying a bundle of ripe sugarcane stalks under one arm and a clay pot in the other. Setting the canes and the pot down on top of the *pila* wall, he called to Donato who was walking back from *Alazán*'s pen.

"Here, I've brought you some fresh canes."

"Thanks. I tried hand-feeding some *quelite* to *Alazán*, but he acted as though he still doesn't know me!"

"He needs more handling. If you help me finish all the ranch chores today, tomorrow we can take *Alazán* on another ride and continue his training."

Donato's face brightened. He didn't want to be assigned ranch chores until Don Tomas returned. "What time tomorrow can we leave?" he asked eagerly.

"We'll start at dawn," Ramón specified offhandedly while gesturing toward the sugarcane stalks. "Use your knife to peel and slice the canes, and then store the slices in this adobe *olla* so they will stay cool. You can refresh yourself by sucking the juice while you are waiting for the *pila* to drain."

Before leaving, Ramón pointed out a burro drinking from the galvanized tub. "The white burro's name is *Pavo*. We hand-raised him from birth. Unlike *Alazán*, he understands and enjoys attention. Why don't you go over and visit with him."

When Donato walked up to *Pavo*, the burro hung his head submissively and let him scratch his chin. After a few minutes however, Donato walked back to the *pila* and peered over the side to see how far it had drained, but the water had only emptied halfway, so he sat down on the cistern wall facing the well, and began peeling and slicing the cane stalks. *Pavo*, who had followed him, stood looking up hopefully, and brayed for a treat. Donato soon took pity upon the endearing burro and offered him a few slices, but these only whetted *Pavo*'s appetite. Eager for more, he nudged the clay *olla* with his nose, knocked it off the wall, and scattered the sliced sugarcane that Donato had worked so hard to prepare, all over the ground.

When Ramón returned, Donato was nowhere to be seen. *Pavo* stood sulkily beside the horse pens, waterweeds dangling from his ears and his sides peppered with pond scum. "What did you do to my poor little *burrito*?" Ramón cried out, laughing at the sight.

At the sound of Ramón's voice, Donato popped his head up out of the *pila* like a creature poking its head out of its burrow and pointed toward *Pavo* with the trowel.

"I was compassionate and offered your burro some sliced sugarcane, but that didn't satisfy him so he brayed for more. After knocking over the *olla* and destroying all I had, I guess he got bored because he walked over to the water tub, stuck one front foot in it and banged the sides, muddying the water." Donato held out his hands to show Ramón the rope burns he had received from drawing water up from the well.

Ramón winced at sight of the raw flesh. "I'll get you some turtle grease when we get back to the hacienda. It will soothe the pain and toughen your skin. For now, I'll shut *Pavo* up in one of the corrals and feed him a nice meal of *milpa* so he will remain nearby and won't pester you. We will need to hitch him to the watermill so we can refill the *pila* this afternoon."

* * *

After Donato finished cleaning the *pila*, Ramón showed him how to harness *Pavo* to the watermill. After saddling him with an old saddletree, he strapped him to the long wooden poles made from split palm trunks that branched out from the well-shaft. These turned a huge worm gear which pulled up a series of water buckets linked together by chains.

After the boys finished filling the *pila*, Ramón showed Donato how to do some of the evening chores, most of which required a lot more walking than Donato had been used to doing in a day's time. He explained what feed to cut for the horses that were kept in at the ranch, when to turn the goats out in the morning, what kinds of firewood to collect for the kitchen, and how to saddle and unsaddle the *bestias* that came and went.

After the drudgery of so much menial work, Donato was overjoyed to have Bruno show up unexpectedly from San Antonio. He announced his arrival with a shrill whistle as he rode in, so that Ramón would know to run and greet him.

"Good afternoon, boys," Bruno said tipping his hat in greeting and then sitting authoritatively back in his saddle. "I bring you orders from Don Tomas. Ramón, he asks that you show Donato how to herd the heifers we turned loose on La Mesa Alta last spring to the *Vacadilla* oasis. He also asks that you boys spy on Señor Bartolo's activities and report back to us when we pass by the oasis on our return from the cattle drive."

"The reason, Boss?" Ramón asked, looking concerned.

"Rumor has it that the Señor needs a new racehorse. Wanting only the best, he is likely to renew his efforts to hunt down and trap the wild Azulejo stallion.

"On our way through San Antonio, Magistrate Don Paco had his *vaqueros* hold our cattle in the arroyo for a couple of days while we rested up at his hacienda. He told us he recently raced his new horse from Tijuana, *Volador*, in a match race against Señor Bartolo's local gelding, *Chispa*. Unfortunately, *Chispa* must have been suffering from sunstroke before Señor Bartolo even entered him in the race because the gelding faltered half way to the finish and then sank to his knees."

"What a tragedy," Ramón replied sadly. Then he turned to Donato. "You should see *Chispa*, Donato. What a big, beautiful gelding! He is *Alazán*'s older brother." Then he turned back to Bruno. "Señor Bartolo must be so mad he could spit."

"Yes, that is why Señor Bartolo will probably try to capture the Azulejo. He not only sponsored the ruin of one of the finest horses in the region, but he lost a large wager in the bargain. He unjustly blames the fiasco on the young boy who has ridden for him these past two years, Zenen. Señor Bartolo has now hired Chico, that detestable creature who once apprenticed under Señor Cuevas."

Ramón made a face. "I remember Señor Cuevas; he is the one-eyed *mulero* who lives on the edge of the no man's land west of Sierra de La Laguna. He is one cold-blooded *hombre* who makes vile cures from noxious plants and insects!"

Bruno turned to Donato, "Don Tomas will soon be taking you to meet Don Paco, the magistrate of San Antonio. His Honor stays abreast of all the local gossip. He informed us that Chico knows how to brew a sedative potent enough to subdue even the wild broncos." Then, lowering his voice he added, "Don Tomas doubts the concoction contains anything all that mysterious. His best guess is that the essence extracted from the leaves of the coyote vine is the effective ingredient. The *bestias* avoid this distasteful plant out in the *campo* because of its disagreeable smell. However, the tea made from the third rinse of the pressed, dried leaves no longer retains a strong odor. This brew can make an animal very sick if it drinks a sufficient quantity. Don Tomas says this news update just goes to prove that Señor Bartolo will stop at nothing in his quest to try and capture the Azulejo."

Donato looked horrified. "How does Chico get horses to drink his concoction?"

"Ah! Chico is very sly. He waits until the weather turns hot and the cattle have polluted the evaporating watering holes with urine which masks the taste and smell of the coyote vine. Don Paco informed us that after Chico has trapped a wild horse in a box canyon, he pours a thin mixture of tea diluted with 'cowhole' water into a pan buried in the earth or natural basin in a granite boulder. Generally, in the dry season, a *bestia* will have become so thirsty in the time it takes to gallop into the trap, it will discover Chico's diluted mixture and drink up every drop. After the sedative takes effect, the creature sinks into a stupor and becomes easier to handle."

Donato was deeply concerned. "How can we protect *Espíritu* from Chico's notorious methods?"

"This, young man, is the reason for my trip. We had hoped that Chico and Señor Bartolo would decide to hold off until the dry season, but rumor has it they are rounding up wranglers competent to help Chico trap the wild horse. Don Tomas thinks the only way to protect the Azulejo now may be to capture him ourselves."

"How can we do that," Donato asked, his eyes shining with excitement.

"Don Tomas is hopeful the wild horse may come down to the corral again the way he did the day you first arrived, to drink out of the water trough. All anyone need do then is shut the gate on him."

"And if he does not show up soon?"

"We will turn Don Tomas' dependable mare, *Cenizas*, loose up in the hills near where the stallion was last seen, and hope he follows her back to the ranch."

* * *

Alazán had grown independent after his long rest and began crow hopping just as soon as Ramón lifted his blindfold. "He doesn't want us to take him on another long trek!" Ramón exclaimed, laughing. "I'll start off by ponying him behind *Rosillo* with all his tack on. The trip will provide a good opportunity to work the quirks out of him."

Ramón collected the supplies they would need for the journey. "A *vaquero* carries little weight so as not to burden his mount," he explained. "During the rainy season, the *campo* provides both food and fodder, so a man and his mount can travel far with few supplies.

All that is needed are a knife, a pot for food, a pot for boiling water, a ladle, spoons, some dry goods, and a water bottle. These things will fit in the front saddlebags with plenty of room to spare. Tie your bedroll and a change of clothes behind the cantle. Last of all, check to make sure you carry a *caracol*. Don Tomas' *vaqueros* always carry one in their saddlebags to summon help in case of need."

Ramón pulled a *caracol reina* out of Donato's saddlebags. This was a giant queen sea conch with a pink- lipped underside that was used to summon help in case of emergencies. With both hands, he lifted it to his lips and blasted Donato with a short, resounding peal.

"That's louder than a car horn! My ears are still ringing!" Donato exclaimed.

"I could blow it longer and louder, but both *vaqueros* and fishermen might show up here thinking we have an emergency at Rancho La Primavera!"

Ramón gave Donato a long-legged blood-bay gelding to ride who wasn't nearly as spectacular as the flashy liver chestnut, *Alazán*. "His name is *Pronto*," Ramón said, pulling his stirrup leather down after tightening the girth. *"Cómo se dice en inglés?"*

"*Pronto* means quickly," Donato replied.

"*Sí*, you must not underestimate Quickly. When he was younger, he won the Puesta de Sol Endurance race that runs between El Santo and San Antonio," Ramón explained proudly.

* * *

The overland trail stretching across La Mesa Alta was well traveled. A few kilometers beyond the tableland, the trail intersected with the old El Camino Real Highway running the length of the Californias. At this point, herds of cattle were sometimes driven down the dirt road to await passage on a freighter bound for the city of Ensenada.

As soon as Donato and Ramón reached the first plateau of La Mesa Alta, Ramón stopped to let the winded horses catch their breath. Unfortunately, stopping gave the *jejénes* attracted to the horses' sweat an opportunity to hover around them.

Ramón explained, "The salt ocean air discourages the gnats down by the ranch, but inland they nest in the vegetation and lay their eggs in the damp topsoil."

Donato was so busy swishing the flies away with a leafstalk, he paid little attention to the changing weather conditions—the sudden drop in temperature and the distant clouds gathering along the southern skyline. Therefore, he was startled when, like the overture to a sinister drama, the clouds let out a long, low rumble. The crack of a firearm discharging in the valley below ensued, followed by shouting voices, as though a group of men were pursuing a quarry.

"*Válgame Dios!*" Ramón exclaimed, watching for movement among the dense foliage at the foot of the butte. "Señor Bartolo and his men must be returning to El Santo along the southern trail from San Antonio. The Señor always carries a rifle to hunt deer, for he likes the meat and uses the skins to make *gamuza*.

"Look! I can see the Azulejo," said Ramón. "The round, white spot on his forehead sets him apart from the shrubbery when he turns this way. Señor Bartolo must have fired off a couple of shots to spook him toward an ambush. See, he and his men are trying to drive the stallion toward Mescal Canyon. The greatest danger to the wild horse will come if he panics and injures himself once he is cornered."

Donato forgot about the *jejéne* flies and squinted his eyes, trying to peer into the distance. "How can you see anything from so far away?"

"You must relax your eyes to see into the distance. Stop squinting and open them wide!"

"But the sun is so bright!"

"We can buy you dark glasses next time we go to Punta Gorda. For now, shade your face with your hands."

When Donato did as Ramón suggested, all at once, he spotted the Azulejo just as the elusive stallion leaped out from behind a thicket of smoke trees and into a red adobe wash. Again, the way his white mane and tail billowed up under the light of the midday sun reminded Donato of foam blowing off the whitecaps on a choppy sea. The sight caused a surge of emotion to well up within his breast like a dormant spirit awakening from slumber, and consumed him with the desire to safeguard and defend this incomparably magnificent wild animal.

"The way he darts in and out of the distant greenery reminds me of his namesake, the flitting azulejo bluebird of my homeland. Surely, Señor Bartolo won't run the risk of shooting and crippling the creature, and will take careful aim," Donato said, groaning at the thought.

Then, as suddenly as he had appeared, the Azulejo dove into a copse of silvery álamo saplings and vanished from sight. Señor Bartolo's men were attempting to frighten him out of the thicket when one of them wheeled his horse around and galloped off in the opposite direction, with the rest following.

"Good! It looks as though the men have given up! But where are they galloping off to now?" Donato asked.

"Look up there on the hilltop that rises up beyond Mesacal Canyon," Ramón said, pointing. "Can't you see him? The Azulejo is looking right at us! His metallic, silvery, blue-black coat blends with the shadowy gray foliage, but you can still distinguish his white forehead marking shining out from between the trees like a tiny moon."

"*Dios mío!* How did the *bestia* get clear up there on top of that hill all of a sudden?" Donato asked.

"Who's to know?" Ramón replied mysteriously. "Some say that like the mother bird leading the cat away from its nest, it is not *Espíritu* at all who leads Señor Bartolo's men on the chase, but the ghost mare."

As Ramón seemed in earnest, Donato decided to keep his thoughts to himself and consult Don Tomas when the time was right. Even though Don Tomas claimed he had seen two identical Azulejos running together, the *vaqueros* apparently thought this explanation less convincing than the phantom theory.

* * *

Since *Alazán* appeared to have settled down, Ramón dismounted *Rosillo* to reposition the colt's saddle and retighten the girth. "Watch the lower mesa plateau for me. When Señor Bartolo gives up trying to trap the Azulejo, he and his men will take the trail passing through the clearing." Then Ramón grumbled that *Alazán* was holding his air and kneed the horse in the belly so he would exhale and allow him to pull the látigo tight.

Suddenly, Donato sat bolt upright in his saddle. "Here they come! Look! The leader rides what looks like an enormous horse with big ears! Following him are three men leading mules with deer slung across their backs, and a boy on a mule ponying a chestnut horse brings up the rear."

Alazán had scuffed gravel into Ramón's boots, so he sat himself down on a nearby boulder to shake them out. "Good!" Ramón exclaimed. "Señor Bartolo has brought *Machismo*, his *fenómeno* mule. What looks like a boy would be Chico, leading Señor Bartolo's sick, *soleado* gelding, *Chispa*."

"Why *is* Chico so small, is he a midget?"

"Well, put it this way, he is no bigger than a boy of ten but is up in his thirties. Also, his voice is like it never changed—but be aware, he is agile and cunning."

"What is a *fenómeno* mule?" Donato asked, wanting to get answers to as many questions as he could.

"A *fenómeno* is a dragon-mule born of a fertile molly mule bred to a horse. Since a mule is half burro and half horse, this makes the dragon three quarters horse."

"The *fenómeno* looks huge—either that, or Señor Bartolo's pack mules are only a burro's size!"

Ramón doffed his hat to Señor Bartolo's little man, Chico, who was handling *Chispa*, and offered his hand by way of apology for *Alazán*'s behavior. "Ramón Castillo at your service," he said acknowledging him in a conciliatory tone.

"Chico Martinez," Chico replied amiably. "Your chestnut is obviously a very fine animal. Perhaps you wouldn't mind letting me try his paces?"

"Be my guest," Ramón answered. "However, I would caution you to wait until he is better trained, for as you can see, he is scarcely green-broke." Then, before Chico had a chance to reply, Ramón turned to Señor Bartolo.

"*Alazán* was only recently brought in from the *campo*," he explained.

Having regained his composure, Señor Bartolo ventured back onto the trail. "Your colt is pretty, but he's obviously not very bright if he doesn't know a gelding from a mare," he replied sarcastically.

Señor Bartolo regarded the sorry gelding, *Chispa*, who had been the cause of all the excitement. "Poor *Chispa*," he said. "I had planned to race him in El Santo next Sunday, but he's succumbed to sunstroke. My only hope now of winning the race is to get myself a new horse." He eyed *Alazán* meaningfully. "I'm afraid, though, if your silly colt were to catch sight of another gelding, he might gallop the wrong way down the racecourse!" Then the Señor and his men burst out laughing and slapped their sides, making more of the joke than was warranted.

Ramón took the opportunity to redirect the topic of conversation toward Señor Bartolo's intentions concerning *Espíritu*. "Surely, there can be no faster horse in these parts than the wild Azulejo stallion."

"I've got better plans for the Azulejo than to squander him on weekend races," Señor Bartolo replied evasively.

Ramón continued to do his best to keep Señor Bartolo focused on the topic. "If you want to hear something extraordinary, the wild Azulejo appears to favor our new arrival, here, Don Tomas grandson. There were signs!"

The light flashed in Señor Bartolo's eyes as he looked across at Donato. He was also interested in getting to know this newcomer to Don Tomas' family. *"Mucho gusto en conocerle, joven,* a pleasure to meet you, young man," he murmured, touching the brim of his hat again. "But you have the look of a city boy about you, son. Tell me, did you travel here from the mainland?"

"From Mexico City, Señor," Donato said, deferentially doffing his hat.

"Ah! The celebrated capital of our country! Tell me, Donato from Mexico City who has a way with wild horses, in your opinion, how do our *bestias* compare with the purebred animals of the mainland?"

"Not even the thoroughbreds and beautiful Andaluz stabled at the Military Academy can compare with your grand *fenómeno,* Señor," Donato responded suavely.

This answer gratified Señor Bartolo. "You have gracious manners and good taste. Come. You must try out my *fenómeno* and accompany us to the *Vacadilla* oasis where I invite you and Ramón to join us for dinner. There will be more than enough venison to go around."

Donato noticed a look of envy on Ramón's face and guessed Señor Bartolo was not in the habit of allowing just anyone to try out his dragon.

As a further gesture to cultivate Don Tomas' relative, Señor Bartolo reached deep into his pocket and pulled out a small bottle of pungent oil. After apologizing for the strong odor, he explained it kept the bugs away and offered to share it. Then he motioned to two men who stood ready to unsaddle *Machismo.* The *fenómeno* had been so well trained it spread its legs when its foreleg was tapped, making it easier for the men to reach its back. After exchanging Señor Bartolo's and Donato's saddles, one of the men offered Donato a leg up on *Machismo* while Señor Bartolo mounted *Pronto* and trotted to the head of the cavalcade.

Donato's view upon the back of *Machismo* made him feel grand. The animal's height set him above the other riders and enabled him to look down on the *campo,* as though he were riding upon some mythical beast. Donato smiled and waved to Ramón, but his friend pretended not to notice.

When the thunderstorm arrived, it showered a torrent of rain down on the procession, clearing the bugs from the air and refreshing both horse and rider. The rain showers continued on and off for an hour. By the time they all dismounted at the lower end of *Vacadilla* oasis, the late afternoon sun was peeking out from between the clouds again.

Trying to regain his friend's good will, Donato pitched in and helped Ramón and Señor Bartolo's men set up camp, but nevertheless felt like an outsider to their activities and conversations. In the meantime, Señor Bartolo reclined under a thatched lean-to with a basket of candied fruit and a pot of unusually dark coffee, which he heated over a small open fire.

The animals were splattered with mud, so the men rinsed them off in the oasis creek. Señor Bartolo's men then stretched lines between the palm trees from which to hang the salted hides and strips of deer meat. They also gathered some of the dry driftwood which had accumulated in the backs of ground-level caves during the infrequent flash floods. After that, they set about preparing one of the deer carcasses for roasting over the campfire coals.

Donato was still struggling to flay the flesh off the back of a deer hide when Ramón and the men took theirs to the creek where they rinsed and salted them before returning to hang them up to dry. As soon as Señor Bartolo saw Donato had been left alone, he caught his eye and beckoned to him. "Why don't you bring that hide over here to me, lad, and I'll show you the easiest way to finish it off. You also welcome to the last of my coffee and I invite you to sample the imported fruit dulces I bought off a vendor on my last trip to La Paz."

It was nearly sundown, so Donato welcomed a hand with his hide-cleaning chore and a hot drink sounded good. Señor Bartolo demonstrated how to flay the skin using a hunting knife designed for the purpose. While he was working, he questioned Donato about

Don Tomas' health and inquired into his plans for the future. In fact, he behaved so graciously, Donato wondered whether Ramón and the *vaqueros* had embellished the sinister tales they told about the man.

As soon as Señor Bartolo had finished with his little demonstration, he handed Donato his knife. "Try practicing my technique. You will find it much easier than scraping the hide with your little machete the way you have been doing."

Before accepting Señor Bartolo's hunting knife, Donato put Don Tomas' knife aside by stabbing it into a small, cardón cactus. However, to his surprise, Señor Bartolo reached behind him and pulled it out again.

"This is an ornate little blade," he said, examining it. "Part machete and part *cuchillo*."

Distrustful of Señor Bartolo's intentions, Donato was defiant. "Stick my knife back in the cactus! My *abuelo* gave that to me as a keepsake!"

The Señor ignored him and smiled craftily. "It is evident your *abuelo* holds you in high regard, my boy, for this is a fine heirloom." Then, as though to test the knife's balance, he took it by the tip and hurtled it end over end until it sank up to the full width of the blade into the trunk of one of the fibrous fan palms growing beside the oasis stream.

"*Maldito, hombre!* Confound it, man!" Senor Bartolo exclaimed, springing up to retrieve it. "That is one bad weapon!" As he worked the knife back and forth to loosen it from the palm trunk, he inadvertently twisted the cap and opened the secret chamber.

"Close that!" Donato yelled, reaching up to grab the knife before Señor Bartolo could discover the contents, but he was not quick enough.

"Control yourself, boy, or you'll cause me to drop the relic into the stream," Señor Bartolo replied mischievously. Then working close to his chest so Donato could not easily interfere, he pulled the first wad of calking out of the knife handle and extracted the first two pearls. After removing his hat, he then tipped them out of his hand and into the crown so he could safely look them over.

"Ah! Just as I thought," he gloated, examining the pearls. "Don Tomas must have discovered oyster beds off Punta Prieta. These are enormous black pearls—the gems for which the waters of Baja California remain famous." Then, by clamping his hat to his chest with his left arm for safekeeping, he was able to use both hands to explore the remainder of the chamber. After extracting the other three pearls, he held up the silvery-blue gem, contemplating it.

"The very fact these were bequeathed to you by your venerable *abuelo* makes them doubly precious, no?"

Donato made no response. Instead, he bit his lip and watched a satisfied grin spread across Señor Bartolo's face as, one by one, he picked the gems up out of his hat and set them down in the hollow of his large palm where he swirled them around. "This land is mine by birthright. I am within my rights to pocket these without giving a second thought to a boy like yourself. However, since you seem determined to feel sentimental about them, I might find it in my heart to put them safely aside until you are older. Given time, we might even agree on their disposition!"

Donato stared back at Señor Bartolo with a look of pain and animosity smoldering in his dark eyes, but the man only laughed. "Come now, my boy! You should thank your Maker for the blessings he bestowed on you. Not only do you have good looks and make friends easily, but also, if what Ramón says is true, even the magnificent Azulejo distinguishes you with his approval. Not all the proceeds from the pearl harvest could purchase such gifts. When the time comes, perhaps you will be able to help me tame the wild stallion!"

Donato was so outraged by Señor Bartolo's presumptuous attitude, he blurted out a curt response. "Don Tomas is the rightful owner of this land, and no, he did not discover these pearls in oysters off Punta Prieta!"

Señor Bartolo's eyebrows fell into line like soldiers in a drill and he tightened his lips. "I see you still have much growing up to do and a great deal to learn!" As the man spoke his last word, feigning anger, he stabbed Donato's empty knife back into the cactus. His viewpoint made clear, Señor Bartolo turned, and silently marched over to the *fenómeno's* saddle, which he had draped over a nearby boulder, and opened up one of the saddlebags.

Donato wrenched his plundered heirloom back out of the cactus and glared after Señor Bartolo. He would like to have paid him back by taking something of his, but common sense told him this type of response would only bring his grandfather's adversary's vengeance down on him.

Since he held it within his rights to confiscate Donato's pearls, Señor Bartolo made no effort to conceal where he put them. Reaching into one of his saddlebags he took out a leather pouch containing a small blue vial, which he casually held up in plain view so Donato could watch what he was doing as he dropped the pearls into it.

When he was done, he corked the vial, slid it into its leather pouch, and stuffed it into his trouser pocket. Next, he opened a small painted tin and took out a handful of wrapped, hard candies, which he also slipped into his pockets. The first stage of his latest scheme concluded, he whistled victoriously and then sauntered off to inspect his hides.

After Señor Bartolo had finished inspecting the deer hides, he walked over to Ramón who was sitting in the hollow of a large granite boulder that was shaped like an armchair, enjoying his plate of beans and venison. Donato watched Señor Bartolo offer him some candies from his pockets and then invite him back to his lean-to to share a fresh pot of coffee.

Donato would have liked to intercept Ramón to inform him of their host's brazen seizure of his pearls, but Don Tomas had kept their existence secret, and Donato was sure Señor Bartolo would deny taking them. The solution was clear. He must conceive a plan to get the gems back on his own.

After dusk, Donato noticed the men preparing places to spread out their bedrolls. So, after he finished his dinner, he collected and trimmed a pile of palm mesh to serve as padding to sleep on, unrolled his bedding, and then pretended to lie down and go to sleep. He planned to wait for everyone else to drop off soundly, and then sneak over to retrieve the pouch containing the vial out of Señor Bartolo's pocket. However, for some inexplicable reason, he found himself struggling to keep his own eyes open.

* * *

When both boys awoke the next morning, they found themselves lying about three feet apart. *Pronto* and *Alazán* were nowhere to be seen, and there was no sign of Señor Bartolo or his men. Only feeble *Chispa* meandered through the mule fat and a small jenny grazed the swamp grasses growing beside the stream.

"*Caramba!* How did I get all the way over by you, and what made us both sleep so late!" Ramón exclaimed, groaning and looking around. "Señor Bartolo must have mixed one of Chico's 'remedies' into our coffee. I've got a terrible headache!"

"What will he do with our horses?" Donato asked, rubbing his eyes.

Ramón rested his head in his hands. "He will free them to find their own way home sooner or later, but it could be weeks before we see them again. And *Alazán! Qué lástima!* Once he is freed, he might take off for the Pacific Coast. It looks as if we've got nothing but bad news for Don Tomas," he said, heaving a sigh.

Now that Señor Bartolo had taken their horses, Donato thought there was a good chance Ramón would believe his story. Accordingly, he showed his friend the hidden chamber in the handle of Don Tomas' knife, and then described Señor Bartolo's shameless seizure of the treasure in pearls it used to contain.

At first, Ramón cursed like a grownup. "I'd ride after the scoundrel and demand he return what doesn't belong to him, but the thief didn't leave us any serviceable riding animals!"

Ramón's eyes fell on *Chispa* and his face brightened. The gelding had left off nibbling mule fat and stood with his head raised and his ears pricked forward as though listening for something faraway. Then it came—Donato and Ramón heard a distant whinny.

"That is *Alazán* calling to *Chispa*. The silly colt must have broken away from Señor Bartolo and is coming back to join the gelding," Ramón reasoned. "Quick! A rope! If we tie *Chispa* up, we might be able to catch *Alazán*!"

To their surprise, instead of showing up alone, *Alazán* arrived ridden by Don Tomas. Behind him came Luis ponying *Pronto* and Bruno leading Don Tomas' white mare, *Cenizas*, behind their horses. The boys noticed *Cenizas* stepping gingerly as though she had worn her hooves down during the long cattle drive. Don Tomas greeted the boys with a knowing twinkle in his eyes.

"How nice of Señor Bartolo to deliver *Alazán* to me right when I was in need of a fresh mount!" Then Don Tomas leaned to the right of his saddle and spat derisively as though speaking the man's name had sullied his lips.

Ramón heaved another sigh and then took it upon himself to report everything that had taken place since they first heard Señor Bartolo fire his rifle along the San Antonio Trail. Meanwhile, Donato looked sheepishly at the ground and scuffed the dirt with his boot.

After hearing Ramón's report, Don Tomas shook his head thoughtfully. "My best friend lost his life trying to safeguard one of his pearls from an avaricious man such as Señor Bartolo."

Donato was very relieved that Don Tomas did not appear to be angry with him. Instead, the old man remained seated on *Alazán* and put his chin in his hand as though thinking over the situation. "All the same, fortune should be on your side, Son," the wise man mused.

A glimmer of hope brightened Donato's face. "Considering Señor Bartolo handed our horses over without protest, do you think you might also be able to persuade him to return my pearls?"

"I doubt it, Son. For now, we will do best to leave the matter in God's hands. Have faith though. Although I know it sounds improbable, I suspect that providence just may bring them back into your life someday. In the meantime, rest assured that Juliano's pearls will never bring good fortune to a dishonorable man such as Señor Bartolo.

"The most urgent question facing us right now is how best to safeguard the magnificent wild stallion the insatiable Señor is trying to capture. I think the time has come when, for the animal's own protection, we would be advised to rope the Azulejo, brand him, and keep him in at our ranch."

*   *   *

In the time that followed, Señor Bartolo's men, as well as Don Tomas' men, searched and searched for the Azulejo stallion, but they never ran across so much as a trace of him. Two years would pass before a Pacific rancher made the long journey to Rancho La Primavera with news that froze Don Tomas' blood. The man reported that he'd found the remains of a feral blue roan with a white mane and tail. A bullet hole in its skull suggested tourists hunting wild sheep had shot the animal.

However, when Don Tomas rode to inspect the carcass, he found the animal's head was of a common type and that the desert sun had yellowed the silver mane and tail. "It's not *Espíritu*," Don Tomas announced with relief.

As time went by, however, it became reasonable to assume that either *Espíritu* had met his end in some undiscovered place or that an outsider successfully snared him and shipped him off to La Paz or the mainland. Over the next four years whenever *vaqueros* met on the trail, it became customary following the greeting, to inquire: "Have you come across any sign of the blue-eyed Azulejo stallion?"

CHAPTER 9

The Omen: Don Tomas' Shadow

EVER since Don Tomas' one-hundredth birthday, on the last day of December of each year, he traveled to San Antonio to indulge in a superstition passed on to him by a *mestizo* elder he knew in his youth. The following day, January 1, 1966, six months before Donato's twentieth birthday, Don Tomas stood facing the east wall of the church, watching for the first rays of dawn as he had done each New Year's Day for the past four years. Now, on the New Year's morning of his one-hundred-and-fifth year, he felt a sudden chill grip him. For the first time the sun had failed to cast his silhouette clearly upon the church wall, and he realized the shaman's omen had finally come true. His death was foretold sometime within the next twelve months.

Coming to terms with the omen, Don Tomas turned and faced the sun until warmth came over him and his head cleared. The sounds and smells of the *campo* coming to life at daybreak filled his senses, reassuring him that his faith in the ways of Nature would carry him through the hard year ahead.

He pondered for an hour or so on the meaning of his whole long life, and what he hoped would happen after he passed. Realizing that he had little time to wrap up his affairs, he decided his first priority was to ensure his legal papers were in order. To this end, he continued down the road to the town square. There, he knew his longstanding ally and friend, Don Paco, the magistrate, would help him with his will.

Don Tomas bequeathed his life's savings along with the house in La Paz to his wife and daughter, and then granted his animals and the Los Terrenos de Punta Prieta property to Donato. After the will was finalized, Don Paco not only notarized it, but he filed the document.

The following morning, Don Tomas headed back to Rancho La Primavera to continue settling his affairs and to have a long talk with his heir. During the journey, he wondered what the future would hold for Donato. He reflected on the many changes that had taken place in Southern Baja during his own lifetime, including the decline of the region's pearl, coper, silver, and gold mining operations. Now was the dawn of the tourist era.

These thoughts brought to his mind an old acquaintance from La Paz, a well-informed entrepreneur who was always looking for ways to capitalize on the tourist trade. Señor Gomez felt Rancho La Primavera would be the ideal setting to build a tourist resort. For many years, he had urged Don Tomas to sell some or all of his vast property and retire in La Paz, but Don Tomas showed no interest. Señor Gomez could not know that Don Tomas had been waiting for an omen.

After receiving the sign, Don Tomas knew the time had come to write his enterprising friend and invite him for another visit. Going into partnership with an influential entrepreneur would provide Donato with an ally in the times to come.

*   *   *

By January 2, 1966, Donato, now nineteen and a half years of age, bore little resemblance to the boy of sixteen standing in front of the cathedral in Mexico City feeding the pigeons. He had grown into a young man with a slim, wiry frame, and a thin mustache penciled his upper lip. His well-defined taut muscles were ready

ran deeper. For some reason, known only to Monsieur Dumas, he assumed responsibility for my education and enrolled me in the little Nuestra Señora de La Paz School for orphans that existed before the cathedral was built. He was a greedy and sometimes violent man, but in time, perhaps he became restless and even regretful of his sins. During the summers, I worked for him diving for pearls.

"I was relived when he left in a vessel bound for France after I turned fourteen. In case the ship foundered during the voyage, he sought to ensure his own salvation by granting a sizable donation of pearls to the church. I expect this contributed to the reasons his Excellency, Monsignor Escalante, had for looking after me.

"After Monsieur Dumas left Baja for good, Monsignor Escalante explained my origins to me. He told me I was the pearl merchant's illegitimate son, Tomas Dumas. Furthermore, he said my mother was a young mademoiselle who died of the plague soon after I was born. When I told the Monsignor that my friend, the town baker, wanted to become my godparent and give me his family name, Rienza, he approved. The Monsignor granted that since my father never openly treated me like a member of his own family, taking the baker's name was permissible. I agreed and he baptized me Tomas Rienza de Amaral. He then calculated my birthday to be October 6, 1861, which was also the historic date when he placed the first stone of Catedral Nuestra Señora de La Paz."

"That makes you the same age as the cathedral, *Abuelo*!"

"Yes, officially, we have the same birthdays," Don Tomas smiled with the recollection. "I was so pleased to finally have a legitimate birthday, I have kept perfect track of my age and have never forgotten when my children were born."

Donato considered how exciting and meaningful having an official birthday would seem to someone who didn't have one. Without a birth date, you were nobody in the eyes of the world. Might Don Tomas' delight in birthdays also explain the mystery of his unusually long life? Donato could picture him ascending to heaven with a smile on his face, saying to Saint Peter as he passed him by, "I held out until my one hundred and fifth!"

Doña Lupe appeared on the veranda carrying a tray set with glasses and a pitcher of tamarind drink. She carried it down the garden slope from the veranda and set the tray down on the small, round, one-post álamo table Donato had placed between the chairs.

"*Refrescos*," she said with a good-natured smile as she filled two glasses from the pitcher.

"*Ah, gracias*," Don Tomas replied, accepting one from her hand. After Doña Lupe left, Don Tomas turned back to Donato and continued his story while sipping his drink.

"After I received my baptism and official identity, Monsignor Escalante sent me to help the resident padres of the mining town of San Antonio with their ministries. In those days, San Antonio was a boomtown because of gold, silver and coper mining. The church in many ways offered the only basic services to the poor souls who had become destitute or needy because of the brutal working conditions.

"It was in San Antonio that I met Consuela, my first wife to be. At the time, I knew her only as the beautiful, well-bred young lady continuously presided over by her mother's watchful eye. Consuela would ride sidesaddle through town dressed in a long, colorful skirt like a dancer—a delicate veil of black lace covering her hair and draped about her shoulders."

The age melted away from Don Tomas' face as he beamed with the recollection. "I thought the Señorita liked me too, for when no one was looking, she would summon me to do small favors for her. I will always remember the first time she asked me to check her white gelding's curb strap. Right then, transported by the scent of her perfumes, I lost my young heart to her and resolved that someday I would marry her."

A shyness overcame the old man as he tapped the side of his glass with trembling fingers. Then he cleared his throat with a gruff sound and went on with his story.

"I found running errands for the unflagging padres quite a tedious occupation and continually looked for excuses to ride their old mule on jaunts into town. I liked to spend some of my free time loitering under the veranda of the San Antonio magistrate's office where Don Paco's great-uncle once presided over mining disputes. There, I listened in on the many interesting tales told by miners, and boatmen passing through town on their way to the coast. My favorite accounts were about a spooky section of the coast haunted by a ghostly horseman and curious, inexplicable lights thought to be the spirits of pirates. They told me fine horses and burros ran wild between the point and the two adjoining northern arroyo deltas. This news instilled in me the desire to travel there and try my luck at catching and taming the wild horses.

"My obsession with visiting the so called haunted wasteland paradoxically populated with beautiful horses so annoyed the San Antonio padres that after a time, they wrote a letter of complaint to Monsignor Escalante in La Paz, describing me as an inattentive daydreamer. However, to their astonishment, instead of sending me an official reprimand, Monsignor Escalante requested I travel to La Paz in person to speak with him."

Speaking in the voice of the monsignor, Don Tomas continued. "'I hear you are interested in catching and taming wild burros and horses,' he said, peering at me from under his *mitra* with penetrating eyes.

"And I replied, 'Yes, Your Eminence, I aspire to teach myself to become an accomplished horseman.'

"Then the Monsignor went on, 'I have an interest in furthering the silver and gold mining operations in the San Antonio area, but we are short of pack animals to transport ore. How would you like to breed mules for use in the service of the church?'

"'I would like that very much, Your Eminence,' I replied, bowing respectfully to him.

"The bishop unrolled some old property maps and looked them over. 'Then your wish shall be granted. From what I understand,

91

the stretch of land the wild horses roam is a haunted, godforsaken wasteland. Since neither of the adjoining deltas have any official name, I shall use my influence to combine them with the valueless, church-owned parcel called Punta Prieta. I will then see to it the entire tract is signed over to you free and clear. Expect an emissary to check your progress with the mules in a couple of years!'"

Donato thought the trace of a satisfied smile crossed Don Tomas' face as he continued. "As it turned out, the mining industry never picked up on a very grand scale; so in the years that followed, I managed my ranch and property exactly as I liked.

"I cultivated the oasis orchard by planting the land around the freshwater spring with the seedlings the padres gave me. I also erected this hacienda, built the corrals, and then set about catching and taming horses and burros from the bands that ran wild. Within a few years, I became known as a dealer of superior mules and saddle horses."

Donato wondered how Don Tomas must have felt settling the remote delta by himself. "Weren't you uneasy about starting out here with nothing but a mysterious ghost rider as your neighbor?"

Don Tomas laughed. "Rather than fearing the shimmering horseman of Punta Prieta, I prayed to him for his protection, and in truth, he seems to have stood by me. However, I experienced difficulty rounding up unsuperstitious *vaqueros* willing to help me manage my ranch, and it was some time before I could offer them competitive wages.

"What worried me most was how to court Consuela. Her mother was a proud woman from the genteel Mendoza family who built small sailing vessels from lumber brought from the slopes of Sierra de La Laguna. I knew better than to expect such a woman to accept an average suitor for her daughter.

"After I had saved up sufficient money from the sale of my *bestias*, I rode to San Antonio and asked for my sweetheart's hand. As expected, I was rejected by her mother. However, during the years that followed, Consuela refused all other suitors. It was not until after her twenty-seventh birthday that her parents eventually sent for me, and we were finally married.

"Nowadays, illness is the outgrowth of refined foods and unhealthy living. Barring injury, difficulties in childbirth, or say, the bite of a venomous reptile, one lives longest on clean air and natural, wholesome foods. But *hijo*, you must understand that even though living in the isolation of the wilderness has its wonders and beauty, the guidelines for survival are harsh and unforgiving. More so in years gone by when educated doctors were almost nonexistent in these parts.

"Even though I employed a midwife to keep her company and later deliver the baby, tragically, Consuela died with the birth of my first child, Sonya. Consuela lies buried up on the knoll behind the oasis. I transplanted a desert orchid tree next to her grave, for it was her favorite flower. I would like to be buried near her."

Donato was touched. "Shall we also plant a special tree beside your grave, *Abuelo*?"

"Yes," he reflected. "I would like my grave shaded by an attractive palo verde. It is a hardy, masculine tree and a complement to the frail, sweet-scented orchid that graces her grave."

"Your second wife passed away on the mainland?"

"Yes, Rosa Lucero from Rancho Salvatierra was from the uneducated *campesino* class. My two sons with Rosa, Fernando and Porferio, found positions on ranches near Guadalajara, and married well. Later on, Rosa also moved there so she could be near them. After she passed away, I took in Doña Blanca and her illegitimate baby, Maria Elena. Doña Blanca was Rosa's niece. I married her after she and her daughter had been with me a couple of years.

"Now, the only one of my children who stays in touch with me regularly is Sonya Balboa, who inherited my tendency to live an unusually long, healthy life. Because Consuela died in childbirth, Sonya was born an heiress to the Mendoza estate. As you know, Sonya's first child, your grandmother, Mercedes Balboa, married Carlos Esperanza, your grandfather on your mother's side. Sonya outliving her daughter, Mercedes, makes you a potential Mendoza heir.

"I have not visited Sonya since you arrived. She married a prosperous cotton farmer living on the outskirts of the large agricultural valley north of La Paz, called Santo Domingo. Perhaps I will arrange for Señor Lucero to drive us up there at the end of the month to visit Rancho Balboa. That way you can meet your great-grandmother, and I can pay her a last visit. I might also see about selling some of my *bestias* in the valley at the same time."

* * *

"Your family's dinner is ready to serve on the east veranda," Doña Lupe announced when she came to collect the empty pitcher and drinking glasses.

"We will be up momentarily," Don Tomas replied. "First, I would like to stroll down to the corrals and take a look at *Carbona*. Santo Domingo plantation owners pay good prices for large, gaited *bestias*, such as this filly."

Donato was relieved to have Don Tomas finally begin talking as though he were not planning to die.

Don Tomas continued, "Should I decide to keep *Carbona* instead of selling her, I was thinking I might try breeding her to Ramón's pacing jack this spring, *Pancho Villa*. The burro is very tall for a jackass and would make an excellent mule sire."

"What will you do if *Pancho Villa* won't cooperate?" Donato asked.

"Then, I shall breed her to my big black stallion, *Pico Blanco*, who I always breed my best mares to," Don Tomas answered. "Hopefully, the resultant horse-foal will inherit its dam's most sought after trait and also be gaited."

CHAPTER 10

Pico Blanco: A Tryst

DON Tomas had named his large, black stallion, *Pico Blanco*, for the triangular white marking extending halfway up his face. The name meant, White Point. Although *Pico Blanco* was a fairly ordinary-looking horse, to Don Tomas, he possessed an attribute that gave him claim to greatness. Not once did *Pico Blanco's* offspring take after him. Instead, they improved upon their dam's best attributes. The only thing Don Tomas did not appreciate about *Pico Blanco* was he occasionally sired unwanted twins. Nevertheless, when Don Tomas wanted a mare to produce a foal gifted with its dam's best qualities, he rounded up *Pico Blanco* and turned them both loose in a small pasture behind his orchard.

* * *

As chance would have it, for four years the wild Azulejo stallion's twin sister paired up with a feral jack roaming the foothills of Punta Prieta. Because of the Azulejo mare's height, this small burro consort was too short to mate with her, but the jack nonetheless somehow served to satisfy her instinct to find a virile mate when she came into season.

During these four years, the mare entered into periodic trysts with this burro, but always returned to her brother's side when they were over. This was until early in the spring of 1966 when, for some reason, Don Tomas' remarkable stallion, *Pico Blanco*, strayed from his usual browsing territory and ventured into the foothills of Punta Prieta. There, he stole the Azulejo mare, now entering the prime of her life, away on a three-month excursion to the Pacific Coast.

During his twin sister's absence, *Espíritu* climbed up the slopes of El Rey to the familiar crater valley to browse alone on the dry amaranth left from the previous rainy season. Once he reached the summit, he continued along its crest, occasionally pausing to scent the shifting breezes for their reports. Their odors might bring news of men out searching for him, and at other times they forecast the weather to come. But, most important of all, *Espíritu* knew the winds would tell him when his sister was returning home.

The only thing *Espíritu* never learned from the breezes was when to expect the guardian spirit of his youth to reappear. Sometimes, the ghost mare, *Azulina* would materialize beside him, as though intent on keeping him company while he browsed on the nutritious amaranth. At other times, he noticed her crossing the foothills below him, ridden by a shimmering ghost rider who seemed to be intent on keeping vigil over the territory.

Not until the last day of June did the winds bring *Espíritu* the news he had been waiting for. His twin sister, now in foal, was at last on her way home.

CHAPTER 11

Pancho Villa: The Drought

THE day *La Perla* returned home to Punta Prieta, came to pass two days before Donato's twentieth birthday. Donato's mission on this day was to dig out three different watering holes located on the southwest border of Don Tomas' land. This property belonged to Don Paco, the magistrate of San Antonio. He allowed Don Tomas to run his cattle on it so long as he assumed the responsibility for maintaining the water sources. Don Tomas only kept a few animals at each location, for he held that overcrowding caused the livestock to dirty the pools and strip the surrounding area of vegetation. Because of this policy, it was enough to have a lone horseman maintain each watering hole.

Two of the underground springs fed granite pools surrounded by meager vegetation. The third was a brackish pond called Terreno Hondo, or Deep Land. When the water table rose, the pool drained downstream through a hollowed-out palm trunk that emptied into a trough for the livestock. The problem was that the banks of this pond were comprised of nasty black silt that cracked in the heat like dried-out pudding. When water became scarce, the cattle tended to congregate and feed near the diminishing, stagnant pools. If a *vaquero* did not relocate them to a new water source, some strayed into the quagmire, which could swallow a struggling animal like quicksand.

This summer, the underground spring at Terreno Hondo had all but dried up, so Donato herded the small band of heifers that browsed the area onto the San Antonio Trail. His destination was the lush Los Cardonal oasis, about half a day's cattle-drive away. This oasis was located at the head of Los Cardenales Arroyo, which originated at the foot of the craggy Montañas del Búho range that marked the northwest boundary of Don Tomas' vast property.

Because the oasis marked the crossroads to many trails, this spot served as a convenient meeting place for the *vaqueros*. Here, beneath the ample shade of a great *higo silvestre*, or wild fig tree, many a campfire was kindled. The fig was a natural wonder that split enormous granite slabs with its serpentine roots; these marvels also provided a comfortable backrest for the weary. As Donato approached the campsite, the familiar smells of a mesquite campfire, coffee, and cigarette smoke filled his nostrils.

With a clatter of hooves and crack of his *ramal*, Donato ushered his bellowing little herd of heifers across the wide granite slabs and past the fig tree to the arroyo riverbed beyond. "*Ándale, vaquillas!*" he cried.

Chevalo, Luis, Bruno and a visiting *vaquero* were there, all on their way from Rancho La Primavera to Rancho Salvatierra. "*Eh! Que trueno del Diablo es esto?* What Devil's thunder is this?" they cried. "It's Donato! The ruffian will run us over and spill our coffee!"

Luis, the quiet one with twinkling eyes, simply sat back and grinned as Donato and the heifers disappeared over the side of the riverbank in a cloud of dust. He knew it was all in fun.

After leaving the heifers to browse on mule fat and swamp grasses down in the arroyo, Donato turned *Alazán* around and rode back up the bank to the fig tree. Now that he was regarded as Don Tomas' heir, the other workers always treated him deferentially and seldom intruded upon his activities unasked. This was why, for the most part, Donato was accustomed to opening their conversations.

"Good afternoon, *caballeros*. What brings you to the crossroads?" Donato queried, untacking *Alazán* and employing one of the fig tree's tall, eel-shaped roots as a saddle rack.

Being Don Tomas' foreman, it was Bruno's place to respond first. "Good afternoon, *Patrón*. You remember young Pepe Lucero from Rancho Salvatierra?"

"*Sí, buenas tardes,*" Donato replied, shaking the boy's hand.

Bruno continued, "Pepe has just returned from delivering a message to Don Tomas informing him that his guests from La Paz have arrived at Rancho Salvatierra.

"After riding to El Santo to purchase some supplies for Doña Blanca, Luis will ride over to Rancho Salvatierra to pick up the mail and escort Don Tomas' visitors to La Primavera. From Salvatierra, Chevalo and I plan to catch the bus to La Paz. There we will take in the sights and look for a gift to send my aged mother who lives in faraway Sinaloa, for her Saint's Day."

Donato was excited. "Señor Gomez has finally brought his friends to visit Rancho La Primavera! But why is Luis escorting them over the inland route rather than the less treacherous coastal trail?"

Bruno explained, "He is doing so at Señor Gomez' request. In the Señor's note to Don Tomas he explained that he is interested in scouting out the feasibility of putting in a road connecting El Camino Real with Rancho La Primavera. To this end, he brought his own riding animals with him by truck from La Paz—an imported American quarter horse and two Andalusians from mainland Mexico.

"The beautiful Andalusians are show horses, originally from Spain, and are known for their bravery in the bullring. Apparently, the Señor believes they are also excellent trail horses. Even so, we doubt animals foreign to the region will feel very secure on the scanty paths traversing the terrain between Rancho Salvatierra and Rancho La Primavera."

Chevalo spoke up next. "We were thinking we might even need to offer our visitor and his *gringo* friends *Pavo* and *Pancho Villa* to negotiate the treacherous pass over the Montañas del Búho foothills!"

After everyone had broken out laughing, Chevalo spoke up again. "Just imagine how inglorious our visitors would feel, exchanging their imported animals for our humbler but more trail-worthy burros!"

Donato left the men joking amongst themselves and led *Alazán* back down into the arroyo bed where he hobbled him and turned him loose to browse. When Donato returned, the men were still discussing Ramón's wild pacing burro, *Pancho Villa*. Ramón had caught and trained him over the last couple of years; the animal had now become a local celebrity.

Bruno was saying, "We teased Ramón that he must have ridden the jack for a good seventy kilometers the first day he rode him. It would take that long to reason with the creature! *Pancho Villa* set his head where he liked and refused to turn unless Ramón spooked him with his hat. This did not achieve much accuracy as to direction, and was probably the reason they traveled so far!"

Chevalo, who had been laughing too hard to catch his breath, joined in again. "Yes, and the burro also chewed through its tether in the night so Ramón tied him up with an old anchor chain he hauled up from the beach on a mule. He wrapped one end around a stump outside his house and then used baling wire to connect the other end to the rings of a short horsehair cinch he strapped around the poor thing's neck. For a long time, the creature could not be tied, except at home, and still took a great deal of patience to ride!"

But Luis defended Ramón's spirited burro. "Yes, that is all true, but now that I have been riding *Pancho Villa* once a week on the trek to Rancho Salvatierra to pick up the mail, he has settled down and become a reliable riding animal. I can rely on the speedy little beast not to stumble, even on the steepest trails. Also, because he does not sweat or require much water, he makes the round-trip faster than any horse; he is now my favorite mount for the trek."

As he kindled his own campfire under the tree, Donato continued to listen to the men. By the time he finished cooking his dinner and preparing his lunch for the following day, the men had all spread out their bedrolls and were lying down to sleep. But Donato had a lot on his mind. He set another log on the fire, leaned back against a fig root, and watched through half-closed eyes until the last campfire log gently popped into flames. He yawned and drew his blanket up, but before dropping off to sleep, he thought back over his conversation with Don Tomas in January, and pondered what the future had in store for him. How many more days might the old man live? Don Tomas had seemed eager for him to meet Elyse Sutton, the young lady from Texas who was planning to visit. Was he hoping a friendship, even a romance might spring up between them? The old matchmaker! And what of the illusive Azulejo stallion? Did he still roam somewhere out in the *campo*? And what about Don Tomas' implausible flesh and blood look-alike mystery filly? Did this creature actually even exist—or had this second Azulejo only been a figment of the old man's imagination?

CHAPTER 12

Whispers on the Breeze: Espíritu's Return

THE men were up at the crack of dawn the following morning and preparing to leave. After telling them farewell, Donato saddled and mounted *Alazán*, and then turned him onto Camino del Diablo, The Devil's Road. This path connected the upper part of the long Los Cardenales Arroyo with the western slopes of La Ballena, Cerro del Fuego, and the plateau called El Hornillo del Diablo, The Devil's Grill. His mission today was to dig out the small pool situated under the perennial falls of La Cañada oasis, a fertile canyon that divided El Hornillo del Diablo plateau.

Upon rounding the last big bend of Camino del Diablo, Donato's view of the gulf disappeared on the other side of Cerro del Fuego, and a mile and a half of startling green trees growing deep down in the bottom of a ravine stretched out before him. The drop down into the canyon made Donato's innards squirm involuntarily as though they felt a spontaneous instinct not to venture too close to the edge of the cliff.

Because *Alazán* deftly picked his way along the outside of the thorn bushes growing at the edge of the chasm, Donato vowed not to let him choose his own path thereafter. "The crazy horse must believe he could sprout wings if the cliff gave way," he muttered.

In dramatic contrast to the green oasis down in the ravine, nothing survived on this part of La Mesa Alta except cactus and stunted bushes bearing spiky thorns a great deal larger than the sparse leaves that appeared briefly during the rainy season. Small rodents and lizards were the only creatures to inhabit this expansive, inhospitable plateau all year round.

A small band of wild burros wound their way up the trail from the freshwater pool deep down in the oasis. These were the same shorthaired, Somali Wild Ass type of burro as *Pancho Villa*, and looked sleek and lively despite the drought conditions of that time of year. Among them was a silvery foal whose dainty velvet muzzle emerged from a dished profile covered in fluff. The eyes too, were large, dark, and luminous. Its ears, though long like a burro's should be, were delicately shaped and hued.

When this kind of burro shed its first coat, the fine hair of the ears turned a delicate rose-gray halfway up the ear, and silvery-white along the tip. These colors met in a faint, wavy line, reminiscent of the patterns Donato had seen on some seashells. As an enhancement to the beauty of this animal's natural markings, this *burrita* sported a white slash down the middle of her face. Because of its shape, Donato christened the little burra, La *Cometa*, The Comet.

Donato took one last look at the shimmering heat waves rising up off El Hornillo in spirals and long, wavy streams. Grateful to be entering the refreshing coolness of the oasis, he turned *Alazán* onto the long switchback trail leading down into La Cañada Canyon. Two thirds of the way down the trail, wonderfully revitalizing air currents invigorated horse and rider and the trickling falls made inviting music as the water spilled into the oasis pool.

Once at the pool, Donato tied *Alazán* to a stout willow tree and then proceeded to cut long, wooden handles for the shovel and mattock heads he had brought with him padded in sacking so they would not rub holes in his saddlebags. He sang the folk songs the *vaqueros* had taught him as he worked to widen and clean waterweeds off the pool, and heard the sound ricochet through the resounding cliffs, which amplified it like the walls of a natural cathedral.

The refreshing coolness of the oasis made Donato feel hungry, so he rinsed his hands and face at the edge of the pool, and then gave his attention to the small wicker basket of lunch he had brought tied in a square of flour sacking. There was a piece of the good white regional cheese, a small blue enameled pot containing cactus tamales, and a packet of candied fruits wrapped in brown paper. His stomach grumbled, and his mouth watered with joyful anticipation as he carried the basket toward a flat rock beside the pool.

Since leaving Mexico City, Donato had not looked at himself in front of a full-sized mirror. This was why he stopped to glance curiously at his image reflected on the pool's smooth, mirror-like surface. He was noticing how mature he looked, when a breath of air blew a fan of ripples across the image. When they cleared, the man looking back at him seemed to have grown even older. Had some trick of time dazed his mind?

Maybe he had been subjected to too much of the July heat and become *soleado* like the little old man in Punta Gorda who muttered of strange visions while tending his citrus trees. The villagers said the sun had taken his reason. Yielding to the spell, Donato imagined the breath of air he heard blowing down the canyon was whispering words in his ear: "The sea chest… Open the sea chest."

"Open the sea chest! What chest?" Donato wondered. If he was going to experience daydreams, let them concern something he was familiar with. He resolved to take better care of his health in the future. Don Tomas had cautioned him that too little food combined with sun exposure could cause delirium. Furthermore, Donato was a *huero*, meaning one with light skin; he must always wear a hat outdoors and keep his sleeves rolled down. He decided that from this day forwards, he would pay closer attention to Don Tomas' warnings.

Donato seated himself on the flat rock to eat his lunch and think over his experience. He decided he should head straight home after he finished widening the pool. Not only would Don Tomas' guests soon be arriving, but also tomorrow, Don Tomas planned to hold a party in honor of Donato's twentieth birthday!

* * *

Donato had finished wrapping the shovel and mattock heads back up in their covering of burlap when *Alazán* began to prance and neigh where he stood, still tethered to the willow tree. From far away, Donato heard a faint reply distorted by echoes. Soon, with his head held high and his silvery-white mane and tail streaming behind him like pennants in the wind, to Donato's amazement and joy, the long lost Azulejo stallion, *Espíritu*, came cantering into view along El Diablo trail above. The mysterious animal trotted down the winding path into the canyon and then came to a balanced stop at the edge of the oasis pool.

"Madre de Dios," Donato whispered to himself, wondering where the mysterious animal could have been hiding out. "Why does the shy Azulejo announce his arrival with such fanfare? Can he be overjoyed to find company after spending so much time alone?"

Espíritu breathed heavily for a moment through distended nostrils—his small, alert ears pricked forward as he surveyed Donato and *Alazán* with an intent expression. The perfect white spot on his forehead and the large deep-blue eyes set far out to the sides of his head suggested uncanny intelligence. Or, did this animal's shy ways, unusual blue eyes, and metallic coloring provide fuel for fantasy?

The Azulejo lowered his head and drank sparingly, showing good sense for a winded horse that probably had not drunk water for some time. When running free, the horses of Baja, adapted as they were to the dry climate, sometimes went two to three days without water, whereas horses from other parts of the world would perish from dehydration.

Because of the scarcity of feed, Donato would have expected the Azulejo's ribs to show under his skin, but he was in surprisingly good flesh. Only his coloring had changed with the season. Remembering the way Don Tomas likened a fine *bestia* to a gem pearl, Donato noticed the Azulejo's summer coat gleamed with a subtle, smoky gloss, just like the two black ones Señor Bartolo had stolen.

"Follow me back to the ranch, *Espíritu*, and I will gather choice green grasses and vines from Don Tomas' orchard for you. They will make your coat glimmer with blue highlights again like the surface of the blue abalone pearl."

In response, as if to assert his independence, *Espíritu* turned and sauntered off to the communal dust-bathing spot, which had existed since the last flash flood. Donato thought it comical how even the most magnificent horses lost all dignity when rolling in the dirt with their legs in the air. When *Espíritu* was done with his roll, he stood up and shook vigorously like a dog after a bath, causing the dirt to fly off in all directions except where it stuck to the sweaty patches on his chest and sides. Then he moseyed back to the pool to take one last long drink of water before resting under a giant *sauz*, or black willow.

Once again, Donato noticed how easily this animal camouflaged himself in his surroundings. In time of drought, instead of fading into the silvery leaves of the *higuera*, *guyacán*, white oak, and *amole* down in the arroyos, he blended into leafless trees, rocky cliffs, and enormous granite boulders.

Donato longed to ride *Espíritu* the way he had dreamed of doing, but he knew he must first win the wild horse's confidence. Therefore, he climbed up the side of the canyon to a spot above the waterfall that livestock couldn't reach, and collected a bundle of wild grapevines. When *Espíritu* noticed Donato gathering the vines, he nodded his head up and down with anticipation. Donato remembered Don Tomas' saying *Espíritu* was actually more timid than spooky, which was proven out by the way the animal stood calmly by without bolting. This was very different from *Alazán's* behavior the day Donato first tried offering him cut grass from Don Tomas' orchard.

Donato tossed a portion of the vines he had gathered to *Alazán*, and then set the remainder down on the top of a large, flat boulder. Unable to resist the offering, *Espíritu* walked tentatively up beside

Donato and began sampling the greenery. When Donato reached out to caress the strong, muscular neck with a closed hand, his knuckles left marks like finger-writing on a dusty pane of glass, revealing the smooth satin coat underneath. Once the stallion permitted him to touch his shoulder with an open palm, to increase his own height, Donato stepped up on a conveniently situated river rock. Once the wild creature had become accustomed to his altered stature, Donato began tugging on handfuls of his mane with even pressure, ending at the less sensitive wither area. When the wild horse was desensitized to the feel of human touch, Donato grasped a lock of his mane firmly in his left hand. Bending at the waist while keeping his left leg straight, in one smooth motion, he swung his right one low over the horse's back and eased into an upright sitting position in front of his withers.

Espíritu snorted and sidled away from his bundle of vines but did not try to buck or gallop back up the trail. With Donato talking soothingly to him, he soon edged toward his feed again. When *Espíritu* was done eating, Donato slid off his back and watched him trot partway up the trail, tossing his head and neighing repeatedly like a mare calling to her foal, as though asking Donato and *Alazán* to follow.

His work finished, Donato decided to find out what *Espíritu* was up to. He recalled the *vaqueros* saying the blue-eyed Azulejo was a *chiclán*, a term indicating a stallion with a retained testicle and poor fertility. Nevertheless, thinking in horse sense, Donato thought *Espíritu* might have gathered together one or two *mestizo* mares and was thinking himself a grand stud. He might begin by showing his acquisitions off to disinterested *Alazán*, who was also a stallion, and then pretend to defend them.

Alazán and Donato galloped behind *Espíritu* along the edge of the canyon, down Camino del Diablo, and into the Los Cardenales Arroyo riverbed where they bogged down for a short while in the deep sand. To Donato's surprise, before nearing Rancho La Primavera, *Espíritu* turned off onto the southern overland trail leading to faraway Punta Prieta.

CHAPTER 13

The Ghost Light: The Robbers

WHOA!" Donato yelled, pulling *Alazán* in a circle. "If you foolish nags keep running like this, *Alazán* will lose weight and Don Tomas will ground me with no riding privileges until the rains come!"

When *Espíritu* noticed his companions had dropped behind, he stopped ahead on the trail. When Donato held him back, *Alazán* responded by champing on his bit and impatiently pawing the sand with one hoof and then the other—his belly low to the ground in the attitude of a show horse standing at attention.

The horses had made good time galloping down from La Mesa Alta, leaving several hours of daylight. Donato felt confident Don Tomas would want him to learn all he could about the mysterious Azulejo's habits and hiding places, so he determined to continue following him.

When at last *Espíritu* reached Punta Prieta, he halted on a little rise to scent the wind and swiveled his ears, listening for unusual sounds. Donato was watching him, wondering what he would do next, when out of the corner of his eye he saw a shadowy horse-like shape flit swiftly and silently up a nearby ravine filled with otherwise noisy pumice. "Have I just seen Don Tomas' flesh and blood mystery-horse? It covers the ground without making a sound!" he whispered to himself.

Whatever the case, *Espíritu* ignored the horse-shadow and continued down the Southern Coastal Trail. Donato would have followed had he not been thrown into the air as though on the crest of a billowing wave as *Alazán* pawed the sky with his hooves. Something smooth and cold brushed Donato's cheek as a red-tailed hawk flapped from under the horse's chest. The bird carried a long black garter snake toward its aerie, located high up in the cuevas *volcán* situated in the cliffs overhanging the trail.

"Madre de Dios, Mother of God!" Donato exclaimed. Then he mused, "Quarry must be very scarce in this drought for a bird to become so emboldened. It seized its prey right from under a horse's chest! The superstitious would say it is a bad omen for a black snake to cross one's path, though surely for a hawk to swoop down and carry it away again is a portent of good. The signs disagree!"

Donato looked ahead on the trail for *Espíritu*, but he saw no fresh tracks on the windswept path. It was not until he turned and looked east toward the line of cliffs overhanging the rocky beach that he spotted the Azulejo standing tense and majestic against the backdrop of the blue gulf—his mane and tail streaming behind him in the offshore wind.

Suddenly, the sound of a rifle shot rebounded in echoes through the cliffs. Donato sat frozen in horror as the Azulejo reared its full height in the air before toppling over the side of the precipice to certain death in the treacherous body of water below. A groan escaped Donato's throat as though it came from someone else. Had the delay caused by the hawk saved *Alazán* and himself from a similar fate?

Getting a grip on himself, Donato dismounted and tied *Alazán* to a tree branch. He crept to the spot where *Espíritu* had fallen over the side of the precipice, but all he could see was dust, and all he heard was the sound of the waves surging against the rocks.

Donato was searching for a safe place to climb down over the section of sheer cliff face, when, further up the shoreline to the north, he spotted four men on a visible strip of the rocky beach. They were carrying a heavy object toward a skiff pulled high up on a sliver of sand. A fifth man stood on a boulder jutting into the surf, a rifle in his hands. Meanwhile, rising and dipping on the glassy swells, a small blue and white commercial fishing boat had anchored dangerously close to the reefs where Prieto Bartolo's ship foundered so long ago. With a rush of outrage rising in his breast, Donato wondered what kind of outlaws would dare to desecrate a grave and shoot a wild horse.

A haze of angry tears clouded Donato's eyesight as he ran toward the robbers along the cliff's edge. He might have pitched head first into an excavation that opened up in front of him had he not grabbed hold of a handy tree branch. A rectangular imprint in the bottom of the pit left no doubt in his mind; the robbers had robbed the legendary nobleman's grave of the sea chest filled with valuables. Human and animal bones littered a mound of earth on the far side.

Looking up he noticed a stout block and tackle swinging from a tree limb. It dangled down the side of the cliff directly across from the rifleman who stood at the water's edge on the beach below.

Only a terrified Prieto Bartolo or a fool of a man driven by greed would have taken the trouble to hoist the chest up or down such a treacherous precipice. Donato's fury and *Alazán*'s sure-footedness must enable him to intercept the grave robbers before they could ferry the nobleman's valuables to their boat.

When Donato returned to fetch *Alazán* where he stood still tethered to the cat's claw tree, the horse sensed his agitation and sidestepped nervously. Donato mounted him, rode up to the head of the precipice, and then for the first time applied the spurs that until now, he had worn primarily for decoration and their jingling bangles.

Startled *Alazán* responded by leaping over the edge of the precipice with no thought as to whether there were earth or air beneath his feet. Sparks flew off the ledges in the cliff as his hard hooves sought the irregularities in their surfaces with swift dexterity.

When the robbers turned to look, they halted their labors and stood slack-jawed with astonishment. Donato and *Alazán* were hurtling down the precipice with the agility of a mountain goat and the power and purpose of a mountain lion descending upon its prey. The membranes of the horse's distended nostrils were tinged with red from exertion as it slid down the last part of the cliff in a landslide of shale and rolling stones. Momentum carried horse and rider over the slippery green stones exposed by the low tide, past the man with the firearm, and into the lip of the sea. The water buffered their forward motion and helped the horse to come to a stop.

While the robbers stood staring, Donato wheeled *Alazán* around and, with the swift and well-practiced ease of an accomplished *vaquero*, tossed the loop of his lariat over the man holding the rifle and drew it taught. Dragging the rifleman through the surf to his horse's side, he snubbed him to his saddle horn with two loops of the lariat, relieved him of his rifle, and tossed it into the sea.

"*Cochinos!* Dirty pigs!" Donato shouted in fury at the stunned robbers.

"The Spaniard's curse will wreak vengeance on you!" he threatened them. "You have stolen chattels that belong to the owner of this property, Don Tomas Rienza." Then thinking of another way to frighten the robbers off his *abuelo's* land, he fabricated a deception.

"Don Tomas and his *vaqueros* are riding along the trail above at this very moment! Neither he nor his men will show mercy to robbers who have plundered the Spaniard's grave and shot a valuable animal, especially the priceless Azulejo stallion! They will lasso you and drag you over the rocks until your bones break, as I plan to do to this horse killer here!"

The sputtering half-drowned crook hung like a sack of wet meal from Donato's saddle horn. Using a rawhide hobble, Donato secured the man's wrists behind his back and then undid the lariat so he could stand upright.

"Now speak! Your mother is a sow, you pig! Talk! Tell me how you came to know of the Spaniard's grave and what made you rob it and shoot the wild stallion! Answer me before I drag your useless carcass over the boulders behind my horse. Or, I might save you for Don Tomas's *vaqueros*. They would drop you from the top of the cliff to die on the rocks like the stallion whose worth was greater than the sum of all your miserable lives combined!"

"Mercy young Señor! I beg you!" the writhing robber pleaded. But Donato had run out of patience.

"All the same, I am too impatient to wait. Look! Your companions have abandoned the sea chest and are scurrying to your dinghy like rats. You must talk fast if you want to join them! The lot of you will never be permitted to return to these parts. You will be arrested, tried, and shot!"

The man choked and struggled, trying to speak in a wheezy, water-soaked gasp. "No, Señor! You have my word we will never return; by my mother's eyes! I will tell you what happened. When Señor Bartolo was drinking in the La Paz cantina, he told us the story of the grave and hinted at treasure, as drunken men will do. He said that whoever sought it must beware of the ghostly stallion with the white mane and tail that possessed strange powers. I do not ignore such warnings nor do I scoff at stories of treasure, for I once found pirate treasure on Espíritu Santo Island. Most of the profits went to the government, and my portion is long spent." He began to whimper, "Please, Señor, untie me and let me go. My wife is ill and I needed the money."

Donato grabbed the man by his belt and snubbed him closer to the saddle horn so his dangling legs would be out of *Alazán's* way. The crook groaned and begged for mercy as they made their way to the dinghy, which his comrades were hastily pushing into the water. There Donato freed his captive from his bonds and dropped him on the stern of the boat right as the prow dipped into the surf.

Taking his right foot out of the stirrup, Donato spurred the last two men to board it in the buttocks, and before they were out of reach, cracked his *ramal* across their backs. The snap of the lash made a satisfying sound, along with the cries of distress it elicited from the robbers.

"Go!" he shouted. "None of you are worth taking the trouble to make into carrion!"

Donato remained seated in his saddle with fierce eyes and a grim smile until the dinghy had reached the ship's landing stage. The grave robbers hurried on board, and then hoisted the dinghy out of the water just as the ship raised anchor and started forward. It then circled around and started out full throttle for La Paz.

With a pang of anguish, Donato thought of *Espíritu*. If the fisherman's bullet didn't kill the Azulejo, Donato was sure his fall onto the treacherous rocky shore below finished the job. Nonetheless, wanting to confirm the stallion's fate, he loped surefooted *Alazán* along the base of the hazardous cliffs, searching for the carcass, until a sheer bluff that divided the beach stood in his way. By then, the sun had dipped behind El Rey, and it would soon be dark.

With a heavy heart, he returned to the spot where the robbers had abandoned the sea chest and turned his attention to *Alazán*. He removed all his tack with the exception of the bosal, and then led him into ankle deep seawater. He used a square of flour sacking to rinse *Alazán*'s legs and belly before wetting his shoulders and haunches, the way Don Tomas had taught him. This sequence of actions prevented cramping of the animal's larger muscles by allowing the blood to cool in the lower extremities first. Next, Donato checked his horse's legs for possible injury resulting from his harrowing descent down the cliff. When he lifted each hoof, he found that except for a few nicks and scratches, the splendid chestnut was as sound as ever.

After Donato finished massaging and rinsing the stallion's coppery red coat, he utilized a smooth chunk of driftwood to scrape *Alazán* dry. Then he led him back up to the abandoned chest and looped his *cabresto* around a large piece of driftwood so the tired animal could stand and rest.

"Now what to do with the heavy chest?" Donato mused. Even though the robbers had left their block and tackle behind, a single man could not be expected to hoist something so heavy back up the side of the cliffs to the grave in the dark.

Only the pale light of the third quarter moon and stars illuminated the unfamiliar landscape. He must wait until dawn, drag the heavy chest to the bottom of the cliff like fabled Prieto Bartolo, and then hoist it up to the gravesite by the morning's light using the robber's block and tackle. "Prieto must have possessed the strength of ten men," he muttered.

Donato stood staring at the chest, praying the nobleman's ghost would understand, when the sound of the quiet surf washing rhythmically over the sand like a surging pulse intruded upon his thoughts. Again, he imagined he heard a whisper like the one blowing down the canyon.

"Open the chest," the swishing waves seemed to say. To Donato, anything seemed possible in this strange place. He wondered, "Could this be the whispering voice of the ghost whose grave had been defiled?"

He took the mattock head out of his saddlebag and used it to scrape the corroded fastenings off the side of the chest. When he pried the lid open, the bending metal groaned as a person might when aroused from a deep sleep.

When Donato looked inside, his suspicions were confirmed. The heavy, well-sealed chest had preserved an assortment of articles once belonging to an 18th century Spanish noble. Lying on top were some ornate clothing, boots, weapons, and a spyglass. The rest of the chest was filled with the gold coins and silver and gold trinkets the robbers, Prieto Bartolo, and the pirates had been after. However, there was also a logbook or diary manuscript, and a leather case containing old documents, maps, and a bundle wrapped in a square of velvet. Curious what the bundle might contain, Donato spread it out on top of the logbook and unwrapped a headstall decorated with tarnished silver rosettes. Tied to it was a small pouch containing a turquoise bead on a thong. Strands of white mane hair remained knotted in it, as though it once adorned an Azulejo's forelock.

The last article in the chest was a box containing a painting displayed in a gilded wooden frame. It was getting dark, but by tipping the painting one way and another, Donato thought he could just distinguish the subject matter. Then his eyes, accustomed as they were to the desert nights, began to focus. Now he thought he discerned the vague shape of a horse and rider. "Ah, yes! A young nobleman sits astride a dark-bodied horse that has a contrasting light mane and tail!" A brass plaque at the bottom of the frame read:

> Don Diego Montenegro en La Azulina

Donato was astonished. Could this be a portrait of the legendary nobleman mounted on the ghost mare of legend? The animal had no white on its forehead, but distinctive white anklets encircled each rear coronet. How intrigued Don Tomas would be to learn of the painting's existence and, at the same time, how mortified to learn about *Espíritu*'s tragic end.

Donato was fumbling in the pocket of his slacks for a match to light, when suddenly he realized he was already seeing the picture more clearly and caught his breath. How could he discern any of the painting's detail in this dim light? Except..., except..., a spooky luminescence in the air seemed to be gradually growing brighter! Donato peered timorously at *Alazán* over the lid of the sea chest. Surely, if anything were amiss, the stallion would spook, but *Alazán* still seemed to be dozing peacefully.

Donato wondered what he would see when he turned around. Would he behold the specter of Prieto Bartolo looking greedily at the chest? Or, might he see the nobleman's spirit wrapped in a ghostly shroud?

Instead, the sight that met Donato's eyes made him think of Doña Blanca's words when she recited the legend:

"To this day, the sightings of strange ghostly lights seen floating over Don Tomas' land are thought to be the spirits of Prieto and the pirates searching for the treasure." Suspended in midair about forty feet above his head like a spider on a thread, a luminous round light appeared to stare down at Donato like a personage peering in at him from another world. Then, as though it had merely stopped by on its way to more rewarding activities, having satisfied its curiosity, the phenomenon swooped abruptly up over the bank and disappeared into the desert sky—leaving the beach once more engulfed in darkness.

The ghost light had just left the beach, when a horseman riding along the coastal trail above in search of Donato, thought it looked as though the moon had flown out of the sea and up into the night's sky. "Madre de Dios!" he exclaimed pulling his horse to a halt. "There goes one of those curious lights!" He pulled his *caracol* out of his saddlebags and blew a long summons.

When Donato heard the call, he also reached for his sea conch. He had just finished blowing two answering peals when *Alazán*, who had been staring intently at the surf with his ears pricked forward, signaled him with an excited nicker. The distinctive sound of a swimming horse blowing through its nostrils answered him. Suddenly, Donato knew. Perhaps miraculously guided by an unseen hand, *Espíritu* must have escaped certain death by plummeting straight into a deep tide pool. Donato was so excited he spoke aloud to himself. "*Espíritu* has been navigating the shore ever since, searching for a passage through the rocks!"

Quickly, Donato seized the mattock and pried up some of the large, slippery boulders at the water's edge. Then to his amazement and joy, the trembling Azulejo scrambled onto the beach and shook himself like a dog after a bath.

Donato no sooner ran his hand over the horse's left shoulder than the animal sidled away. He could feel the warm moisture of blood on his fingertips.

Guessing *Espíritu* had swallowed seawater, Donato poured the contents of his water bottle into a cooking pot he carried in his saddlebags and then let the horse drink it up in long, noisy gulps.

Pedro shone a flashlight over the cliff's edge above and looked down. "What a strange place to spend your birthday, *Primo*! What are you doing down there, fishing for octopus?"

"*No, tonto!* Stupid. *Espíritu* was shot by robbers and then fell over the side of the cliff!"

"*Qué bárbaro!* What evil news is this?" Pedro muttered.

"We need help down here! It's a miracle! The Azulejo survived his fall! Bring water!"

"*Qué milagro!* Alright, but how do I get there?"

"Ride south along the cliff's edge to the spot where the robbers plundered the nobleman's grave. You can let yourself down by the block and tackle they left hanging just north of there."

"Alright, I'll be right down."

Now the respectful custodian of the sea chest and curator of its contents, Donato felt a solemn responsibility to sense what Don Diego would want. While Pedro was figuring out how to climb down, he quickly hid the painting, the diary manuscript, and the headstall in one of *Alazán*'s spacious saddlebags.

When Pedro showed up, he helped Donato drag the chest into the back of a small, dry cave. Then Pedro rode *Alazán* and Donato followed on foot, leading *Espíritu*. When they reached a spot further north where the high bluffs dropped down to a low bank, they climbed it, backtracked along the cliff to fill in the nobleman's plundered grave, collected Pedro's horse, and then started on the long journey home.

CHAPTER 14

The Birthday: Elyse

DONATO awoke to see Ramón's cheerful face looking down at him. "Happy birthday, lazybones! It's mid afternoon already and everyone is eager for your birthday party to begin! I intended to wake you an hour ago, but everything happened at once. I was hanging up decorations for your fiesta when Luis and our important visitors rode up, Señor Alejandro Gomez and his American friends. Luis asked me to drop what I was doing, unpack the mules, and carry our guest's luggage to their rooms. Such a lot of stuff they brought too—bags and books, a typewriter, binoculars, cameras, and a tripod. You would think they planned to stay for a year!"

Ramón held up a white embroidered dress shirt and a pair of jeans sewn out of brushed, black denim. "Here is your first *regalo*, a gift from Doña Blanca. *Que elegante, no?* She had these clothes specially tailored by Señora Hernandez in Punta Gorda. Doña Blanca said not to worry if you should soil the shirt. Today is your birthday! Relax and be happy, amigo! Here, I'll lay your new clothes out on the bed for you."

Donato wished Ramón would stop talking and let him wake up slowly so he could remember his dream. Then, all of a sudden, Donato realized it was not a dream at all he had been trying to remember but events from the previous day. He sat up at once, "How is *Espíritu* doing?"

Ramón's eyes sparkled, "The Azulejo is doing well. Imagine having him in a corral! I helped Don Tomas give him a drench for infection and pack his bullet wound with lomboy. Now he's acting as though he'd rather be left alone."

"*Pobrecito*! Poor thing!" Donato exclaimed. "He isn't used to being handled and will probably turn his back on me too now."

"Also, we branded him."

"Branded him?"

"Yes, Don Tomas says that without a brand, the Azulejo remains at risk. Should anyone else want to claim the stallion, all they would need to do is steal him and do the same. We must pony him to San Antonio next week to get his markings and the fresh Rancho Primavera RP brand legally recorded with Don Paco, the magistrate of San Antonio, who records the ownership of all Don Tomas' animals."

Donato gave a sigh. "The thought of disfiguring the magnificent Azulejo's sickens me, but I suppose Don Tomas knows best. Now tell me about our visitors from La Paz."

"They seem nice enough, especially the girl. Actually, I am a little envious you speak her language so well. Ramón dropped his tone to a confiding whisper. "The Señorita is fun and *muy bonita*! She has been asking a lot of *preguntas* but does not understand Spanish. Señor Gomez has been acting as her interpreter, but since he has also been trying to discuss business with Elyse's father, Mr. Sutton, Don Tomas has suggested that you show her around the ranch grounds."

Donato was fully awake now and laughed, "Why don't you escort her around? This would give you an opportunity to practice some of the English I have been trying to teach you."

"Yes, I have learned some new vocabulary, but not nearly enough. I learned that binoculars are *gemelos*, and panniers are *aparejos*. 'Where is my father' means *donde està mi papá*, and 'What is this' is *Que es esto*? How is that for a start?"

"That's very good, Ramón! Also, *muy bonita* means 'very pretty'!"

"That's what I said; she is very pretty," Ramón answered with a twinkle in his eye. "Don Tomas seems to think you and the Señorita will get on really well."

"Don Tomas assumes too much," Donato muttered, looking embarrassed. "I don't intend to let some frivolous *gringa* turn my head!"

"I wouldn't be too sure if I were you," Ramón observed playfully. "Don Tomas is gifted with uncanny insights." Ramón chuckled at Donato's annoyed expression, then left through the door.

"Why don't you go dunk your head in the creek before you get dressed?" he suggested. "You still look half-asleep. I must tend to the *caballo*s that came in—I mean horses. The *pobrecitos* have been standing out there cooling down for a couple of hours now."

Donato realized that with Bruno and Chevalo gone on their vacations, he would be celebrating his birthday party with the women of Don Tomas' household, Don Tomas, Pedro, Luis, Ramón, and the newly arrived strangers. Suddenly, he had to admit to himself how nervous he was feeling about meeting Elyse, especially as he was sure everyone would be watching them to see how well he and she would get along. Besides that, he hadn't heard fluent English spoken for some time—what if he couldn't think how to reply to her.

After going and rinsing his head in the creek, Donato returned to his room, dressed hurriedly, picked up the sack containing the manuscript, the painting, and the Spanish headstall, and then tucked the package under his arm. After leaving his room, he tiptoed down the hallway leading to the east veranda, stopped in front of the curtain that hung in the doorway, and peeked out.

The rafters were hung with tinkling chimes and bright crepe-paper streamers fluttering in the breeze, while beyond the porch, a colorful burro piñata dangled from a tamarind tree.

Don Tomas sat at the head of the smaller of two dining tables. Stacks of presents wrapped in brown paper and tied with colored cord were piled in front of him. To his right, Pedro was sitting back in a rocking chair, still looking half-asleep. To Pedro's right, the tall impressive mustachioed bulk of Señor Alejandro Gomez reclined in a comfortable palm-rope hammock suspended from the rafters. Farther down the veranda, the women and ranch hands chattered around a larger dinner table loaded with tasty dishes. Donato's attention, however, had focused on the activity directly in front of him where Mr. Sutton and his daughter, Elyse, stood talking just outside the veranda.

From Donato's perspective, the pale blue background of the distant gulf framed Elyse's comely form. True to what he expected a *gringa* naturalist might wear, she was dressed in light hiking boots, khaki slacks, and a plaid sport shirt. However, a green and yellow scarf rolled into a headband and the sparkle of a small diamond pendant featuring a white pearl, added a feminine touch. As she moved her head, copper highlights sparkled in her glossy auburn hair. Now and then, when she tossed it back over her shoulders, Donato caught a glimpse of her winning smile and sparkling green eyes. Even though Elyse was quite a bit older, her reddish-brown hair, poise and gestures, reminded him of his auburn-headed little sister Anna. He had tried not to dwell on his personal losses, but he still secretly mourned his family's passing. In time, could this attractive American girl also come to seem like family to him?

Donato was just bending down to lean his package against the inside wall of the curtained veranda doorway, when Maria Elena emerged from the entrance to the kitchen behind him, carrying a platter of cheese and fruits intended for the visitors. Donato greeted her with a smile, pulled the curtain aside, and ushered her ahead of him through the entryway.

"You look very elegant!" she whispered, returning a dimpled smile as she passed him with a rustle of skirts. "Happy Birthday!"

"Thank you," Donato replied, glancing bashfully down at the earthen floor while following her out onto the veranda. Halting outside, he braced himself to look up and face the assemblage. "Good afternoon," he announced, shyly doffing his hat.

Don Tomas immediately stood up and proudly introduced his heir to the newcomers. Although Elyse and her father didn't understand very many words of Spanish, Don Tomas addressed them as though they did, and Señor Alejandro Gomez—acting his part as gracious guide to a remote part of the world—interpreted for them.

Trying to attract everyone's attention, Don Tomas picked up a little brass bell sitting near him on the table and gave it a short jingle. "Let me introduce our birthday boy, my grandson Donato Perry! Donato is heir to my estate. He is also the young man who so valiantly apprehended the grave robbers yesterday. Let us sing him, Happy Birthday, *Feliz Cumpleaños!*"

Señor Gomez, Don Tomas, and Pedro began singing a rendition in Spanish and then the group sitting around the employees' table further along the veranda joined in. When the locals had finished singing, Señor Gomez motioned to Elyse and Mr. Sutton to join him in English. When everyone had finished singing, Donato removed his hat, bowed, and then self-consciously brushed his curly brown bangs away from his forehead.

Don Tomas motioned to Donato to pull chairs up to the table for the guests and to seat himself next to Elyse. Donato hoped she would attribute his shyness to embarrassment at the mountain of presents stacked on the table in front of Don Tomas.

Elyse, on the other hand, had expected Don Tomas' heir to be a weatherworn *vaquero* well over middle age. Instead, here was a good-looking young man with an athletic build, courteous manner, and well-spoken English.

Fortunately for Donato, Elyse initiated their conversation. "Glad to meet you! Your last name is Perry—an English last name!"

"Yes, my father's parents were English and German immigrants to the United States who settled in Texas."

"How about that! I am also from Texas. You have been to Texas?"

"When I was thirteen. When I was twelve, my father took me to visit a Mayan dig located in the jungles of Southern Mexico, hoping that like him, I would become interested in the study of archeology. However, while we were there, he noticed that instead of becoming interested in archeology, I liked to study the wildlife. This was when he wondered if I might like to become a veterinarian. Later in the year he took me along on a business trip to Texas to meet and talk with my uncle Stanley, who is a dog, cat, and exotic animal vet in Austin."

"Your father is an archeologist? How interesting! Where is he living now?"

"My parents and two sisters passed away in an automobile accident in Mexico City in 1961 when I was sixteen. This is the reason I came to live with Don Tomas in Baja California. Believe it or not, he is not really my grandfather, but my great-great-grandfather!"

Donato was about to mention to Elyse that she reminded him of his younger sister, when Don Tomas interjected a suggestion in Spanish.

"Donato, Señor Gomez and our guests from the United States might be interested to learn of our local legend and about the details of your recent trip to Punta Prieta."

"Alright," Donato replied, acknowledging Don Tomas and then turning back to Elyse. "My *abuelo*, that is my great-great-grandfather, thinks you, your father, and Señor Gomez might be interested to hear our local legend. Also, about the experiences I had yesterday that substantiate the local folklore. I can switch from English to Spanish so as to include everyone in the conversation."

Mr. Sutton and Elyse listened attentively as Donato related the legend. Their reaction reminded him of his own incredulity the day he first heard the tale from Doña Blanca. He ended by recounting the details of his meeting with *Espíritu*, the grave, the robbers, the chest, and the inquisitive, luminous orb.

Pedro perked up at mention of the light. "I also witnessed the phenomenon," he began with Donato interpreting. "It sailed off into the night sky like a celestial spirit going up to Heaven. It was a most curious sight!"

Don Tomas nodded, "That might be one explanation. However, what you describe reminds me of the lights we used to see out at sea when I was a boy diving for pearls. The fishermen called them *lucernas*.

"Remarkably, they seemed unaffected by the wind or the forces of nature. They would sometimes hover motionless above our heads, or vanish and reappear at will as though governed by some contrary science. Then, like a vision from another world, just when they had beguiled our interest, they would disappear completely. Although children and simple folk sometimes saw them, for some whimsical reason, these shy curiosities never revealed themselves to anyone who might be able to offer a scientific explanation."

Judging by Señor Gomez' expression, Donato guessed he did not give folklore much credence, but Elyse and her father seemed more open-minded.

"How intriguing!" exclaimed Elyse. "I wish the orbs would show up sometime when I am around. I would like to get a look at them!"

After Donato interpreted, Don Tomas winked. "Perhaps someday they will!"

Donato wondered whether he ought to show Don Tomas the artifacts he had taken from the nobleman's chest in front of the guests, but he knew they would also be interested after hearing his account, so he got up and retrieved the package from the doorway. After pulling the manuscript, headstall, and painting out of his sack, he set them down on the table in front of Don Tomas.

"What treasures have we here?" the old man asked with delight and amazement.

"Relics I borrowed from the sea chest the robbers dug out of the grave," Donato replied.

With childlike delight and keen perceptivity, Don Tomas studied the painting, nodding his head knowingly as he examined it. "The horse's coloring and body type are similar to the Azulejo stallion. It is her longer legs, the shape and length of her ears, and the outline of her head that differs." He pointed to the ornate bridle. "Look! The Azulejo mare in the painting wears a headstall just like the one you discovered in the chest. Donato! Why don't you ask the Señorita whether she would be willing to take photographs of *Espíritu* wearing his magnificent Azulejo grand dam's headstall?"

Elyse was delighted with the idea. "I will set up my tripod and use a telephoto lens. This will enable me to photograph your wild stallion from a distance without intimidating or scaring him."

"Maybe Ramón can clean this old headstall up for us," said Don Tomas.

Ramón, who was eating dulces at the end of the ranch help's dining table, noticed Don Tomas beckoning to him. Stuffing one last sweet into his mouth, he got up to find out what his employer wanted.

"Do you think you could polish this headstall for us, lad?" Don Tomas gave a wink, "It will be a good test of Donato's horsemanship to see whether he can bridle the Azulejo stallion with it!"

"Well, I'll be. This certainly is an elegant piece of tack," Ramón commented, holding it up reverently and looking it over. Then he studied the painting the same way Don Tomas had done, and afterward reexamined the headstall. "They are the same!"

"Yes, don't let news of these relics reach Señor Bartolo's ears! Donato borrowed them from the sea chest the robbers pulled out of the grave yesterday. We think that in all likelihood, this painting depicts the legendary ghost rider and his mare."

When Ramón dropped the headstall on the table, crossed himself, and stepped back, Don Tomas laughed. "Nothing to fear, lad! Don Diego's spirit will do you no harm. I am sure it gratifies him to have us honor his splendid mare's memory. You can safely pick the headstall up again!"

"You sure?"

"Yes, sure!" Don Tomas leaned closer to Ramón, and then motioned to him to bend down so he could whisper something in his ear. "Psst! Take your time. I will see to it the cooks save you plenty of food!"

Next, Don Tomas addressed his guests, "Now, let us all watch Donato break open his piñata and unwrap his presents!"

Everyone gathered round the tamarind tree while Maria Elena positioned Donato near the piñata. After tying a blindfold over his eyes, she spun him around a few times, put a stout stick in his hand, and then directed him toward the target with a push. However, every time Donato tried to hit the piñata, it only swung away from him.

Pedro urged him on. "Come on, *Primo*! Break the piñata before nightfall or we won't be able to find the candies! You have four hours; do you think you can do it?" In the end, Donato gave up, but Pedro, who was more practiced, broke it open with a blow across the top, scattering candies everywhere.

Ramón soon brought the headstall back looking like new. He had polished the buckles and Spanish rosettes using a fine clay paste. He had also lined the underside of the heavy cheek-straps with soft deerskin, which he secured in place with woven Turk's Heads. To keep the bit he had attached to the headstall from injuring the wild horse's sensitive mouth, he added a rolled leather bosal and *cabresto* to lead him by. A separate rawhide headstall supported the bosal.

Ramón handed the tack to Donato and then spoke softly in his ear, "Be careful, amigo, *Espíritu* is no longer the tired pony you brought in last night and has turned *mañoso*. I put him over in the sandy corral where we break the young broncos."

Don Tomas' household all gathered behind Elyse's camera tripod to watch Donato and the Azulejo stallion from a respectful distance. *Espíritu* was pacing around the corral, seeming to divide his attention between the *campo* over the fence and Donato who cautiously approached with the newly refurbished bridal, added bosal, and horsehair cabresto. With his searching looks and occasionally throwing his nose up to scent the air, *Espíritu* seemed annoyed by the approach of the horseman.

Although Donato's attention was on the task of the animal's capture, at the same time he began to understand. He wondered about the shadowy form he had spotted in the ravine at Punta Prieta. Was it possible *Espíritu* sensed a wild mare nearby, or possibly even the presence of the phantom?

Donato, now an experienced horseman, knew that dealing with obsessive behavior in a stallion called for discretion. His priority was getting the animal to give him his undivided attention. To this end, he left *Espíritu* to continue his pacing and walked up to the stockroom located on the west veranda. There, he picked up a short, stiff, rawhide lariat that was too thick to tangle around the animal's legs. As he was walking back toward the corrals, he secured the honda so it would not slide. Next, he entered the bronco pen and tossed a wide loop over *Espíritu's* head so it would settle low on his shoulders, intentionally allowing the free end to trail behind the horse on the ground.

"*Cálmate, Espíritu, cálmate*," Donato called quietly to the agitated stallion. The moment *Espíritu* felt the trailing end of the lasso tickling his flanks, he stopped to snort and kick at it. Finally, when receptive to help, he turned to face Donato.

Donato took a few steps toward *Espíritu*, causing him to back up and drag the lariat in front of him along the ground. The stallion's eyes flashed as he threw his nose defiantly in the air, "sky nosing," while Donato picked up the end of the lariat and walked toward him trying to back him into a corner of the corral. As soon as Donato was close enough to do so, he reached out and touched his neck the way he had done at the La Cañada oasis.

"*Bonito potro, cálmate, cálmate*," he soothed, looping the lariat into a simple rope bridle, which he secured around *Espíritu's* nose. Next, Donato took the refurbished tack from over his shoulder, drew it up over the animal's nose and ears, and then using his thumb to open his mouth, he slipped the bit behind the horse's teeth. Once he determined the animal's headgear fit properly, Donato stepped back to admire the thoroughness with which Ramón and Don Tomas had tended to *Espíritu's* injuries.

They had extracted the bullet from the stallion's left shoulder and packed the wound with a poultice of aloe and medicinal herbs to ensure it would heal cleanly from the inside out. They also sealed the abrasions on the animal's left side with a sticky coating of lomboy sap and then covered the wound over with a layer of fine, dry, sterile ashes to discourage screwworm flies from laying their eggs in the open flesh. The only blemish not intended to fade was the RP brand on his lower flank. This had also been carefully treated and then dusted with ashes.

After unthreading the lariat from around the stallion's neck and head, Donato led the Azulejo out of the corral gate by the *cabresto* and stood him in front of the veranda with his unblemished side facing the spectators. When the little group stared in wonderment at the proud animal showing off the ornate Spanish headstall, the sound of their voices trailed off into silence.

A dreamy look also seemed to come into the Azulejo's eyes. Now that he wore his grand dam's headstall, might he also be reliving her memories? One could imagine he sensed the tension of armed conflict, heard the call of the bugle, the simpering speech of noblemen, the clang of steel, and the boisterous shouts of conquistadores. Over his head in the crisp cold Spanish sky, colorful pennants may have floated while a white pigeon flying between two towers carried a message to somewhere...

Espíritu, who seemed to have genuinely been reliving a bygone moment in time, spooked when Señor Gomez cleared his throat, breaking the silence. As would be expected, the bosal and attached rawhide strap caught him sharply around the head when he tried to break free, causing him to rebounded in the opposite direction. Failing to break free, he planted his feet, snorted with indignation through wide, distended nostrils, and defiantly surveyed the spectators with a regal bearing.

Don Tomas beckoned to Elyse and the other visitors to draw a little nearer so that they could converse with him about the stallion. "I hear the Señorita knows a great deal about horses. Does she have any observations about this one she can share with us?"

Señor Gomez spoke to Elyse and then translated her response. "The Señorita says your Azulejo doesn't resemble the robust Spanish horses, but rather a lean, fine boned desert type. In particular, she sees classic Arab influence in his fine head and arched neck. But why do you refer to him as an azulejo, she wants to know?"

"Because of his coloring. The word refers to a deep shade of blue. In horses, azulejo also means 'blue roan.'"

"In that case, the Señorita points out that the silver-white roaning predominant in your Azulejo's mane and tail is unusual. Most roans are bay with a solid black or salt and pepper mane and tail. She also remarks on the unusual metallic sheen in his coat. This is a characteristic of the rare Akhal-Teke breed of horse thought to descend from the chariot horses depicted in Egyptian frescos. Famous for its better-known metallic golden shade, this ancient breed has sometimes been called The Heavenly Horse. It was a Russian general who named it 'Akhal-Teke' for the Turcoman tribe that safeguarded it. According to what Elyse has read, when the tribesmen's horses were first termed a Russian breed in the early nineteen hundreds, royalty imported them. She further states that how your rare blue-eyed, white-maned metallic roan came to inherit such a diverse mixture of exotic traits is very intriguing!"

Don Tomas smiled. "Tell her that when it comes to the noble Azulejo, nothing surprises me! He has always been a creature of deepest mystery."

"What are your plans for this phenomenal individual?" Elyse inquired of Don Tomas through Señor Gomez.

Don Tomas furrowed his brow. "Unfortunately, because of the Azulejo's elegant bearing, desirable size, and unusual coloring, he would have always remained a trophy for horse hunters. This is why, although it breaks my heart, I chose to mark him with my brand. The penalty for horse thieving is very severe in these parts. After we have recorded the stallion's capture and ownership in San Antonio, no one will dare steal him. I would like to use him for breeding, but unfortunately, we have reason to question his fertility. In any event, the wonderfully prolific mares in these parts are more likely to reproduce look-alike offspring than my stallions are. Discovering an Azulejo mare that looks just like *Espíritu*, now that really would be a find!"

CHAPTER 15

End of an Era: The Valley is Silent

DON TOMAS and Señor Gomez decided to scout for a suitable site to clear an airstrip where Mr. Sutton's private plane could land, so Pedro and Luis saddled fresh horses for the guests.

After choosing a low plateau facing the prevailing northwesters, Mr. Sutton unwrapped a colorful windsock and handed it to Donato. "Can you find some way of securing this to the top of the tall cardón cactus over there? It will mark the spot where workmen may begin clearing the strip, and point the wind's direction."

"No problem!" Donato replied amiably. Next, he showed off by positioning *Alazán* under the cactus, and then leaped up on the well-trained animal's back. With one foot planted in the middle of his saddle and the other on his rump, he was just able to reach the tallest arm of the cardón, shave off the spines, and secure the windsock to it. After he was done, everyone applauded Donato and *Alazán*'s performance, and then they all began the ride back to the hacienda.

Mr. Sutton had noticed Elyse's eyes following Donato and rode up beside her. "He is a nice looking young man, don't you think?" he whispered.

"And heroic!" she replied, blushing. "Did you see the way he leaped up on his horse's back like a circus rider?"

"Yes! He is evidently a very accomplished horseman."

That evening, Luis played his hand-carved bamboo flute while Donato and Pedro sang folk songs and strummed their guitars. About an hour or so after it turned dark, one by one, everyone except Donato, Elyse, and Don Tomas got up to go off to bed.

Donato decided he would like to take a closer look at the old diary manuscript from the Spanish nobleman's sea chest, so he fetched it from his room. When he returned to the veranda, he invited Elyse to sit beside him under the light of a large kerosene lantern sitting on the dining table, and opened the old logbook. Don Tomas listened in on their conversation from his comfortable seat in an adjacent high-backed wicker rocking chair. Donato's sharp eyesight and the Castilian Spanish he picked up from reading the classics in school enabled him to understand some of the nobleman's writing.

"Look here, I think I may have found a reference to the mare in the painting! Listen to this," exclaimed Donato, reading aloud. *"White anklets on the back feet were preferred among the Arabs for they held them to be a sign the animal was fast. The trouble was with the uncharacteristic metallic sheen on the coat and the unusual dark blue eyes. This foal had not been sired by a purebred Arab, but perhaps by a Russian or Turk.'*

"Now listen to the next paragraph. *'As the months went by, the smoky filly with white mane and tail grew into a fleet, long-legged courser that ran like the wind. Unfortunately, when news of the filly's superior abilities reached King Phillip's ear, he desired her on a whim and had a warrant issued for my arrest.'"*

Elyse could not contain herself. "This validates what I said. Your Azulejo most likely throws back to the long-legged Turkmenistan horse bred by the Turkmen tribe—later named Akhal-Teke. What still perplexes me though is how your animal came to inherit the metallic coat—a recessive characteristic not generally reported in crossbreeds."

Eager to learn more, Elyse and Don Tomas waited patiently while Donato continued perusing the manuscript. After mumbling to himself for a few pages, he summed up what he had been able to read. "It looks as though a relative at court forewarned Don Diego about the king's warrant. Becoming fearful of retribution, Don Diego masqueraded as an imperial dignitary leaving for an assignment in Mexico. Taking his mare and her filly with him, he left for the New World on board a ship already laden with supplies and a cargo of unusually fine horses.

"However, his writing becomes more difficult to make out as the journal progresses. An illness may have enfeebled him or maybe he injured his writing hand. The final paragraph refers to a storm. Even though our own legend seems to tell the end of the story, it would be interesting to read about the village and perhaps learn how he impersonated the dignitary. When I go to visit my uncle in Mexico City, I can take the manuscript to one of the curators at the Museo National de Antropologia. A man who was a good friend to my father works there. I expect he would know how to preserve the old manuscript.

"Yes, and I would like to have a copy translated into English! How could Don Diego have assumed an important dignitary's identity? If he were found out, ships would have been dispatched across the high seas to arrest him and bring him back to Spain!"

"You would think so. Maybe the captain and ship's crew hadn't yet met their distinguished passenger; maybe he mysteriously vanished en route to the docks without anyone other than Don Diego being the wiser!"

"That sounds like a possible explanation. I can't wait to study Don Diego's entire diary!"

Earlier in the evening, Donato had noticed Don Tomas looking unusually youthful, as though Elyse's charming company had revitalized him. At first, the old man had gotten up from his rocking chair to sit between them at the head of the table, occasionally interjecting questions and comments into the conversation. However, after a while he got up and went over to the hammock Señor Gomez had been resting in earlier, lay down, and closed his eyes. After putting the manuscript away, Donato moved his chair closer to Elyse so they could talk quietly without disturbing the old man's sleep.

133

"How do you like living in the United States?" Donato asked. "I would like to have seen more of your country during my short visit there, but there wasn't time."

"Oh, it is very hectic in Dallas where I attend Baylor University during the school year, but I stay at my parent's Arab horse ranch in San Antonio during the summers. I prefer country living to the city!"

Donato was about to ask Elyse to tell him about her family's horses when Don Tomas roused himself, so he turned to speak to him. "Why don't we all call it a day, *Abuelo*, and go inside for the night?"

Don Tomas smiled. "Don't worry about me, I'm alright. I like breathing the fresh air and enjoy listening to the sweet intonations of Elyse's voice. Tell her never to be a stranger; I sense that even the spirits of this land will always welcome her," he said dreamily.

Elyse liked to indulge Don Tomas' spontaneous fondness for her, and looked appreciatively at him after Donato translated what the old man had said. "Tell him it touches me deeply that he should say so."

Don Tomas smiled with gratification at Elyse's answer and then drifted off to sleep again.

Around midnight, a strong wind began blowing down the Los Cardenales Arroyo. Donato got up to bring a jacket for Elyse and to get a blanket for Don Tomas. However, when he returned with the blanket and looked down upon his *abuelo* again, tears filled his eyes. Don Tomas looked like no more than a husk. Somehow, Donato knew the moment had finally come when his youthful spirit had flown the body that had grown too old to house it.

Since the days when his classmates had teased him about going to Baja to live with his aged relative, Donato knew the old man would die one day. Still, as Don Tomas had already lived so long, those close to him went on about their daily lives as though they believed he would live forever.

Donato took his grandfather's hand. "Bless you Grandfather and thank you for teaching me your ways."

"Feel his pulse," Elyse suggested. "The elderly can sometimes give you a scare by appearing to have passed away in their sleep when they haven't."

"I don't need to. My *abuelo* is dead. Even he knew he would pass away this year," Donato said, sobbing. "And now he has! It was so touching the way he liked birthdays. Why, of all days, did he have to die on mine?"

Elyse put an arm around Donato to comfort him. "Don't take it too hard. I am sure his time had come. Your *abuelo* was very old. Look at his face; he passed away with a smile on his lips! Even though I only knew him a few hours, he shared so much it seems like a lifetime. I wonder if he was waiting for us to get acquainted before leaving."

Donato and Elyse stood looking down at the old man a few moments before Elyse spoke again. "Now he's joined the beneficent spirits of this land."

* * *

By morning, the wind that had come up just before Don Tomas' passing, turned into a whistling summer gale, which lasted two days and three nights. It erased all the trails, footpaths, and superficial contours that had distinguished the Los Cardenales Delta during Don Tomas' lifetime. It filled in the water channels, piled wind-drifts against the west side of objects, and cast a pall of red adobe dust over everything.

Despite the terrible weather, Donato and Pedro interred Don Tomas on the second day of the gale. As he had requested, they buried him up on the hill above the orchard so he could rest beside his first wife, Consuela. The fine, red earth had blown back into the grave almost as fast as Donato and Pedro could dig out the pit, so they determined to wait until after the storm had passed to erect Don Tomas' cross. Later in the year, after the rains watered the *campo*, Donato would select a hardy, wild *palo verde* sapling to plant

135

beside the grave—one that promised to spread ample shade over Don Tomas' resting place.

During the remainder of the storm, the ranch hands mourned Don Tomas' passing in silence while the women of his household dressed themselves in black and lit votive candles in his memory, shielding the flames against the wind. The guests waited the unseasonable weather out in their rooms while Ramón and Luis turned all the animals except for *Espíritu*, Don Tomas' mare, and *Pancho Villa*, loose to find shelter for themselves.

The day following Don Tomas' burial, Donato decided to turn his spirited white mare, *Cenizas*, out of her sheltered oasis pen into the sugarcane fields for the duration of the storm and move *Espíritu* to her pen. This small corral was comprised of the tall, bristly *garambullo* cactus no self-respecting animal would pass.

When Donato returned to the hacienda, he noticed Elyse standing on the east side of the veranda shaking the dust out of a duffel bag. He knew the wind would snatch the sound of his voice away if he tried calling to her, so he walked up behind her and tapped her shoulder. She was so surprised to see him materialize out of the inhospitable dust storm, that to Donato's delight, she flung her arms around him and gave him a big hug.

Donato shouted to her over the wind. "Follow me. I want to show you a very special place!" Pointing to the empty duffel bag, he said, "Hold that around your head. It will help shield you from the dust." He then took her hand and led her back through the sugarcane fields to the shelter of the Ojo de Agua, or Eye of Water. This oasis spring ran out of a small mesa flanking the northern fringes of La Primavera ranch.

Elyse was astonished by the climate change and the breathtaking beauty of the orchard, which seemed magical in its abundance. Myriad trickling waterfalls poured out of the face of the vine-covered mesa cliffs into twenty lily-filled pools. And many small bushes bearing huge clumps of fragrant white and purple flowers perfumed the air.

"I wish you'd told me to bring my camera. Entering this place is like entering paradise!" Elyse exclaimed, her eyes bright with amazement.

Donato laughed, "Come back and visit our land after the rains have turned the *campo* green, and you will find the entire desert has turned into a paradise. This 'mother spring' flowing out of the face of the mesa cliffs is the origin of the creek watering the crops," he explained. "Don Tomas always cultivated herbs here in time of drought." Donato plucked a reddish-green leaf off a bush. "Smell it, it smells like cinnamon. It is called Santa Maria and is used to treat fever."

Elyse breathed in the smell. "You are right. It does smell like cinnamon! Visiting this magical place makes me want to remain in Baja forever and forget about studying for my degree! I only have one more year of college to go though, so I would be foolish not to finish. What are your plans now that Don Tomas has passed away?"

Donato sat down on the nearest boulder and rested his chin in his hands before replying. "Maybe you could help me start my own resort?"

Elyse broke into laughter.

"No, I am serious," Donato affirmed, standing up again and gripping her hand. "I don't want to return to Mexico City where nothing but sad memories awaits me. Now that I have inherited Don Tomas' property, it is my choice whether to sell it or continue to live on here and manage it on my own."

Elyse looked serious, "Are you suggesting my father go into business with you directly instead of leasing the land from Señor Gomez? I expect both men have completely lost interest in this piece of property after experiencing this terrible storm."

"The windstorm shouldn't discourage anyone. It is a phenomenon to do with Don Tomas' passing I think. The old man had an amazing reciprocity with the forces of Nature. I expect it is Nature's way of clearing his land for a new era."

"Yes, but Don Tomas' absence also leaves me with a sadness and restlessness I cannot explain," Elyse said sighing. "I feel like we should try to preserve the values and way of life he cherished. Señor Gomez' idea of developing this land into the usual kind of resort would not accomplish this. Maybe I will return for another visit after I have graduated. By then you should have your grandfather's property transferred into your name and be in a position to discuss the possibilities. If I do come back, will you promise me you'll let me ride *Espíritu* on an expedition out into the *campo* so you can teach me about the native herbs?"

"*Mama Mía!* You won't return unless I promise to let you ride the wild stallion in the bargain? *Espíritu* has been a range animal for many years. No one has any idea how well he will take to being saddled and ridden; he can react unpredictably and might never become dependable enough for a lady to ride. Anyway, Ramón is a more accomplished horseman. Why don't you make him that proposition? He might take you up on it!"

"I'll bet on you nevertheless," Elyse said coquettishly. "What I would love most is to own an azulejo foal just like *Espíritu*; then I could hand-raise it so it would become tame and grow attached to me."

Elyse smiled so sweetly that Donato's heart filled with generosity. He replied. "I suppose I will simply have to have a talk with every one of Don Tomas' mares explaining my need for that special foal. One of them just might surprise me!"

Elyse threw her arms around Donato's neck and thanked him with a kiss. "You promise? Really?"

"Yes, alright! I promise I will give the assignment my best effort!"

"Didn't you say you brought *Espíritu* here to a corral in the orchard?" Elyse asked. "Let's go and see him!"

"Yes, I put him in the impregnable old cactus pen Don Tomas used to keep his spirited white mare, *Cenizas* in." Then, on the pretext of guiding her, Donato wrapped his arm gently around Elyse's shoulders. "Come on, this way." When Donato and Elyse arrived at the cactus pen located just inside the northern orchard fence, there was no sign of *Espíritu*. The rope holding the gate closed had frayed against the post as it flapped back and forth in the wind, and flying sand had obliterated the animal's tracks.

"Donato shook his head ominously. "*Caramba!* What am I to do? I can't track an animal in this dust storm! And, unless I recapture *Espíritu*, I can't legally record his brand with Don Paco, the magistrate of the township where Don Tomas registered all his animals. The stallion's injuries might also make him easy prey for Señor Bartolo and Chico who would know how to obliterate Don Tomas' freshly applied brand."

Donato sat down on a boulder again and rested his head in his hands. His spirits drooped like a wilting flower. "What more can go wrong? Señor Bartolo has taken my pearls, Don Tomas has passed away, and *Espíritu* has disappeared again. Uncle Mario might be right when he says I should return to Mexico City and catch up on my studies."

"It is too soon to give up," Elyse counseled him encouragingly. "I am sure you will find *Espíritu* again and everything will still work out. But in the meantime, tell me about your pearls. This is the first time you've mentioned them to me."

As Elyse was an outsider, Donato did not expect her to understand that in his mind, the real worth of Don Tomas' cherished pearls lay in their spiritual significance. "Don Tomas gave me some pearls as keepsakes. Now they are gone, there is nothing more to tell."

"But your anecdotes are so fascinating, and the pearl is my birthstone! See! I wear one in a pendant around my neck! Come now, tell me about your pearls."

Elyse was so persuasive Donato decided to set his misgivings aside and tell her the whole story from beginning to end.

"What did you plan to do with your keepsake treasures before Señor Bartolo made off with them?" Elyse asked after Donato had finished telling her about the pearls.

"Don Tomas seemed to think they were going to play some sort of auspicious role in my future. He said that exactly what that was,

139

I must discover for myself. By endowing each pearl with unique symbolism he also bestowed a bit of magic on it. For example, since the pink one was his best friend's greatest find, he said that gem stood for good fortune."

Elyse acted so eager to hear more about the pearls, Donato could not resist toying with her a little. "Myself, I thought maybe I'd set the pink one into a piece of jewelry and present it to the first pretty girl who agreed to marry me. The rest, I thought maybe I'd save to pass on to our four daughters."

Elyse realized Donato was teasing her and giggled as a flush reddened her cheeks. "But what if your girl didn't want to bear so many children and preferred the blue pearl over the pink one?"

Donato became serious. "The blue one is very special. Don Tomas told me that when he discovered it off Cerralvo Island, the strong current passing the southern tip nearly swept him out into the Pacific Ocean. He prayed to God for the strength to swim back to the pearling boat, so to him the blue pearl symbolized courage. A Señorita would have to be very deserving to be entitled to that one!"

Elyse laughed and then put a forefinger to her lips to suppress an amused smile. "I see you have discriminating taste both in gems and in women. But seriously, I realize that symmetrical abalone pearls are extremely rare. Since your pearls had personal significance to your grandfather, maybe his spirit will help to return them to you one day."

Now it was Donato's turn to laugh. "Dream on, my sweet! Until the rains come, all I own is this drought- stricken property and Don Tomas' thin horses."

CHAPTER 16

The Azulejos: Lost on the Delta

TWO days and nights had passed since *Espíritu*'s return to La Primavera. On the morning of the third day the wild horse was more anxious to break free than ever. He shook his head with annoyance as he paced back and forth in the *garambullo* corral. He was sure that somewhere out on the delta, his Azulejo sister searched for him. She was currently sixty days in foal to Don Tomas' premier stallion, *Pico Blanco*, and carried precious cargo. Now he felt an instinctive need to protect her more than ever.

Although his shoulder ached, *Espíritu* was determined to find a way past the spiny cactus barrier encircling him. He sensed the risk in trying to jump the heavy, six-foot wooden gate in case he impaled himself upon the spiky upright posts and later died of his wounds.

Then suddenly, as though Nature herself had responded to his resolve, the winds came and went in unusually short, fierce, gusts, fraying the rope that tied the flapping gate shut. When it swung open, *Espíritu* galloped out of the corral and toward the beach, repeatedly neighing for his twin sister. He seemed to know that if she were in the eastern part of the delta ahead of him, the sound of his whinnies would be carried to her on the wind. Then when he and she were reunited, he planned to lead her galloping down the seashore toward Punta Prieta, where together they would escape the unseasonable dust storm by ascending the sides of El Rey until they reached the sheltered crater at the top.

However, it was not until the wind shifted direction that *Espíritu* heard a distant reply to his whinnies. He came to a stop and looked around. "Call to me again, my sister," he neighed shrilly, replying to her with that furtive nuance in his voice characteristic of lonesome horses. He stood in the midst of the flying dust and sand listening for an answer, but the only noise that reached *Espíritu*'s ears was the moaning and whistling sound the wind made.

CHAPTER 17

The Freighter: A Rude Awakening

ON the third night of the storm, Donato lay awake too anxious to fall asleep. It seemed providence had been both charitable and heartless at the same time. On one hand the lovely young lady who had come into his life had offered him comfort after Don Tomas' death. On the other hand, his beloved Azulejo seemed to have been spirited away by the dreadful storm as though by a demon, and the young lady would soon be leaving.

Donato finally dozed off shortly after midnight, only to be awakened around three in the morning by an eerie silence. The wind had ceased at last, and a profound stillness settled in over the delta valley. Off in the distance, he could hear the rhythmic swishing of the faraway surf and an occasional snapping sound made by a small animal stepping on a dry twig out in the *campo*.

Feeling too restless to fall back to sleep again, Donato got up and lit a kerosene lantern. Now that the wind had dropped, he could leave at dawn to search for *Espíritu*'s tracks. But first, he must write Elyse a goodbye note. Señor Gomez and his guests might decide to leave La Primavera before he returned.

Suddenly, like a clue from a fortuitous dream, the piercing cry of the seagulls nesting in the cliffs overlooking the Northern Coastal Trail to Don Tomas' property exploded on the still air. Donato immediately wondered why anyone would choose to travel that remote part of the delta at that late hour. His fear was that intruders might have found and captured injured *Espíritu*. He dressed himself quickly and ran to wake Ramón.

"Come on, get up!" Donato exclaimed, shaking Ramón out of a sound sleep. "Something disturbed the seagulls nesting along the Northern Cliffs a few minutes ago. I heard them squawking. Let's go down and investigate."

"*De veras!*" exclaimed Ramón, rubbing his eyes. "Alright, you go and let Pedro and Luis know, and I'll fetch *Cenizas* and *Pancho Villa*."

In his new capacity as heir of Don Tomas' estate, Donato gave out orders. "Pedro, make use of the hours before the guests get up to sweep the wind-drifts away from the hacienda, then attend to our visitor's needs. Hopefully, I'll be back in time to help you, but if I'm not, you and Luis must go ahead and erect a cross over Don Tomas' grave. I know he would expect me to make finding the Azulejo my first priority."

Donato turned to Luis. "Bring in the *bestias* we turned loose during the storm, drain and fill the *pila*, and then clear the dirt and debris out of the irrigation canals. The trees and plants will all need watering after experiencing such a wind."

The only available mounts were *Pancho Villa* and *Cenizas* who had been turned out in the oasis orchard. "I had planned to retire *Cenizas* after Don Tomas passed away," Donato said sadly, addressing Ramón. "But the need is pressing. You ride her and I'll make use of this opportunity to try out your popular burro."

Ramón was astonished. "Why *Patrón*? Surely, it is your place as heir to Don Tomas' estate to ride his mare."

"No, riding his horse would only make me feel as though I were stepping right into the old man's shoes and being irreverent of his memory. Besides, I have never had the chance to try out the celebrated burro. How well does the little beast keep up with *Cenizas'* ground-covering trot?"

"The pacing burro keeps up just fine," replied Ramón. "Why only last week he carried me from here to Rancho Salvatierra to pick up the mail, back to Rancho La Primavera, and then on to San Antonio all in a day's time!"

"Let's hope we won't need to travel that far today. I would like to get back to the ranch before the guests leave so I can say goodbye to Elyse. I didn't even have time to finish composing her farewell note."

There was a sliver of a moon, and a dusty haze hung in the air after the storm, dimming the light of the night sky. At first, *Cenizas'* white rump moved ahead of Donato like a beacon in the darkness, but when Ramón turned off the trail and cut across the *campo*, Donato knew what lay ahead by paying attention to the angle of his mount's ears. When *Pancho Villa* pricked them straight up like a jackrabbit's, this indicated there were no tall bushes ahead. When he laid them flat against his head, Donato took it as a signal to cover his face with his arms to protect himself from the long broomweed and *chamizo* branches that whipped back into his face.

It was the crack of dawn when Donato and Ramón came out upon the sandy beach—that magical hour when the stars fade and then disappear into the morning sky.

"Look at the sand over there above the surf line," said Ramón, pointing to some tracks leading from a headland with big caves in it sometimes used by wayfarers and seasonal fishermen. "It looks as though one of their horses must have been acting up!"

Ramón dismounted to rub some of the sand between his fingers. "The earth from the tracks is still damp. If we hurry, we should be able to verify whether these men have *Espíritu*."

Donato and Ramón were so intent on following the intruder's tracks they never noticed the touch of pink spreading across the eastern sky behind them or the ship resting at anchor on the glassy water off the shore of the delta. Instead, they followed the prints left by the cavalcade past the outcroppings of rock where the raucous seagulls liked to roost, and beyond to intersecting inland trails.

"Shut up, you noisy birds!" Donato admonished the screaming gulls as they rode by.

The bluffs that rose up over the beachfront were solid sandstone, so on this section of trail the horse's tracks were hard to make out. The right-hand branch of the path winding along the shore at the foot of the cliffs eventually connected a series of fishermen's huts and then petered out into an isolated stretch of goat trails ending in a no-man's-land. This was why the young men took the left-hand fork. It intersected with innumerable trails to El Camino Real, inland ranches, and the townships of San Antonio and El Santo.

At the top of the headland where the rock turned to earth again, Donato and Ramón were surprised to see skid marks end abruptly at the base of two adjacent Copal trees. When the young men looked up, to their horror, they saw a body in tattered garments wedged between their trunks. The man's right hand had been pulled high over his head with its extended fingers still entangled in what remained of a frayed lariat. His other arm hung limply downward and gently waved back and forth in the coastal breeze as though signaling his killer's route of escape.

"What a ghastly way to die," Ramón murmured, turning away from the grisly spectacle. "It looks as though this luckless fellow was dragged to his death by a wild horse. Come on, hurry!"

At a run, *Cenizas* was faster than *Pancho Villa*, but even so the mare never left the remarkable burro very far behind. Ramón pulled her up at the crest of the next promontory and waited for Donato to catch up.

"A group of horsemen just disappeared over that distant ridge," he said, pointing. "They were ponying a dark-bodied horse with a white mane and tail. No way can we catch up with them before they make camp for the night. They are traveling too fast."

"The horse thieves must not get away with this!" exclaimed Donato. Then he furrowed his brow, looked down at the path and examined the hoofprints. "I don't see *Machismo*'s prints. If Señor Bartolo were involved, I should think he would want to follow behind his prize so as to keep an eye on it. Where do you suppose these men are headed?"

"I don't know. Why don't you let me track down the poachers, *Patrón*, and you go home and say goodbye to your girlfriend? I should be able to guess whether they are Señor Bartolo's men when they reach the El Santo turn off. Should they turn north instead of turning south to El Santo, they are most likely drifters traveling the back trails from La Paz. I will follow and identify them, make a guess at their intentions, and then report back to you so you can prepare a plan. In any case, I should make a quick stop in El Santo to report that poor *vaquero's* untimely death to the authorities."

"Are you sure you feel comfortable pursuing these horsemen on your own? It seems like my responsibility to accompany you. I could catch a bus to the Cape in a week or two and meet up with Elyse and her father at the Los Barriles resort before they leave for Los Estados Unidos. That way I might be able to fill Elyse in on the latest news regarding *Espíritu*, and tell her goodbye at the same time."

"Don't worry about me, *patrón*. I will be fine. You go on back and say goodbye to your girlfriend before she leaves the ranch. First though, I'd like to exchange mounts. The burro attracts less attention and will hold up better than the mare on the long ride."

Although Donato felt torn, he felt an urgent need to see Elyse again before she left the ranch. He reasoned that Ramón was not only fully capable of ascertaining the identity of the robbers and finding out what their intentions were, but riding alone on *Pancho Villa* he might actually conclude their mission more successfully.

Donato unbuckled the wristwatch Don Tomas had given him for his birthday and handed it to Ramón. "When you reach El Santo, give my new watch to Paiza Ramirez who runs the country store. Tell him to provide you with food and lodging for the night. I will reward him handsomely the next time I visit El Santo. The best of luck, my friend; may the Virgin keep you safe!"

Ramón looked down the trail the way they had come. "On your way back, why don't you lay that poor devil's body out in a shady cave to await burial? He won't keep for very long hanging out there in the hot sun. Soon, the vultures will be wondering what he'd taste like for lunch!"

Donato made a face, "I'll send Luis. I want to get back to the ranch as soon as possible. It just occurred to me that when Señor Bartolo gets wind of Don Tomas' death, he may show up and begin trying to throw his weight around."

While galloping down the switchback cliff-side trail leading back to the delta, for the first time, Donato noticed the freighter anchored offshore. He reasoned that no ship's captain would choose to drop anchor along that stretch of unprotected coastline unless he were experiencing engine trouble or needed to unload cargo of some kind. Might the captain have business with Señor Bartolo?

Donato became so anxious to get back to the ranch before Elyse left, the fate of the unfortunate *vaquero* wedged between the trees slipped his mind. *Cenizas,* startled by the dead man's clothing fluttering in the wind, shied and skidded off the narrow path.

*   *   *

The next thing Donato knew, he was lying face up on a wooden table in a small, tiled pantry. Someone had removed the shelf over his head, giving him room to sit up. To his right stood a small coffee table strewn with an assortment of first aid supplies.

A chubby, redheaded teenage girl wearing an unbecoming bright-orange dress sat in a rocking chair just outside the doorway, as though she had been stationed there to keep an eye on him. She was chewing *chicle* and reading a magazine to pass the time. This sudden change in Donato's reality seemed so far-fetched he intentionally brushed some of the medical supplies off the bedside table and onto the floor to see how or even if the mysterious teenager would react.

Startled, the girl looked up and stared at him dispassionately for a moment before calling aloud to her mother. "Mamá, the young man is awake!"

Soon, a heavy woman who looked like an older version of the girl appeared in the doorway, and they both peered in at Donato as though thinking he were nothing more than a curiosity of some kind. Then, agreeing that the stranger really was awake, they left without introducing themselves and disappeared across the courtyard in the direction of the clattering sound of dishes and clanking pots and pans.

Donato felt an uncomfortable throbbing sensation in his head when he tried to sit up. When he put his hand up to his forehead, he found his head was swathed in a bandage. Then looking down at his legs, he realized to his dismay that he was wearing nothing but boxer shorts and a T-shirt. How humiliating! Who had undressed him? Had it been these two uncommunicative women?

Donato was trying to figure out what he ought to do next, when a dark-skinned, shy servant girl entered the room carrying a cup of broth, which she set down on the makeshift table beside him. Donato tried to speak clearly enough to ask her who had taken him in, but his throat was so dry the sound did not come out right. Although the girl seemed to guess what he was trying to say, she only offered a short reply.

"The Señor will soon be returning to speak with you," she answered.

Awakening in this unfamiliar place with strangers looking in on him made Donato feel despondent. How he wished he could see Elyse's reassuring face again! But how was he going to manage to catch up with her before she left for the United States? He didn't even know what town he was in! And who was this mysterious Señor who had offered him hospitality, he wondered? Might this esteemed country gentleman be in some way connected with the unidentified freighter he had seen anchored off Los Cardenales?

Donato sat up and reached for the cup the servant had set beside him on the table, and then leaned back against the head of his makeshift bunk and sipped his broth. From this perspective he could see through the pantry door beyond into part of an enclosed Spanish style courtyard that looked as though it once displayed a lavish patio garden. The bricks were old and crumbling now and small weeds had rooted themselves in the cracks and crevices. Since Donato could not immediately see a gate, it looked to him as though the shortest way out of the enclosure might be over the garden wall.

He could hear the tolling of a bell in the distance and wondered what he might see on the other side of the garden. Would he spot the rustic bell tower of El Santo, the small church of San Antonio, or the busy city streets of La Paz? He comforted himself with the hope that after receiving a little more nourishment, he could summon the strength to clothe himself, sneak out through the patio and escape over the wall.

Meanwhile, his thoughts drifted back to Elyse. Would she even remember him after she returned to the United States? And what of *Espíritu*? Would he ever see the Azulejo again? With these discouraging thoughts weighing heavily on his mind, he heaved a sad sigh and succumbed to a powerful need to lie back down and rest. He had no sooner fallen asleep than he found himself talking to Don Tomas about the Azulejo's disappearance. The old man's counsel seemed absurd, the way things often do in dreams. "The way to get the better of Señor Bartolo is to outwit him in a wager," the old man had suggested.

Donato heard his own voice answer as though it belonged to someone else. "But I thought no *bestia* in the territory could outrun the fleet-footed Azulejo."

Don Tomas gave a knowing smile. "If it is your destiny to win, the animal you ride will be of little consequence, *mi hijo*."

* * *

The next three days passed in much the same way for Donato as the first. The servant girl remained tight-lipped and the other two women looked in on him curiously from time to time. It was not until the morning of the fourth day that a couple of gentlemen showed up. One appeared to be a visiting *gringo* doctor and his six-year-old daughter toting a small medical bag, donating their services in the impoverished area. The other was Señor Bartolo, looking quite different from the man Donato first met mounted on his *fenómeno* dragon out on the trail. He smelled of cheap cologne, was clean-shaven, and dressed like a gentleman cattle rancher. His clothes showed signs of wear but were smartly tailored. He wore a stylish deerskin vest over a spotless white shirt and a fashionable red neckerchief clasped by a leather bolo. Dangling just below the second button of his shirt, an ornate crucifix characterized him as a devout man.

Donato wrapped his knees in his arms and bit his lip. Was this what Señor Bartolo dressed like when he was in town? Why should he, of all people, choose to put Donato up at his house? The last thing Donato wanted was to find himself beholden to Don Tomas' old adversary. He resolved to find out what news Señor Bartolo was willing to share concerning *Espíritu*, and then leave El Santo in time to catch up with Elyse before she left the country.

The doctor was extending his hand, introducing himself. "My name is Dr. Burton, I understand yours is Donato."

"*Sí, mucho gusto,*" Donato replied as the doctor began the process of unwinding the bandage from around his head.

"How is our patient coming along?" Señor Bartolo inquired.

In turn, the doctor questioned Donato. "I see the swelling on your head has gone down and the sunburn on your face is beginning to heal nicely. How do you feel?"

"Well enough to go home," Donato replied hoarsely. "Hmm, hmmm," the doctor continued, checking Donato's pupils and pulling his lower lids down to check for yellowing of the mucosa around his eyes. The doctor explained that had this last symptom been present, it would have suggested liver toxicity brought about by severe sunstroke and dehydration. The doctor finished up by checking the color of his gums. After finding Donato to be in passable health, he turned to Señor Bartolo.

"Moderate exercise, good food and rest are the best prescription."

"Thank you, Dr. Burton," Señor Bartolo acknowledged. "Come back on Monday, will you?"

"It will be my pleasure," Dr. Burton replied, tipping his hat in assent before taking his daughter by the hand and ducking out of the doorway.

Señor Bartolo's eyebrows flew up, and his piercing black eyes opened wide while a satisfied grin spread across his face. "Didn't I tell you, you were a lucky boy? But for the will of God, you might have met your death at the base of the canyon cliffs. Instead, a ledge sticking out about halfway down broke your fall."

"Indeed, I am beholden to you for rescuing me, Señor," Donato replied in a low voice. "But tell me about Don Tomas' mare. What fate befell her?"

"A pitiful tragedy; judging by the position she was lying in at the bottom of the canyon, she probably broke her neck."

"*Qué lástima! Qué dolorido!*" Donato exclaimed, hiding his face in his arms. "Not beautiful *Cenizas*! It's not possible!"

"There, there, lad. All things considered, you are not only very lucky to still be alive, but the *gringo* doctor just happened to be passing through El Santo with his little girl."

Donato felt anything but fortunate, however. He wanted to ask Señor Bartolo what business led him to travel the same trail as the unidentified dead man, when a manservant appeared in the doorway carrying the old satchel Donato had brought with him from Mexico City.

Señor Bartolo gave the man directions. "Set that bag down in my son Telmo's room, will you, Alfonso?"

Then he addressed Donato again. "See how thoughtful I have been? I've brought clean clothes for you all the way from Rancho La Primavera. In addition, as luck would have it, my son, Telmo, left for La Paz this morning with his wife and children, so you can move into their room. My stepdaughter, Carmen, will show you the way," he said, gesturing toward the chubby, redheaded girl now standing just outside the doorway.

"Come join me in my family room as soon as you are presentable. We have much to talk over. It is down the hall to the right."

Donato wanted to question Señor Bartolo about the Azulejo, but he knew his host was accustomed to providing answers where and when he felt like it, so he thought it prudent not to annoy him. Instead, Donato resolved to do his best to get along with him and made up his mind to speak only when spoken to. However, now that *Cenizas* was *dead* he needed another fleet-footed horse to ride away on! And what about Ramón? Where was he, and had he heard news of his accident yet?

CHAPTER 18

A Jewel of a Mare: La Perla

UPON entering the doorway, Donato thought Señor Bartolo's adobe family room looked very spacious and inviting, but somewhat Spartan. He noticed his host was already seated in a comfortable, homemade leather armchair positioned against the east wall, looking over some documents. In front of him, hanging over the west doorway leading out to his veranda, prints of the Last Supper and the Madonna and Child were displayed on either side of a painting of The Crucifixion. On the north wall were two oils of bullfight scenes painted on black velvet. Below them, a couple of ostentatious *charro* outfits complete with big sombreros hung from lacquered steer's horns mounted on blocks covered in cowhide. Donato imagined Señor Bartolo probably wore the costumes in parades.

After stepping into the room, Donato turned to glance at the pictures on the south wall, and stopped in his tracks. To his disbelief, the portrait he had recovered from Don Diego's sea chest hung between two nicely framed prints of classical Spanish horsemen. Below them were displayed photographs of Señor Bartolo's family.

Señor Bartolo waved Donato to a handmade leather sofa that faced his chair; beside it a tempting dish of fruit pastry rested on a side table. "Help yourself to the *dulces, joven*," Bartolo said.

Donato walked across the room and seated himself on the sofa Señor Bartolo had indicated. "Thank you," he said, helping himself to the *dulces*. "Why have you hung my painting on your living room wall?"

"Why did I hang it on my wall? You left that mistreated work of art carelessly propped up in a corner of your room. I almost stepped on it accidentally while I was packing up your clothes. Instead of questioning me, you ought to thank me for rescuing it and displaying it where it can be appreciated! Clearly it is a portrait of a man mounted on a blue-eyed azulejo with a white mane and tail. How extraordinary! Where did you obtain it?"

Donato was defiant. "Where I got it is none of your business! I suppose you also appropriated *Espíritu* and brought him here to your estate?"

"Shh, lad. You know not what you say. I have some very disheartening news for you. I ran into a group of fishermen the other day in the La Paz *cantina* who bragged they'd shot the animal at Punta Prieta. Although none of them admitted to finding evidence of a burial site, one of the men claimed to have been relieving himself behind a bush, when quite by accident, his urine stream exposed the corner of a chest.

"It is generally held by all accounts of the Punta Prieta Legend I have heard, that the Spaniard's valuables were buried with him and his horse in a single grave." Then Señor Bartolo furrowed his eyebrows. "But you already know of this. You are the ferocious young man who rode down upon the fishermen on the fiery-red stallion, intent on recovering the chest they were trying to carry away."

Donato smiled self-consciously at Señor Bartolo's description of his conquest on that day. "There's nothing more to tell," he replied, trying to sound indifferent. However, secretly, he was trying to figure something out. If Señor Bartolo believed the Azulejo was dead, what dark-bodied horse with a white mane and tail had he and Ramón seen the unknown group of men ponying up the trail?

Señor Bartolo riveted his piercing eyes on Donato as though he believed he could peer right into his soul. "You can credit me with saving your life, *joven*. You now owe me a good turn. I want you to show me the location of the Spaniard's grave and fill me in on what you did with the sea chest. His ghost will never be at rest until the last rites have been said over his remains and a cross and headstone distinguishes his resting place."

Since Donato knew the legendary Spanish nobleman was no relation of Señor Bartolo's, he felt justified in embroidering the truth a little. "I did the honorable thing and concealed the dead man's valuables in a secret place some distance away from the grave so that no one will ever be able to find them again. I also buried everything during the night by nothing more than the light of the stars and a half-moon, so I doubt I could locate the spot."

Señor Bartolo went poker-faced.

"Then, by your own admission, you are able to show me both the location of the grave and the chest the fishermen removed from it?"

"I am afraid that's easier said than done. You, yourself, know that the landmarks out on the point all look alike in the dry season. There is nothing to see out there now but barren rocks and hills, and cat's claw bushes. Not only that, but by this time the wind will have blown away all traces of the disturbed earth."

Señor Bartolo ignored Donato's prevarications and continued to press his objective. "Then we must hasten to Punta Prieta to search for landmarks that will jog your memory."

The last thing Donato wanted was to get into a heated dispute with Señor Bartolo, so he did his best to humor him. "If you insist, I might be able to recall the general direction," he admitted. Then, trying to steer the conversation back to the topic of *Espíritu*, he continued. "But before we discuss anything else, first explain to me about the Azulejo Ramón saw your men ponying down the trail," Donato added, slyly implying that they had actually identified Señor Bartolo's men on the trail.

Señor Bartolo leaned back in his chair with a self-satisfied expression on his face. "You are in for a real treat my boy! Chico and I have captured a veritable prize, a very pearl of perfection! I've named her *Mi Perla Azulina*, My Blue Pearl."

Again, Donato found himself sitting bolt upright on the sofa. "You captured an azulejo m-mmare?" he stammered, immediately putting all other topics of conversation out of his mind. This news was more exciting to Donato than opening all his birthday presents had been. It suggested Don Tomas really had seen a second blue-eyed azulejo down in the arroyo; a filly! Now, the means to procure an azulejo foal for Elyse had revealed itself. He must look the animal over, and if he liked her, devise a scheme to either win her in a bet, or, in time, negotiate ownership of one of her look-alike foals!

"Does she look like *Espíritu*?" Donato asked, suddenly drawn to Bartolo on account of their mutual interest in the mysterious Azulejo mare.

"Very similar."

"How do you mean?"

"The color of her coat and her forehead marking are identical to *Espíritu*'s, but her ears are more noticeable. Also, her body is of a leaner build and she appears to stand taller. In addition, when she is standing still, a layer of dark guard hairs falls down over her luxurious mane and tail. It is when she moves freely, and these dark strands blow up to reveal the crystal-white layer underneath, that she becomes *Espíritu*'s spitting image."

"This suggests the Azulejos would have looked exactly alike when running wild through the *campo*!"

"Yes, it would have been difficult to tell them apart when they were galloping."

"Since they continued to run together even after they reached maturity, maybe the two Azulejos were twin foals who remained companions."

Señor Bartolo shook his head. "It is obvious they trace back to similar breeding, but all the local ranchers maintain that twins born out in the *campo* would never survive—much less mature into fine specimens."

Donato furrowed his brow as he tried to imagine another plausible explanation. "Don Tomas maintained that stranger coincidences occur in nature than we realize. I wonder if a wild mare might adopt an orphan simply because it looked like her own foal. If the foals grew up side by side, they might continue to run together after reaching maturity. When threatened, the colt would have been the first to emerge into the open, trying to lead their pursuers away."

Señor Bartolo furrowed his brow. "You are right. I believe the two Azulejos worked as a team. When the colt tired, he took cover behind the underbrush. Then it became the filly's turn to appear some distance away and lead their pursuers in another direction."

Donato shook his head unbelievingly. "Considering she would have been the more reclusive of the two, it's amazing you caught her!"

"Yes, my men and I were camping in the caves located at the north end of Los Cardenales Delta, taking shelter from the dust storm, when she stumbled onto the beach, half-blinded by flying dust and sand. Imagine our amazement when we realized she was an azulejo!"

Donato remembered how anxious *Espíritu* had seemed when pacing the corrals at La Primavera and nodded, "I expect she was a handful."

"Sure, but my man, Chico, is skilled at handling the wild broncos. After lassoing her, he and his men hogtied her and then drenched her with calming granadilla potion. After washing the sand out of her eyes, Chico then laid my brand on her flank."

Donato found it so difficult to downplay his excitement about finding the mare, he changed the subject. "Why were you and your men camping out on Don Tomas' land?"

"Let us stick to facts now, son. First off, no one owns the beaches; they belong to the government. Therefore, not only was the mare wild and unbranded, but we captured her on government land no one can dispute. Secondly, my men and I were awaiting a friend of mine, Señor Fidel Martinez, scheduled to arrive on board a freighter passing by on its way from La Paz to Ensenada. If you will agree to be patient, I can fill you in on the details."

"Go on," Donato replied with resignation.

"In the predawn hours of the morning following the day we caught the mare, the wind died down and a freighter called, Dorado, came in to anchor offshore. Knowing that her captain would be eager to get under way again, I signaled the ship with my flashlight. The crew immediately lowered a skiff to pick me up so I could board her and discuss plans with Señor Martinez.

"After concluding our business, the Dorado's skiff again returned me to shore. This was when I learned that while I was away, my men had taken off with my Azulejo mare and left a dim-witted fellow behind to look after the pack mules. He is Raul, the *mulero* who brought in your satchel. The man is a little slow but loyal to me. Not understanding the import of what had really taken place, Raul told me the Azulejo mare had frayed her tether on a rocky ledge, and that the rest of my men had ridden after her to recapture her and bring her back.

"I suspected foul play the moment Raul told me the story, so I left him to look after the pack mules and rode after my men. When I came upon my foreman, Salazar, wedged between the two trees, I imagined he'd met his just rewards. Then, I spotted the place where you and the mare slid off the trail, and stopped to rescue you from the ledge, which so luckily broke your fall down to the bottom of the canyon.

"It wasn't until I arrived at my ranch carrying your unconscious body across my saddle that I encountered your pal, Ramón, waiting for me to show up. After helping me tend to your needs, he updated me on my men's activities. He told me they had blistered the Azulejo mare's fresh brand with creosote to disfigure it and then spirited her away to Rancho Salvatierra. He said their scheme was to waylay an empty cattle truck returning from the Cape, and then escort her to the Minister of Agriculture in La Paz. Inasmuch as she is one of a kind, they expected the minister would be willing to pay a very generous price for her.

"Needless to say, before my men had time to follow through with their deception, Ramón and I arrived at Rancho Salvatierra in the company of Don Chepe, the sheriff of El Santo, and his two deputies. We set matters straight with the owner of the ranch, Señor Manuel Lucero, and then charged Chico and his cohorts with the crime of horse thieving. Don Chepe also led an inquiry into Salazar's death. He interrogated my men, Ramón and myself. He may wish to question you as well. It appears that Salazar entangled his hand in the wild mare's lariat and she dragged him to his tragic end.

"My greatest quandary throughout this fiasco has been how to proceed with the Azulejo mare," Señor Bartolo explained, shaking his head doubtfully. "She rears up on her hind legs and strikes at anyone approaching her with her front feet, just the way a stallion would do. Even Ramón was unable to win her over; luckily he escaped over the corral fence before she trampled him to death under her hooves!"

Señor Bartolo took a pack of cigarettes out of his pocket. "Cigarro?" he asked, pulling one out and offering it to Donato.

Donato held up his hand. "Not for me. Don Tomas maintained that smoking is a very unhealthy habit," he replied curtly.

Clearing his throat, Señor Bartolo withdrew the proffered cigarro, lit one for himself, and then took two long puffs. Next, he lowered his eyebrows along with his voice. "Didn't I hear a rumor somewhere that you were gifted with a natural ability for working with the wild *bestias*? Subduing this mare might afford you an opportunity to show off your talents!"

Donato thought back to the day he and *Espíritu* had spent together at La Cañada oasis. "I don't see why you should expect my help gentling your vicious mare. She was a peaceful wild creature before Chico mishandled her. Not only that, but you ponied her across my *abuelo's* land without notifying me."

Señor Bartolo smiled indulgently as one who is confident he has the upper hand. "Once more, let us be sure to stick to facts, son. It is permissible to relocate livestock over all the trails traversing privately owned, unfenced land. Also, it grieves me to be the one to inform you, but the only reason I have waited so long to lay claim to Los Terrenos de Punta Prieta was out of consideration for Don Tomas."

Donato was indignant, "Don Tomas willed Los Terrenos de Punta Prieta over to me free and clear. Don Paco has his will and all the other pertinent documents on file in San Antonio!"

Señor Bartolo picked up an envelope lying beside him on the coffee table, drew out some papers, unfolded them, and handed them to Donato to read. "Don Paco would never have questioned Don Tomas' legal right to the property," Señor Bartolo replied coolly. "He and Don Tomas have been buddies for years."

As was the acceptable form for contracts in rural areas, Donato noticed Señor Bartolo's documents had been scribed in blue and red ink, and stamped with an official red seal. What lent the stiff, yellowed pages a particular look of authenticity however, were the deep creases indicating that they had been folded and filed away for many years.

Señor Bartolo continued. "See where the legal landowner signed his name there on the first page? My grandfather, Señor Tito Bartolo de Joaquin, signed that land grant. Now turn to the second page and read the last paragraph where the name of the legitimate heir is indicated in red ink."

Señor Bartolo studied Donato's face, wondering how well he might have taken the young man in. "You do know how to read?" he smirked, pointing impatiently to the document.

When Donato finally replied, his expression was blank and unbelieving, and even in his own mind, his voice sounded faint and far away. All of a sudden, his life seemed to have come full circle and he felt no more powerful than the young boy standing in Plaza Zocalo feeding the pigeons had felt.

Donato nodded, "Yes, I see what it says. It says: 'Señor Aliseo Bartolo de Casas.'" What Donato did not know, however, was that years ago, when Don Tomas had reached his eighties, Señor Bartolo himself counterfeited these documents and forged his own grandfather's signature. In view of the fact that Don Tomas had no official heir and the property had been named after Aliseo's great-great grandfather, Prieto Bartolo, Señor Aliseo Bartolo doubted the authorities in La Paz would even think to question his phony document's authenticity. That was, until the day when Donato showed up unexpectedly as a potential heir to Don Tomas' estate, and complicated his plans.

"I must get back to the ranch," Donato replied stubbornly. "My job now is to settle Don Tomas' affairs."

Señor Bartolo turned a deaf ear to the young man's concerns. "Don't be a stupid boy and harbor a grudge now that you are aware of the true story, son. It behooves both of us to work together. I have just entered into a contractual agreement with Señor Fidel Martinez to form a partnership. Our new company will, among other ventures, mine the La Ballena caves for the opals. Señor Martinez is in fact the mining engineer I hired years ago to prospect those caves for the potential gems. His report back to me indicated that a full-scale mining operation had the potential to yield considerable profit.

"When I went to visit him last month in La Paz, he informed me he was planning to arrive at Los Cardenales Arroyo Delta on board the freighter with a crew of workers. He requested I meet him at the beach with a string of pack mules to transport workers and supplies up to the mine site."

Señor Bartolo reached into his trousers pocket and drew forth what Donato thought looked like a lump of congealed, glistening red lava. "Cooperate with me as you did with your *abuelo*, and together we can both make our fortunes," he said, holding the translucent red mineral up to the window so it caught the light.

"From La Ballena?" Donato asked dryly as if to question the validity of the whole affair.

Señor Bartolo nodded, "Remember, I also agreed to safeguard the pearls. I'll bet you'd like to impress your *gringa* girlfriend with one of those gems," he said, winking.

It incensed Donato to have Señor Bartolo presume to know so much about his private life, but mention of the pearls refocused his attention. Once again, he found himself sitting bolt upright. "You mean you've held onto my pearls all this time?"

Señor Bartolo indicated his living room with a sweeping gesture of his hand. "You don't see me surrounded by riches, do you? I thought we both agreed I'd set the pearls aside in a safe place until you had grown a little older."

Donato was beginning to feel really nervous. In the space of one short conversation, Señor Bartolo had laid claim to all the things he valued most in this world and then offered to return a percentage under his own terms. Donato was considering how to respond, when Señor Bartolo reached for a second sealed envelope sitting beside him on the coffee table.

"It is a letter from the Americana," he announced, studying Donato's expression again while handing it to him.

Donato recognized the feminine handwriting on the envelope and caught his breath. He carefully opened the letter and began silently reading. After perusing the first few lines, his heart quickened. Elyse was genuinely worried about him!

Dear Donato,

> *When you and Ramón didn't return, I experienced the same restless feeling I felt after Don Tomas passed away. I was afraid something terrible might have happened to you and that I should check on you. Then Ramón showed up with the terrible news. He told Señor Gomez that you had suffered a concussion after falling down a ravine when your mare skidded off the trail, but that luckily, a rancher named Señor Bartolo rescued you. Ramón seemed to think this was fortunate since at Señor Bartolo's you could recover under a doctor's care.*

> *For my part, after hearing your story about Señor Bartolo stealing your pearls, I could not help feeling uneasy during this uncertain time following your grandfather's death. So, believe it or not, I decided to check on you and have accompanied Señor Bartolo back to El Santo!*

Love, Elyse

Señor Bartolo leaned back in his chair and smiled at Donato like a benevolent old grandfather. "I told you, you were a lucky boy! Only true love would have motivated such a refined and well educated young woman to strike off in the company of a stranger she had only just met, just so she could check up on her young man!"

Donato scowled. "The Americana's letter contains nothing personal—just a message from her father offering me a proposal concerning the land. But where is Elyse now?" Donato asked, afraid the hoarseness in his voice might betray his emotions after telling Señor Bartolo the little white lie.

Señor Bartolo gave him another charitable wink. "You tell Señor Gomez he should direct all inquiries about the land to me, lad. As to your girlfriend's whereabouts, last time I saw her, she was amusing herself by taking pictures of my aviary birds. Come. Why don't you invite her to accompany us to Rancho Salvatierra this afternoon to see my wild Azulejo mare?"

CHAPTER 19

Rancho Salvatierra: Donato Loses His Hat

SEÑOR Bartolo pointed along his long shady veranda, which opened into the bright sunlight on the west end, where Elyse stood beside his bamboo aviary. She was focusing her camera on two vivacious orange-headed conures and did not notice her visitors. Donato guessed she had bought the blouse she was wearing at one of the local outdoor shops called, *tiendas*. She looked as fresh and charming as ever, even after the long ride from La Primavera.

Señor Bartolo winked again at Donato and then beckoned with his hand. "Come along now son, don't be bashful. Greet your girlfriend. After you two finish visiting, I will show you my aviary. I buy tropical birds from the mainland vendors: conures, songbirds, mariposa canaries, and redheaded Amazon parrots."

Donato felt his heart skip a beat at the prospect of visiting with Elyse again but wished the circumstances were different. "The Americana is just a friend," he insisted. "I've only known her a few days."

Señor Bartolo grinned, "You can't tell me this young lady traveled all this way just so she could admire my pretty birds. Her father and Señor Gomez tried to persuade her to go to the Cape with them, but she would not listen to reason. So, make the most of your good fortune my boy. She is charming and pretty and, I am sure, well-off to boot." Señor Bartolo cast a salacious smile in Elyse's direction and then stepped up to his aviary to look over his birds.

Elyse paid no attention to Señor Bartolo, for she only had eyes for her love interest. Studying his face, she thought the stress of recent events had worked a sophisticating change in Donato, making him handsomer than ever. Forgetting herself, she let her camera drop on its shoulder strap, and ran to greet him.

"Donato! I am so glad to see you are feeling well enough to walk around. I apologize for showing up without an invitation, but I wanted to set eyes on you one last time! I see you hit the side of your head. Does it hurt? Ramón reported you took a nasty fall."

For the first time in days, Donato felt his spirits lift. Elyse's vivaciousness, her warmth and concern, and the refreshing fragrance of her perfume made him feel that somehow everything was going to turn out alright after all.

"Don't worry yourself about my injuries; they will soon heal. Indeed, I am very glad to see you. Thanks for your note. How is everyone back at the ranch getting along?"

"It was hectic the day all those men showed up with the train of pack mules to feed and water, but things seemed to be settling back down to normal by the time I left." Elyse gestured toward Señor Bartolo who stood with his back to them. "He really enjoys his birds doesn't he? They bring out a gentler side in him, somehow."

Donato ignored her comment. "Did he treat you alright on the trip?" he asked.

"Oh sure; he didn't take any liberties and behaved like a real gentleman the whole way. It was back when he first arrived at Rancho La Primavera that I witnessed his obnoxious side. Naturally, he was deferential to Señor Gomez, my father and myself because we are guests. But where your workmen were concerned, he stepped right in and ordered them around. He directed the women to fix food for his men and ordered Luis and Ramón to pack a couple of mules with our things—stating ostentatiously that he had agreed to personally escort me to El Santo and that he didn't want to be kept waiting!"

"Where are your father and Señor Gomez?"

"Ramón escorted Señor Gomez and my father back over the northern trail leading to Rancho Salvatierra, along the route where Señor Gomez is thinking of putting in a road. They planned to leave his horses off at the ranch, and then drive on down to the Cape."

Elyse's face brightened as though something had just occurred to her. "Has our host brought up the subject of your pearls yet?"

"Yes. He assured me he still has them. He even insulted me by hinting that if I cooperate with him, he might give a couple back to me right away!"

"What a con artist! Listen, I arranged for a taxi to show up here at three o'clock. Why don't you accompany me to town where we can look for a quiet place to talk and get something to eat?"

"You came across a taxi in El Santo?"

"Yes, the driver drove down from La Paz and knows some English from talking to the tourists. He is on holiday, visiting his family, and seemed eager to make what extra money he could while he is here."

"I would love to go with you, but I agreed to accompany our host to Rancho Salvatierra this afternoon to take a look at the Azulejo mare he captured. Why don't you come along with us instead?"

Elyse was unbelieving, "An Azulejo mare?"

"Yes, Señor Bartolo captured her somewhere near the big caves that lie along the Northern Coastal Trail above the Los Cardenales Arroyo Delta, during the dust storm. He says she has the same markings and coloring as *Espíritu*."

"A mare? That would be my dream come true! Of course I would like to accompany you and take a look at her. If she looks like *Espíritu*, don't you want to see if you can buy her from Señor Bartolo?"

"With what, my good looks?" Donato replied, jesting. "He would never part with her anyway. Señor Bartolo says she is even taller than *Espíritu* and sports the same exotic coloring and identical markings."

"So where is *Espíritu* now? Did you find him?"

"No, may the Lord be praised, *Espíritu* still runs free." Donato furrowed his brows and looked toward the imposing, distant outline of La Mesa Alta that rimmed the skyline east of El Santo. "Even

169

Don Tomas never knew where *Espíritu* went when he disappeared. I somehow know that he is out there up on one of the plateaus right now scenting the winds for news of his companion."

Donato looked at Elyse and his expression relaxed with gratitude to see her standing there beside him. "Tell me, how long do you plan to remain in El Santo?"

"I told my father I'd catch the bus to the Cape Thursday afternoon. He and Señor Gomez want to look over some more beach properties just as soon as I join them."

"Thursday—that is only the day after tomorrow!"

"I know. I wish I could stay longer, but it would upset my father. You and I will simply have to make the most of our time. Also, before I forget, I brought Don Diego's diary manuscript with me. I wondered if you would mind if I had it restored and translated in the United States? Señor Gomez said that he could take care of the paperwork for the government; we will have to post a bond ensuring we will return the original to Mexico after its restoration."

"No, I wouldn't mind. That actually sounds like a good idea! Who knows when I will be going back to Mexico City? So tell me, where are you planning to stay while you are here in El Santo?"

"Señor Gomez told me Señor Bartolo invited me to stay here at his hacienda, but advised me to rent a room at the little hostel called Los Misioneros instead. What is your advice?"

"It is up to you, but we would see more of each other if you were to take Señor Bartolo up on his offer. The local people would consider it improper for an attractive young lady to have made an unchaperoned trip with a lone *caballero*, and there will certainly be talk if you remain at the same gentleman's house. However, since you are a foreigner, most will ignore your indiscretions."

"I didn't especially like the idea of taking off on my own with a strange man either, but it was the only way I could arrange to see you again before leaving. In any event, like I said, our host acted like a perfect gentleman the whole trip, so I really don't see any harm in taking him up on his offer."

"Yes, the Señor can be very charming when he wants to be. I thought so myself when I first met him—that is until he confiscated my pearls!"

Donato and Elyse both looked up when they heard Señor Bartolo close the door to his aviary behind him. "It sounds as though our man has finished inspecting his birds," Donato whispered. "Let us continue our private talk later, after we return from seeing the mare."

Señor Bartolo tossed an old wooden *charro* saddle, saddle blankets, and other equipment Donato might need into the back of his truck. Generally, he took this particular truck on trips to La Paz to pick up supplies; it was a big, blue, battered stake-bed.

On the way to Rancho Salvatierra, Donato found it difficult to sit with his long legs straddling the gearshift, so Elyse was obliged to sit between him and Señor Bartolo. At first, nobody said anything as the noisy truck rattled down the hard clay washboard leading out of El Santo onto the old El Camino Real dirt highway. But before long the well-traveled road dipped down into a riverbed where the scenery whizzed quietly by. Donato thought it felt strange to be flying past the broomweed in a truck that seemed to be traveling only slightly faster than a horse could run—the difference being a horse could not keep this speed up for very long.

Looking past Elyse at Donato, Señor Bartolo spoke first. "So as to demonstrate how fair-minded I can be, I have been thinking how you and I should divvy up our pearls. In view of the fact I am now the proud owner of the one and only 'blue mare,' *La Perla, Azulina,* I have decided I ought to let you keep the magnificent, blue abalone pearl as a consolation prize! Also, now that I see how well you and your girlfriend are getting along, I was thinking of allowing you to select a second one to present to her."

"You think only getting one or two of my mementos back will satisfy me? Each of Don Tomas' pearls has sentimental value!" exclaimed Donato. "For example, he said the yellow one signifies friendship. The others have meanings too. Courage and love, and the two black ones together represent perfection."

"Vaya! Oh go on!" scoffed Señor Bartolo. "A pearl is but a piece of grit an oyster has digested. What significance can anyone bestow on a grain of sand?"

Donato was defensive. "My pearls are memorials to a young boy named Juliano who died trying to safeguard a single, precious gem he brought up from the deep. Don Tomas gave him his solemn promise to hold onto their collection and forever treasure them as keepsakes."

Señor Bartolo frowned, "I suggest you take a lesson from Juliano's fate and put your silly notions about Don Tomas' promises out of your head. Boys invariably run into trouble when they meddle in men's affairs."

*   *   *

Aside from the shards of broken multicolored glass crowning the stone wall surrounding Rancho Salvatierra, the architecture of the ranch settlement was a tribute to the Spanish settlers. The two heavy wooden gates at the entrance scraped as Señor Bartolo pulled them open. Inside, a quiet hacienda, thatched huts, and a large rectangular stone corral were visible just beyond the mango trees. The celebrated Azulejo mare was eating from a wooden trough positioned beside a goat pen situated alongside the cistern. Farther down, Señor Alejandro Gomez' imported horses stood alone in a stake run.

Señor Bartolo continued up to the house to talk with Señora Lucero, and left Donato and Elyse studying the Azulejo mare from the vantage point of the fallen stones that lined the perimeter of the corral wall. Donato rested his elbows on the stones at the top of the wall and then whistled and tossed a pebble behind *La Perla* to provoke her to turn around and face them.

"De veras!" he exclaimed. "She has the exact same ears and head as the mare in the Spanish nobleman's painting. Like a gem covered with dust, the sweat and dirt covering her make one even more eager to see what her metallic, blue-black coat looks like underneath!"

Elyse was as eager as a child on Christmas morning. "Back at the ranch, you said you could predict what kind of disposition a wild horse was going to have by the look in the eye and shape of its head."

"Yes, first off, you can interpret a great deal from the eyes, but what really gives the temperament away is the size and shape of the ears. A prime example of this would be the long ears of the burro family. They resist doing what they don't want to do, and will only give in when coaxed to obey. They never change their headstrong attitude!"

Donato gestured toward the mare. "According to Don Tomas, those exotic ears combined with the Azulejo's long, thin muzzle and somewhat petulant expression suggests she is a 'pouting' mare, apt to hold a grudge for any and all wrongs done to her."

"I don't see it," countered Elyse. "Those clear, liquid, deep-blue almond eyes, long lashes and the shapely ears set forward on her forehead like an Akhal-Teke's give her a distinctive, classical beauty."

"Just the same, Don Tomas maintained that the most challenging kind of horse to train was a very hot-blooded *bestia* with inherited willful character traits thrown in. When a mare like *La Perla* is badly handled, she is liable to retaliate by turning into an outlaw. Something else to consider is if she's not bred wisely, she might produce untenably temperamental offspring!"

Elyse looked disappointed, "Are you saying you think she might not make a good broodmare?"

"No, I am not saying that. It is obvious she is an exceptionally fine mare. I am simply advising she be crossed with a good-natured stallion. Breed her intelligently, and horsemen everywhere will offer good prices for her progeny."

A faraway look came into Donato's eyes. "If it were up to me, I would breed her to *Pico Blanco*, the coal-black stallion Don Tomas used on his finest mares. *Pico Blanco* is a rather ordinary-looking horse, but he has a very tractable temperament and brings the very best qualities out of the mares he is bred to."

"Are you sure we couldn't persuade Señor Bartolo to sell *La Perla* to us if we offered him a high enough price for her?"

"You are asking me whether he would sell a mare whose worth he compares to a gem pearl? I don't think that's likely. Though, like in a dream I had a few days back where I was receiving advice from Don Tomas, I suppose Señor Bartolo might be persuaded to risk almost anything in a wager."

Donato felt a thrill run over him as Elyse slipped her hand into his before replying. "It sounds as though your *abuelo* is still giving you good councel! Didn't you say Ramón's burro, *Pancho Villa*, could cover long distances faster than any horse? Why don't you bet Señor Bartolo that *Pancho Villa* can beat his *fenómeno* in an endurance race across La Mesa Alta?"

"That wouldn't work. No self-respecting *mulero* would stoop to pit his fine mule against a lowly burro, no matter how fast the little beast is. For the moment, what I need to do is figure out Señor Bartolo's motives. First off, why is he trying so hard to cultivate my loyalty?"

"It is my guess he wants your help with the mare."

"Yes, I can see that. Still, I doubt he is motivated by anything that simple or straightforward. What's more, he wants me to show him where I hid the Spanish nobleman's sea chest. But there is also something deeper I can't quite put my finger on."

"You'll figure it out in time."

"Yes, I won't know the best way to further my own objectives until I do."

Donato slipped through the corral gate, removed his hat, and knelt down on one knee, trying not to threaten the wild Azulejo mare. Studying her expression, he marveled at the quixotic play of emotion in her dark blue eyes. When she pricked her quaint ears forward, she looked curious and innocent. However, as soon as she laid them back, devilish lights leapt into her eyes.

Donato sensed that so long as he remained kneeling, the mare would neither threaten nor approach him. Wishing to evoke some sort of reaction, he stood up slowly, replaced his hat, took three steps in the mare's direction, and then held a loose fist out to her, hoping she would step forward to sniff his hand. *"Vente potranca chula, potranca maldita*, come here you pretty filly, you ornery filly," he enticed.

However, to his consternation, the mare laid her ears flat against her head, and with glaring eyes, reared her full height into the air so that every rib stood out, making her look like an instrument of death. As soon as Donato saw those ears go so far back, he sprung backwards, and then turned and hurdled the corral wall. He could still hear *La Perla*'s hooves clattering against the stones when Elyse helped him to his feet on the other side. Shortly, he glimpsed the tips of the mare's ears appearing and then disappearing as she stamped the ground and tossed her head up and down victoriously.

Elyse was concerned, "You didn't injure yourself again scrambling over the wall, did you? Are you alright?"

"I'll be fine," Donato grumbled, glancing back at Señor Bartolo's vindictive mare. She had pranced over to the spot where the nice white hat Ramón purchased for him on their first trip to Punta Gorda lay on the ground, and was ripping it to shreds—rampant fury flashing from her eyes.

As soon as *La Perla* turned her left side toward him, for the first time, Donato clearly saw Señor Bartolo's disfigured brand. "Ah, that wound will be one of the many wrongs that have contributed to her attitude. Don Tomas claimed that not even a maddened bull can match the ferocity of an enraged horse."

When Señor Bartolo returned, Donato and Elyse still stood watching the champing mare pace the corral fence. Taking the animal's hostile behavior for granted, Señor Bartolo remarked instead on her appearance. "So far, the only feed she has deigned to eat has been yucca vines from my orchard and chopped goatnut mixed with corn chaff. Before she got so dirty, because of the nutritious wild foods she prefers to eat, exquisite metallic highlights glimmered in her coat.

"The goats strip the jojoba plants of goatnut this time of year, so I have to send boys to gather the pods from the steep cliff sides even goats can't climb." Then Señor Bartolo looked up at the dark clouds gathering on the horizon. "I heard an early storm advisory over the radio. The outskirts of a tropical depression is expected to pass over the area by midday tomorrow. Do you feel competent to load the mare into my truck? Señor Lucero will want to run some animals into the protection of his corral."

"Imprudent handling of your wild mare has turned her into a rebellious outlaw," Donato scoffed. Señor Bartolo rested his elbows on the corral fence to observe *La Perla* tossing spiteful glances up at her audience. Without acknowledging her dangerous behavior, he gave Donato a black look. "I thought I heard a rumor somewhere that you were gifted with an unusual ability for gentling wild horses, but I guess it was wrong. If you are unable to tame this mare for me, my only recourse will be to get my man Chico out of jail." Then, turning on his heel, Señor Bartolo walked off toward his truck.

Elyse, disappointed over the impasse they seemed to have come to with the Azulejo mare, looked up at Donato with concern in her eyes. "What do you suppose Don Tomas would suggest you do with *La Perla* if he were looking on?" she asked.

Donato could not help feeling a little hurt that Elyse seemed more concerned with the fate of this dangerous mare than with his own safety, but he humored her because he cherished her genuine love of horses.

"I suppose he might have said something like this: 'Imagine the humiliation this magnificent animal has undergone, being manhandled by Señor Bartolo's insensitive men. She no longer has pride in herself after losing her dignity and she feels cross with the world.'"

Suddenly, Donato's face brightened, "Thank you, Elyse! Now I know what to do!" Donato stood up and called to Señor Bartolo who was about to get into his truck. "Stop! I have a plan," he said pointing. "Go up and persuade our gracious lady of the hacienda to lend me a comb and some jojoba oil, and then back your truck up to that tall bank over there so the bed is on a level with the ground."

Señor Bartolo grumbled something about Don Tomas never having taught this rude young man to address his elders respectfully. Nevertheless, he backed his truck up against the bank as Donato had directed. He then sauntered off towards the hacienda to ask Señora Lucero for the shampoo and jojoba oil.

Donato studied the layout of the stone corral. Some goats were confined within it, inside a stick pen constructed up against the *pila* wall. He guessed that if the Azulejo mare were pressed, jumping the lower *pila* wall behind the goat pen would look like her easiest escape route to freedom.

Eager to lend Donato a hand, Elyse fetched the tack from Señor Bartolo's truck. At Donato's request, she removed the stirrup leathers, leaving only the bare saddletree and cinch, and then set everything down on top of the *pila* wall.

Meanwhile, Donato had stepped back into the corral armed with a bullwhip. Elyse watched with admiration as he cornered the mare alongside the goat pen. He had employed this exercise to teach *La Perla* not to come at him. But as he anticipated, rather than submit to the lesson, the mare leaped over the low stick fence that encircled the goats and ended up standing among them.

When the billies crowded *La Perla* against the *pila* with their horns, the distraught mare jumped into the long, broad cistern to land half-swimming and half-sliding among the slimy waterweeds growing on the bottom. She leapt through the chest-deep water until she was almost near enough to the far cistern wall to jump it, when suddenly, Donato's whistling lasso closed around her neck and pulled her up short. At first, she flailed at the end of the line like a snared marlin, but because she could not maintain her footing, Donato soon managed to halter her to the overhead crossbeam that supported the bucket used to draw water out of the reservoir. Utilizing the bucket, Elyse helped him pour water gently over the mare—being careful to avoid getting any in her ears.

More than rinsing the dirt away, the cleansing shower also seemed to douse the anger from the mare's soul. Little by little, her breathing slowed as she resigned herself to the revitalizing bath and nurturing attention. Soon, with her ribs showing through her wet coat, she looked as slick and gangly as a newborn filly. Within minutes, the hide on her neck began to dry, and the beautiful metallic blue highlights Señor Bartolo had mentioned began to appear.

As a finishing touch to the gentling process, Donato enclosed *La Perla*'s quaint ears in the palms of his hands and stroked them slowly upward with a soothing motion that assuaged her fury and anxiety even more. Next, right there in the water, he slowly and carefully saddled her with the saddletree and bosal and then strapped a leather blindfold across her brow so it would be ready for use. While the mare succumbed to the feel of her tack, Donato worked the jojoba oil Señor Bartolo had brought him into her mane and tail, and combed out the tangles.

Donato and Señor Bartolo were still discussing the best way to load the mare, when Señor Lucero arrived in a flatbed truck piled high with sacks of feed. After a heated discussion, Señor Lucero ordered his farm hands to pile weevil-infested costales of bran designated for hog feed up against the inner and outer sides of the cistern wall. This created safe footing for the mare to climb over. Then everyone lent a hand. Some of the men tugged on a butt-rope from her left side while others hauled the animal's tail forward on her right side, and together they pulled her back out of the cistern.

Next, Donato lead gentled *La Perla* up the bank behind where Señor Bartolo had parked his truck. He pulled her blindfold down over her eyes and then coaxed her to step backward into the truck bed padded with a deep layer of spongy sugarcane pulp, and cross-tied her between the stake sides.

To ensure the Azulejo mare's safety on the bumpy return trip to Señor Bartolo's ranch, Donato and Elyse rode with her in the back of the truck. By the time they reached El Santo, the sun had disappeared behind ominous clouds and a strong breeze had sprung up.

CHAPTER 20

The Storm: Señor Cuevas

THE approaching storm became the immediate concern of everyone, including Donato. He wished he were back at Rancho La Primavera helping Doña Blanca, but instead he was stuck at Rancho Los Santos, assisting the Bartolos. Intermittently, strong gusts of wind produced loud swooshing sounds as they blew flying debris clattering across the small town and surrounding *campo*.

Señor Bartolo gave orders out to his household. He instructed Señora Bartolo and the maid to move all furniture away from the windows so the rain leaking through the shutters would not ruin it. Next, outside in the yard, he instructed the gardener to dig trenches around the house so the rainwater pouring off the hacienda's eaves would drain to lower ground. He asked Donato and Elyse to help Carmen transfer the aviary birds to individual bamboo cages, stack them in the hallway running beside the kitchen, and then cover them over with a tarp. After that, he drove his truck across town to pick up his sister, Manuela, and her two daughters, Tila and Veronica. He would bring them to his hacienda to weather the storm and leave her husband, Tito Dominguez, and their two boys behind to look after their fragile *ranchito*.

Though Manuela had not married into money the way her brother did, she displayed the heritage and manner of gentry. When Donato met her two daughters, he thought they were both very pretty. He also noticed they batted their eyelashes at him when their mother introduced them, which made him feel self-conscious in front of Elyse.

After Señor Bartolo's family had settled into their rooms, everyone gathered around the dining room table and sat down to a dinner of beef stew, seasoned rice, and tamales. Driving rain started pelting the hacienda during the meal. The wind began to howl, and the palm crossbeams supporting Señor Bartolo's roof creaked like the timbers of a ship at sea.

Everyone retired early except Señor Bartolo, who invited Donato to sit up with him while he kept track of the storm. Señor Bartolo sat back in his armchair and smoked cigarettes one right after the other while Donato entertained himself by weaving quaint little figures of people and animals out of palm fronds the way Ramón had taught him. He intended to paint faces on them the following day while waiting for the storm to die down and then make a gift of them to Elyse.

Looking at the palm-leaf dolls, Señor Bartolo smiled knowingly. "Your fondest wish has come true, my boy; your girlfriend will have to remain here awhile. Whether she likes it or not, the bus to the Cape won't be able to negotiate El Camino Real until work crews have repaired the damaged roads after the storm. Elyse must remain in El Santo until the storm passes and the water pooled in the washes and arroyo beds has substantially dried up." Donato's thoughts raced through his mind. For the first time since Don Tomas' death, providence finally seemed to be on his side. This change of events would allow him the opportunity to visit with Elyse so they could continue to get better acquainted. It would also afford her the time to take photographs of *La Perla*, which they could later compare with the ones she took of *Espíritu*.

While Donato was secretly rejoicing over his good fortune, Señor Bartolo changed the subject and began to talk about upcoming events. "It will interest you to hear that the last weekend of July, Don Chepe will be retiring, and I am taking over as sheriff of El Santo. Not only that, but Sunday morning of the same weekend, my wife's niece is getting married. The celebrations will last until the afternoon when we plan to hold a horse race through the center of town. Don Paco will be bringing his part quarter horse over from San Antonio— *Volador*, who beat my gelding *Chispa* four years ago."

Señor Bartolo did his best to continue their conversation during the lulls in the storm, droning on about the damage the wind and rain would do to his ranch property, and the havoc it would wreak in town. However, there were spells where they no longer heard each other over the howling of the wind. Noticing that Donato was no longer trying to listen, Señor Bartolo stopped talking and lit another cigarette.

During these interludes, Donato would look up at the paintings on the walls. Sometimes he imagined the warm flickering light of the lamp brought the figures to life. The enraged bull in the bullfight scene would suddenly glare at him as though it planned to rush headlong into the room, while the elegant Spanish nobleman riding prancing *Azulina* poised to step out of their picture frame.

Momentarily, when the roof shuddered as though about to come loose from its moorings, both Donato and Señor Bartolo sat bolt upright in their seats. "Madre de Dios," Señor Bartolo cried, looking visibly shaken as he pointed up at the creaking crossbeams directly overhead. "That gust nearly blew our roof away!"

Listening to the increasing fury of the wind continued to heighten Donato's senses, as happens when potential danger threatens. He was prepared to jump up at a moment's notice to handle any emergency, but as time passed and the wind began to subside, deeper concerns preoccupied his heart and mind.

Donato knew that Elyse would soon be returning to her home in Texas, and that he only had a few precious days left of her good company. After all, her interest and enthusiasm had fortified his spirits and ensured his recovery from a bad spill on the trail. It also occurred to Donato that after her departure, reliance upon his two closest friends for comradeship and loyalty would become increasingly important in the days ahead. He had faith in Pedro's maturity and decision-making ability, especially in regard to caring for Dona Blanca and the family. He was somewhat less sure of Ramón's loyalty, though he respected his know-how when it came to the "nuts and bolts" of running La Primavera. Ramón had taught him almost everything he knew about horsemanship. He also valued the times they had spent training the *bestias* and riding the trails that traversed Don Tomas' vast, pristine parcel of land.

Just before midnight, the wind all but stopped, and a monotonous downpour ensued outside. Lulled by the hypnotic sound of rain splashing on the roof, Donato slipped into a dream about *Azulina* and the nobleman until the booming tones of Señor Bartolo's resonant, basso voice brought him back to the present.

"It is time we took a walk through the hacienda to check the ceiling and windows for leaks. I can hear water splashing on the kitchen floor. Go and find a big pot to set under the drip!"

*   *   *

It took three days for the storm to die down, during which time the Bartolo and Dominguez families hovered around Elyse and Donato, as though they thought it their duty to chaperone them. It was not until the women of the Bartolo household began occupying themselves with preparations for the upcoming festivities in town that Elyse and Donato found an opportunity to sneak out to check on the mare, *La Perla*.

Donato was so overjoyed to be alone with Elyse again, he felt like a happy child. "I love the energy in the warm summer storms," he cried excitedly holding his hands out to catch the raindrops. "When enough rain falls, the dry earth soaks it up, the plants branch out in leaf, the wild flowers bloom, and the animals fatten and become sleek again."

Elyse joined in Donato's merriment and decided to tease him. "I am sorry the mare trampled your hat, but you look cute with your bangs falling in your eyes." Then she laughed at the embarrassed look on his face.

"I can see I must hurry and pick up a new hat at Paiza's Almacén," Donato replied bashfully.

Elyse flashed a winning smile. "Let me pick one out for you. I'll choose one that'll make you look like a movie star cowboy and then take pictures of you while you are working with *La Perla*!"

Señor Bartolo kept his animals in a two acre fenced pasturage bordering his small oasis orchard. There were four stake pens situated in a clearing near his front gate. In one of them stood the *fenómeno*. There was also a large stone corral similar to the one at Rancho Salvatierra. Now, the only animal in it was *La Perla*. She stood huddled at the east end near the south wall, basking in a patch of sunlight.

Elyse was disappointed. "She is all muddy!"

"Although she rolled in the mud during the storm to hold in her body heat, her coat will still be cleaner after the bath we gave her at Rancho Salvatierra," Donato explained. "When the day heats up, the mud will dry, and she will shake it off. Later, we will give her a thorough grooming to clean off the remaining dirt and then continue with her training."

When Donato glanced up at the sky, he noticed the clouds had broken up and the sun was shining brightly. "Let's take a walk over to Paiza's Almacén so you can pick out my hat."

Elyse chose for Donato a hat made of gray canvas adorned with a black and white horsehair band that had a spray of dark blue cock's feathers stuck into it. A blue and white tassel dangled from the back.

"This one goes with *La Perla*'s coloring, not *Alazán's*," Elyse announced enthusiastically. Then she whispered, "You see, I still have faith you will figure out a way to best Señor Bartolo in a wager and win possession of her!"

"Alright," Donato said, ignoring Elyse's hint and trying on the hat. "I'll buy this one if it pleases you. It's a little on the fancy side, but it'll age nicely after a few trips out on the trails. Just the same, I'll probably replace that gaudy cock's plume with a hawk feather. Also, because it feels a little loose, I'll have to sew some padding inside the sweatband."

By the time Donato and Elyse returned to the corral, not a cloud was in the sky. Donato put his hat aside to work on later and then captured the mare by offering her a small bunch of freshly sprouted *quelite* he found growing among the mango trees as bribery and enticement. Next, he showed Elyse how to coax her into being groomed; he talked as he worked.

"This kind of attention develops a bond of trust between the horse and his handler. If *La Perla* had been handled gently in the beginning, she would never have become vicious and would want to cooperate with everything we asked of her."

"I remember you said you preferred training wild horses to ones that had been badly handled or even someone's spoiled, backyard pet," added Elyse.

"Yes, an untamed wild horse's natural timidity keeps it from taking its handler for granted, and it listens better."

When they were done grooming *La Perla*, Donato turned the mare loose again in the corral. "What will happen if Señor Bartolo wants to handle *La Perla*? If she turns vicious again, won't he be furious?" Elyse asked.

"He might lose an ear to her teeth or get kicked or both if he isn't careful," Donato said grinning with eyebrows raised. "But seriously, if he treats her right, she should cooperate with him as well as she does with us. Lord knows I've experienced my own mishaps while practicing the challenging art of horsemanship. But look, here he comes, accompanied by a party of his friends: the gray-haired sheriff of El Santo, Don Chepe, and the two lean deputies who work under him. There is also the portly proprietor of Los Misioneros and Chico's mentor, curious old Señor Cuevas, the one-eyed *mulero*."

The company of men stopped by the front gate to greet Donato and then spread out around the corral to rest their elbows on the stone wall and observe the Azulejo mare. At first, *La Perla* surveyed the group from the middle of the compound as though trying to figure out what they might want with her. When Donato whistled to egg her on, she broke into a magnificent ground-covering trot—eliciting whistles of admiration from Señor Bartolo's friends as strands of her crystal mane and tail cascaded around her.

Señor Cuevas moved close to Señor Bartolo. *"Qué curiosidad!* Indeed, it is very curious to find a wild-caught *bestia* in such good flesh this time of year!" he remarked in a confiding tone. "She is a little ribby but not malnourished, and her chest and haunches are exceptionally well muscled. Now that you have trapped this exquisite Azulejo mare, I'd hunt down the Azulejo stallion and put a bullet through his head if I were you. That creature is the familiar of the shades of Punta Prieta, and if left alive, will cause you nothing but trouble."

Señor Bartolo responded. "Actually, on my last trip to La Paz, I overheard some fishermen claim they'd shot the animal, and so believed he was already dead. That was until the other day when I visited Rancho Salvatierra. Señora Lucero told me her men spotted him briefly, standing outside of the ranch compound, looking over the fence at the captured Azulejo mare. They also testified that like a spirit horse, the creature disappeared again in a twinkling and they never saw it again."

Señor Cuevas peered intently through his one eye. "Did anyone check the ground for hoofprints? Señora Lucero's men may have seen the Spanish phantom. Listen, Chico can use a project to occupy him while he serves out his jail sentence for trying to steal your mare. As additional penance, I will provide him with the supplies to make your Azulejo a beautiful bosal and main hair *cabresto*. I will also have him create a fine, woven browband made of *gamuza* decorated with consecrated rosary beads. This tack will serve as a Talisman to safeguard your priceless Azulejo from unpropitious influences on the occasions when you choose to ride her out in the *campo*."

Señor Bartolo thought Chico and Señor Cuevas normally charged him rather high prices for their good-luck amulets, but considering native muleskinner shamans earned very low wages and Chico's work was excellent, he tolerated their prices. He knew that fine, hand-woven deerskin bosals and *cabrestos*, such as Señor Cuevas described, could not be purchased from the usual vendors. These elegant hackamores were treasured as heirlooms and handed down from father to son through generations of horsemen.

Donato was standing beside Elyse just outside the corral, a rawhide lariat coiled over his shoulder. He had finished tacking padding behind his new hat's sweatband and was now attaching a chin thong.

"Hey boy, stop fiddling with your hat!" shouted Señor Bartolo. "Come and show off your skill to our visitors. Saddle up the mare for us," he commanded, walking up to Donato and slapping him on the shoulder. Then, turning again to Señor Cuevas who was following him, he added, "This young man has a real gift for taming horses."

Señor Cuevas acted interested. "Ah, so this is the youth I've heard you talk about. Let us see how well he handles your wild-caught mare!"

Donato put on his new hat and then tipped it in assent to Señor Bartolo before starting for the corral gate. In view of his circumstances, placating his host seemed like the only option. At the very least, he felt proud to show off the skills and horse sense he had picked up from Ramón and Don Tomas.

However, the moment Donato entered the corral, the old familiar flicker of malice rekindled in the dark depths of *La Perla*'s changeable blue eyes. Donato had not worn a hat since she trampled his at Rancho Salvatierra, so he found himself looking over at the cowboy hats worn by the spectators encircling the corral. Trying to think like *La Perla*, he wondered whether his new hat might have elicited her hostile reaction. Did she associate this style of hat with the harsh treatment she had received at the hands of Señor Bartolo's men? Yes, that must be it! She viewed all cowboy-hat-wearing individuals as participants in some sort of horse-abusing cult.

"My new hat still feels too big and I'm afraid it might fall off and frighten the mare," Donato announced to the onlookers in a matter of fact way. He then called to Elyse in English. "Elyse my pet, my hat still doesn't fit and I am afraid it might fall off. I'd rather not risk ruining it the first day. Could you come take it from me?"

Donato's false explanation elicited a chuckle from a few of the onlookers who knew enough English to understand. Since they never guessed the real reason Donato had dispensed with his new hat, everyone whistled and hooted in applause when the wild mare allowed him to walk right up to her.

Donato was still in the process of strengthening that fragile bond of trust so crucial to winning over a skittish wild animal, so he did not appreciate the intrusive applause that made the mare edgy. On the other hand, propriety cautioned him not to give orders out to Señor Bartolo's guests without first consulting him. On the other hand, Donato believed that the only way to make steady progress with *La Perla* was to take charge of the situation.

He turned to the spectators. "The wild mare will need more handling before I can show her off properly. Now that you gentlemen have all seen her, I request you leave us alone for the time being and return in a couple of days. By then I predict I will have Señor Bartolo's wild Azulejo mare so well trained even my Señorita will be riding her!"

A murmur of disappointment rose from the spectators as they turned to leave. Señor Bartolo saved face by backing Donato up, but scolded him after his guests had left. "It is becoming clearer all the time that Don Tomas never taught you manners, boy! The proper course of action would have been to confer with me before giving orders out to my guests!"

After Donato's impropriety, Señor Bartolo became suspicious that he and Elyse were plotting to undermine his interests where the mare was concerned. However, Señor Bartolo's more far-reaching designs required patience and cunning, so he kept his cool. The crafty Señor was used to pushovers in his underhanded dealings, especially with a *joven* like Donato. However, in Donato's case the stakes were higher. There was a year long statute of limitations pertinent to the transfer of Los Terrenos de Punta Prieta that Señor Bartolo wanted to exhaust. Since his counterfeit documents seemed to have effectively shaken Donato's confidence, it now simply became a waiting game.

It served Señor Bartolo's objectives to keep Donato preoccupied with the mare as long as possible. Further, he hoped to foster his trust by tricking him into believing he genuinely intended to return a couple of the pearls. If his tactics worked, the young heir would not act until it was too late for him to claim the land legally; that way he would naively lose all. Señor Bartolo therefore continued to play the part of a congenial host and invited his two houseguests to accompany him back to his hacienda for lunch.

After lunch, Donato and Elyse returned to the corral. Continuing to employ the techniques Ramón and Don Tomas had taught him, Donato made miraculous progress with *La Perla*, who being very sensitive, quickly learned everything he taught her.

Señor Bartolo bided his time to check Donato's progress until the following morning. So far, the mare had never permitted the Señor to so much as feel her smooth satin coat. Consequently, it irritated him to find Elyse was riding his mare while Donato gave her pointers from his seat on the corral wall.

After entering the corral, Señor Bartolo motioned to Elyse to ride the mare over to him, but when he reached out to touch *La Perla*'s fine crystalline mane, she gave him a distrustful look and sidled away. Making a gesture of disgust with his hand, the Señor turned on his heel and strolled over to Donato, who was still sitting on the corral wall. *"Felicitaciones!* Congratulations! Your Señorita appears to be having no difficulty riding my mare."

"You are right. *La Perla* has taken more readily to Elyse than she did to me at first. My guess is the inept treatment she received at the hands of your *muleros* provoked her to harbor a lasting grudge against all men. However, watch while I demonstrate the good news," Donato volunteered, jumping down off the wall. He turned over an old galvanized bucket sitting on the ground, and then began beating the bottom like a drum. "See, *La Perla* only swiveled her ears. She will make a very steady parade horse!"

Señor Bartolo leaned back against the wall, lit a cigarette, and pondered the best way to negotiate with Donato. "Get *La Perla* to allow me to ride her in front of my friends tomorrow, and I'll agree to take you to the coast this weekend. After you locate the sea chest and show me the Spanish nobleman's grave, we can pick up the pearls." Then, slyly, he added, "I still think the pink one would be the best choice to bestow on your girlfriend. If you play your cards right, you might even be able to persuade her to get engaged to you before she leaves the country!"

"You don't keep my pearls here at your hacienda?" Donato queried.

Señor Bartolo scrutinized Donato with piercing eyes. "What sort of numbskull do you take me for? I concealed my pearls in a secret hideaway out in the *campo* where no one else would ever be able to find them!"

"Why should I believe you genuinely intend to give two of them back to me?"

Señor Bartolo acted offended. "Stand by me son, and I'll share my fortunes with you. It's that simple."

Donato felt himself being maneuvered into a trap but saw no choice but to play along while Señor Bartolo continued to hatch his schemes.

"Why don't you take my mare on our trip?" suggested Señor Bartolo. "This will afford you an opportunity to get her used to the ride through town as well as to train her out on the trails."

Since Donato wanted to hold onto his advantage with the mare, he heaved a quiet sigh and assumed a pleasant expression.

"That sounds like good advice. Let's let bygones be bygones and work together to achieve our mutual goals. I will agree to ride your mare on the trip. But first, I noticed Elyse admiring the detail on your traditional *charro* outfits the other day. Why don't you wear one of them tomorrow? That way Elyse can take pictures of you wearing one of your elegant costumes while you show your mare off to your friends."

Señor Bartolo, who was accustomed to winning people over for his own purposes, was very glad to see Donato was coming around. He liked the idea of having his picture taken and he looked forward to riding his flashy new mare in the La Paz Independence Day parade, so he willingly agreed to the proposal.

* * *

The following afternoon, Señor Bartolo showed up at the corral accompanied by his friends, looking very dapper in his black and white *charro* outfit and wide-brimmed Mexican sombrero accented with white brocade. Sure enough, as Donato had predicted, *La Perla* did not associate this gaudy outfit with the bad treatment she received and didn't even sidle away from him.

"She acts as though someone charmed her with a spell," muttered Señor Bartolo, at last running his long fingers through her luxurious mane. "How fine her tresses are! The white strands sparkle like glistening foam upon the sea."

"Yes, I have been saving her mane and tail hair out of the comb after grooming her. I will make elegant white tassels out of it," replied Donato, gathering *La Perla*'s reins up in his left hand and then holding her stirrup so Señor Bartolo could mount. Meanwhile, once Señor Bartolo was aboard, the spectators hooted in admiration and Elyse took pictures.

"*Qué distinguido es el Señor en su yegua Azulina!*" the spectators cried. "How distinguished the Señor looks riding his Azulejo mare!"

To begin with, Donato walked beside *La Perla*'s left shoulder, leading her by his lariat. He kept her at a walk at first, and then urged her to pick up her magnificent trot. Next, he halted her again, coiled up the lariat, and tied it to the saddle with a thong, leaving Señor Bartolo to continue riding on his own.

The mare was so cooperative Señor Bartolo was moved to congratulate Donato. "I've got to hand it to you, young man. You've certainly brought this bronco mare a long way in a short time!"

Señor Bartolo turned to the spectators. "The good Lord must have put something extra into his work the day he created this extraordinary animal. She not only covers as much ground in a single stride as my *fenómeno*, but I can hardly distinguish her footfalls beneath me."

Here, Donato spoke up. "Don Tomas maintained that the harshest test of a *bestia*'s quality was to observe how well it moves in the dry season when it is thin. An animal not encumbered by conformational faults travels straight and picks its feet up even when it is out of condition."

"Your *abuelo* would applaud your knowledge and skill as a horseman, lad," called Paiza Ramirez of Paiza's Almacén.

"Ah sí, que listo! The boy is gifted!" the remaining spectators echoed.

CHAPTER 21

The Vision: The Phantom on the Trail

THE citizens of El Santo paused in their morning labors to watch Señor Bartolo, Elyse, and Donato progress through town on their way to La Mesa Alta. Señor Bartolo's jaw was set, and the rifle he carried to shoot deer hung across his leg. Looking austere and statuesque, he led the way on his grand *fenómeno*. Behind came Elyse, looking as pretty as a picture on flashy *Alazán*. The white cowboy hat Donato had picked out for her and the coral peasant blouse she bought at Paiza's Almacén complemented *Alazán*'s white blaze and red chestnut coat. Donato brought up the rear of the procession riding *La Perla* with the ease of a natural horseman. He still rode bare-headed so as not to upset her, and continued to use the excuse that his new hat did not fit properly.

As Donato watched Elyse's auburn hair swish back and forth in time with *Alazán*'s pinkish-blond tail, he wondered how events would unfold and hoped he hadn't bitten off more than he could chew. Matching wits with Señor Bartolo was one thing, but confirming his legal ownership of Don Tomas' land, while at the same time winning Elyse for his own, was beginning to seem like wishful thinking. "One day at a time" he thought, "or problems will multiply and I could lose everything!"

At first, the prospect of getting at least two of his pearls back encouraged him. However, as he thought over everything that had taken place, he began seriously questioning whether someone like

Señor Bartolo intended to leave himself with only the three lesser pearls. This concern, along with his misgivings about the mare, the land, and the safety of the nobleman's chest, all combined to manifest as a hollow feeling in the pit of Donato's stomach. Even if Señor Bartolo should actually part with a couple of pearls, the idea of presenting Elyse with a gem not appropriately displayed in an attractive jewelry setting felt wrong to him. A poor *campesino* might well offend such a respectable young lady by offering her a hasty, poorly presented gift!

Elyse, on the other hand, assuaged Donato's discouraging thoughts by periodically giving him a backward glance and a heartening smile. As she watched him ride the trained Azulejo mare through town restrained in native trappings, Elyse thought about the folklore surrounding the Azulejos. Did the ghosts of Don Diego and *Azulina* look after *La Perla* the way Donato believed they looked after *Espíritu*? If so, supernatural means might liberate her once she was back in the *campo*. Suddenly, Elyse feared for Donato's safety.

"The Señor rides in charming company today," the onlookers remarked. "Behold the charming Señorita riding the flashy liver-chestnut stallion and the handsome young man astride the showy Azulejo! Indeed, she is a jewel of a mare. These horses hold their heads high in the manner of parade horses and prance like dancers under their riders."

Others whispered inauspicious prophecies in the background. "Donato and the *gringa* may have a way with the Azulejo mare, but one can still glimpse cold fire in those spooky blue eyes—a throwback to an ancestor who met with an unfortunate end. Surely, such an animal must be accursed!"

* * *

After the storm, the breezes carried the scent of new life across the plateau of La Mesa Alta. The tufts of green, leafy shoots pushing up through the baked earth not only offered a promise of hope, but they served to remind Donato that his heart was in this land. Returning to Mexico City seemed unthinkable now. For now, he must still tag along after his host and see events through to their conclusion.

Señor Bartolo, on the other hand, considered the trip an opportune time to familiarize *La Perla* with the sound his rifle made as he fired it at targets along the way. At one point, he leveled it at a band of wild burros crossing the plateau and then acted amused when Elyse pleaded with him not to shoot one. "I'll agree a whole burro might be a bit much to carry, but the meat is excellent," he rejoined, chuckling.

Donato was not sure what gave Señor Bartolo more enjoyment, killing wild things or watching Elyse's expression when he went to gut them with his hunting knife. She made such a revolted face while he was skinning a fox that he broke out laughing. He turned to Donato. "Tell her if she agrees to cook a couple of these jack rabbits I've shot for our dinner, just to please her, I'll content myself with practicing on the satisfyingly tall Cardon cactus fruit for the rest of the trip!"

By the time the tall, green palms of the *Vacadilla* oasis came into view, late afternoon shadows stretched across La Mesa Alta. The riders were nearing the trail winding down into the lower end of the canyon when *La Perla* stopped to scent the breeze blowing across the mesa, and swiveled her expressive ears as though listening for faraway sounds. Following her gaze, Donato looked toward a nearby upland where, silhouetted against the scarlet and gold clouds overhanging the horizon, an Azulejo stood. Its body was the hue of the patches of dark blue sky that framed the outer edges of the deepening sunset above, and its sparkling-white mane and tail swirled around it like strands of wispy cloud.

Elyse and Señor Bartolo also halted up ahead. Again, Donato heard Elyse plead with Señor Bartolo to put his rifle down. She need not have gone to the trouble, however, for shortly, where the apparition had stood, all that could be seen were the outline of a granite boulder and a clump of scraggly cat's claw bushes.

195

Donato was still admiring the sunset and thinking back on the beauty and mystery of the spectacle he had just seen, when Señor Bartolo's cursing as he rode back up beside him intruded upon his thoughts. It seemed to Donato as though the man purposely positioned his giant mule in front of the colorful sky so he could look down upon him from the anonymity of his silhouette.

"Keep a tight rein on the mare," ordered Señor Bartolo. "Mark my words. No *bestia* made of flesh and blood would choose to browse that desolate plateau. That was the ghost mare come all the way from Punta Prieta to provoke *La Perla* into breaking away from us and returning to the freedom of her former feral life in the *campo*."

Donato was not certain the apparition had actually been a phantom. In his heart, he also knew *Espíritu* was following *La Perla*, but corroborating Señor Bartolo's assumption seemed like the most prudent thing to do.

"Yes, only the phantom would have vanished into thin air," he agreed.

"Alright, now that's settled, let's get going," commanded Señor Bartolo. "If we want to allow enough time to look for the pearls, we must start on our return trip back from Punta Prieta by noon."

"What do you mean 'allow enough time to look for the pearls'? You assured me you hid them somewhere safe! Didn't you?" Donato challenged.

In reply, Señor Bartolo shrewdly threw Donato's own argument back at him. "Wasn't it you who so eloquently pointed out that the desert all looks alike when the trees are leafless? You must also allow me time to get my bearings and locate my landmarks. Besides, you of all people must realize that the storm will have obliterated all the familiar paths."

As they entered the canyon, the travelers heard the sound of men's voices rising above the lowing of cattle down in the riverbed. Before long, they also spotted the flickering light of a campfire and smelled the smell of wood smoke coming from the direction of

Señor Bartolo's old campsite under the palms. But Señor Bartolo led Donato and Elyse to a thicket of black willows bordering the stream further up the canyon.

After dismounting and tethering *Machismo* to a willow branch, Señor Bartolo turned to Donato. "Take care of the *fenómeno* for me, will you, Donato? I am going back down the canyon on foot to talk to those *vaqueros*. I also run cattle in the area and they can update me on the condition of the water holes after the storm."

Glad for an opportunity to finally be alone with Elyse, Donato acted agreeable. "I will hobble both *Machismo* and *Alazán* in the upper canyon, and then turn them loose for the night. I must tend to *La Perla* first though; she has never been tethered out on the trail before and will require careful handling."

To Donato's disappointment, Señor Bartolo took his time unpacking the *fenómeno* and then hung around to see how he managed *La Perla* for the night. Señor Bartolo and Elyse both looked on while Donato unsaddled and watered the Azulejo mare at the nearby stream, and then observed with interest as he tossed the end of her lead over the high limb of a suitable willow tree.

"This way she won't tangle herself in her rope," Donato explained. "I have tied the end to a low branch that is within easy reach. That way, in the event she panics and tries to pull free, I can easily release her by pulling on the quick-release knot."

Next, Donato secured a rawhide feed bag to the willow's trunk, which he filled with a small handful of jojoba nuts mixed with grain and a quantity of digestible dry chaff for *La Perla* to eat.

Donato was sure *Espíritu* was nearby but knew that wild horses tended to keep quiet whenever they felt uneasy. This was why it didn't surprise him when the mare never whinnied but instead fretted and pawed the ground until she dug a hole.

Señor Bartolo tried stepping up to *La Perla* and crooning to her the way he did to his birds to calm her, but Donato still had not let him in on her secret hatred of cowboy hats, so the mare only became all the more upset by his presence.

197

Señor Bartolo quickly lost his temper. "If you don't settle down, you daughter-of-a-motherless-goat, I'll whip you till you behave and then let you earn your keep as a weekend racer!"

Now, the hollow feeling in the pit of Donato's stomach felt as though it suddenly had no bottom. He must not allow the conflict to continue. After all, Señor Bartolo might do the mare great harm with impunity, and without remorse.

"Why don't you allow me to try and calm her down," Donato suggested from where he stood looking on.

Señor Bartolo scoffed, "I doubt Ramón would cater to the mare the way you do. She just needs to be taught who's boss!"

In the end, to Donato's great relief, Señor Bartolo finally gave up the mare and left on his aforementioned walk down the canyon to visit with the *vaqueros*.

While Donato had been otherwise preoccupied with Señor Bartolo and the agitated mare, Elyse made use of her time selecting a secluded, level spot behind a large granite boulder to set up her campsite for the night. She then searched the nearby shrubbery for a sturdy, leafy sprig with which to sweep the ground and clear a space for her sleeping bag.

La Perla settled down after Señor Bartolo left, but Donato blindfolded her anyway. He wanted to find out whether Elyse needed help setting up her campsite or unloading her bedroll from behind *Alazán*'s saddle. "If sleeping on the hard ground bothers you, we can gather and trim the dry leaves and palm mesh that lie scattered beneath the palms for padding," he suggested.

"That sounds like a good idea. Can you show me how?"

"By all means." Donato replied amiably. "But first, would you be so kind as to lend me a hand leading *Alazán* and the *fenomino* to the upper canyon? I want to hobble them there for the night."

"Of course. I would also like to see how you do that."

"Wrap the hobbles you mean?"

"Yes."

"Sure. I use a long, flexible rawhide latigo to hobble them with. I'll show you…"

When Donato and Elyse had finished hobbling the animals and gathering and trimming a pile of spongy palm mesh with which to pad the ground under Elyse's sleeping bag, Donato showed her what kinds of wood to collect for their campfire.

"Dried hardwoods stripped of bark and termites are best because they don't smoke. Mesquite, cat's claw, and dried cactus woods burn well but not torote or ciruelo. Some of the best kindling is made from mule fat twigs."

Next, Donato taught Elyse how to kindle a fire between three stones and set water to boil for wild damiana tea. After the logs burned down, Donato showed her the best way to roast Señor Bartolo's game over the coals.

Señor Bartolo awakened Donato and Elyse before dawn. "I plan to stop by the mine on our way to Punta Prieta to check on Señor Martinez' progress. Let us partake of an early breakfast of coffee, leftover rabbit and tortillas, and then be under way before sun up."

After an hour's trek over shale-strewn trails, the south side of the High Mesa came into view. Like its namesake, the mountain called La Ballena, where Señor Martinez was supervising the mining project, stood perched on the lower plateau of La Mesa Alta like a great, beached whale. The diggings were located at the northwest end where the mountain bordered the west banks of Los Cardenales Arroyo. Here, damp soil and rock provided a protective environment for the soft fire opals. The reason this location was called La Boca, or The Mouth (of the whale), was due to the large cavern at the opening, which in turn led into the smaller interior caves. It was here in this location that the most accessible opals could be found.

Since Elyse's interests embraced all the whimsical desert flora and geology of the dramatic terrain, she elected to hang back and admire the fascinating mountain from a little distance while Donato and Señor Bartolo rode up to speak with the engineer.

The first curiosities to catch Elyse's attention were the amazing hanging cacti, or *pitayita*, that dangled over the entrance to the lower caverns like clusters of mythic snakes. Above the cactus, she noticed the indomitable succulent live-forever, or *siempreviva*, which thrived almost solely on the desert air. However, the mountain's outer layer of loose shale struck her as the most fascinating feature of all. It was composed of a different substance than the primarily granite caves and surrounding terrain, as though La Ballena had erupted from under this layer of dissimilar rock when the land rose out of the sea. This shale looked as though it had slowly been slipping along its sides ever since, like layers of runny icing on a cake.

Ever since Donato first learned about Señor Bartolo's partnership with Señor Martinez, he had difficulty imagining the sort of entrepreneur who would choose to collaborate with him on the hazardous opal mine venture. But the picture came together for him as soon as he met Señor Fidel Martinez. The engineer was a sprightly middle-aged man with reddish hair and a bushy mustache who wore wire-rimmed glasses and a baseball cap. Donato supposed he was equally comfortable working in an air-conditioned office as he was prospecting for minerals out in the desert.

The engineer dug into a pouch hanging from his belt and offered Donato a handful of uncut fire opal samples to look at. "We call the red ones *ópalo cereza*, cherry opals," he said, resting the palm of his hand on *La Perla*'s satin neck as she twitched nervously under his touch.

"She is a young mare," Donato explained. Señor Martinez only shrugged, and then walked a few feet away to where Señor Bartolo sat upon *Machismo* to hand him the best stones.

"I expect to find more of these red ones deep within the damp, inner parts of the mountain where underground streams feed the small veins of moisture interlacing the rock strata. This variety displays the richest color."

"How far inside have you managed to excavate up till now?" Señor Bartolo asked, delightedly examining the translucent red samples as he held them up to the light.

Señor Martinez shrugged again. "We are dealing with two types of rock, one of which is very dense; so progress is slow. This is why I plan to detonate strategically placed sticks of dynamite in the backs of some of the caves. I can save time by blasting through the flinty stuff."

This was when Donato spoke up, "Using explosives in such close proximity to loose shale sounds risky. La Ballena is known for rockslides!"

Señor Bartolo turned on Donato with annoyance, "I expect the engineer knows his business better than you do!" Señor Martinez was less defensive. "Rest assured there is little cause for concern, *joven*. The landslides you see around the mountain indicate it has experienced a few earth tremors over the millennia, nothing more. It would take nothing less than a major quake to unsettle the larger pieces lying halfway up the side, and these big quakes only occur once or twice in a century."

Since the engineer's logic sounded more like ambitious planning than sound reasoning, and no one seemed interested in what Donato had to say, he decided to ride *La Perla* back down the bank and show Elyse the stones Señor Martinez had given him.

"How exciting to find beautiful minerals concealed within such a stark mountain!" she exclaimed, holding the fire opals up to the light. "They look edible, like chunks of red Jell-O."

When Donato recounted his brief conversation with the engineer, Elyse was astounded. "It sounds to me as though he's not taking the obvious threat of landslides very seriously. Let us get away from the mountain before he detonates his explosives! See that gully we just crossed? That looks to me like a fault. If quakes haven't taken place for a long time, setting off dynamite could precipitate a temblor!"

"I trust your wish to leave the area is granted! Here comes Señor Bartolo. He looks as though he is also in a hurry to get going."

Donato and Elyse were anxious to leave La Ballena before the engineer set off the dynamite, and Señor Bartolo was eager to reach Punta Prieta and wrap up the business of the day. So the company urged their mounts into an extended trot and proceeded toward the Southern Coastal Trail leading to faraway Punta Prieta.

On the journey, Donato reflected how according to the legend, the reason Prieto Bartolo had buried the Spaniard's valuables in the grave in the first place, had been to appease his ghost. Nonetheless, Señor Bartolo acted as though 'the powers that be' had ordained him lawful warden of the nobleman's legacy by birthright.

Donato thought hard upon the matter, but could not come up with a plausible scheme to keep Señor Bartolo from learning where he and Pedro had left the nobleman's chest. The only remedy he could think of was to offer up a prayer to the ghosts of Don Tomas and Don Diego to intervene. While still actively praying to his guardian spirits, Donato took the lead at Punta Prieta and leisurely rode *La Perla* through the coastal scrub growing at the cliff's edge, as though searching for a particular spot.

"If I could only locate the place where I rode down upon the robbers, I might recognize some familiar landmark, recall the location of the grave, and then remember where I concealed the chest," he explained to Señor Bartolo.

At one point, Donato halted *La Perla* and was looking over the side of the cliff when, suddenly, Elyse screamed, "Donato, look out!"

Donato's heart skipped a beat when next he heard Señor Bartolo cocking his rifle behind him. When he turned around, he found himself looking down the bore of the barrel. However, as though it had only been a joke, Señor Bartolo grinned and, raising the firearm a fraction over his head, fired it at a seagull flying over the cliffs.

"I had you going there for a minute, didn't I?" he chuckled. "Come on, then. Let us not waste all day here. I want to stop at the mine site again on our way back. By then Señor Martinez should have set off the explosives and unearthed more of the quality stones."

Donato could only interpret Señor Bartolo's little joke as an unspoken warning not to double-cross him. He was sorting out how to respond when he was startled by a luminous glow materializing before his eyes. Appearing mercurial silver in the full glare of the morning sun, three luminous orbs took shape above a cat's claw thicket that stood about twenty yards distant, and then began slowly gliding toward him over the top of the shrubbery like itinerant souls drifting through space.

Reminded of the phenomenon that had visited him on the beach that night, Donato again recalled Doña Blanca's words when she recited the legend:

"To this day, the sightings of strange, ghostly lights seen floating over Don Tomas' land are thought to be the spirits of Prieto and the pirates searching for the treasure."

"What's the matter?" Señor Bartolo asked, trotting the *fenómeno* up beside Donato. "Don't tell me you still can't figure out where you rode *Alazán* down the side of the cliff!"

Donato silently pointed in the direction of the sun at the three luminous orbs drifting toward them. When Señor Bartolo caught sight of the spectacle, all at once, he stared, gulped, and blanched as white as the chalky sandstone lying round about. "Madre de Dios!" he gasped, clutching his crucifix. "They look like three featureless faces lit from within! They are staring at us and moving this way—I swear they are!" Wondering what the phenomena intended, Donato and Señor Bartolo both sat motionless in their saddles as though melded with their mounts, awaiting the next development.

Then, as though intent on scaring the horsemen off their customary haunting grounds, in unison, the dazzling cluster sped up suddenly and swooped toward them. Next, to the onlookers' astonishment, as though unwillingly plucked back into the netherworld by the Devil's own hand, the orbs unexpectedly dematerialized into thin air. A wailing sound and the eerie patter of ghostly hooves fading into the ether followed.

The men looked about them for any remaining evidence of the unearthly display, but once it had revisited its birthplace in the infinite, they no longer heard or saw any trace of the phenomenon. Instead, the native cry of a hawk shattering the silence as it flew over the *campo* brought Donato and Señor Bartolo back to the present.

Donato pretended to share Señor Bartolo's fear and spoke softly. "This place has always given me the creeps. Strange sightings have been reported down here before. You said you planned to pass by the mine again on our way back; this does not leave us much time. Why don't we call it a day? I am sure the nobleman's sea chest is still quite safe, and I can't seem to identify the spot where I rode down over the side of the cliff and apprehended the robbers."

The color had begun to return to Señor Bartolo's face. "Yes, it looks as though you will need to devote a couple of days to exploring the area. We'll come back when we can spare the time to camp out."

Elyse had ridden *Alazán* up to an overhang that shaded a high spot on the Southern Coastal Trail, and watched the men's activities from a distance. "What did you find out?" she asked Donato after they rejoined her. "You both look as though you'd seen ghosts!"

"Didn't you notice the three lights like the one I described at my birthday party, sailing toward us above the cat's claw thicket over there?" Donato asked, studying the nuances in Elyse's skeptical expression as he pointed out the direction. "They made an eerie wailing sound right before they disappeared."

While Donato and Elyse were talking, Señor Bartolo dismounted his *fenómeno* and led him to a knoll overlooking the beach, as though searching one last time along the precipice for a spot where Donato might conceivably have ridden down upon the robbers.

While Señor Bartolo was otherwise occupied, Donato moved close to Elyse and spoke in a low tone. "I had hoped our host would view the manifestation of the ghost lights as an omen he ought to think twice about meddling with the mysteries that were the bane of his ancestors. But look, I think he is still trying to figure out where I might have hidden the chest. He is peering down the side of the drop off, examining the cliffside."

Elyse frowned, "Considering you had to have been facing the sun, how can either of you be so sure of what you saw? You might not have seen anything more than sunspots before your eyes. It is also normal for gusts of winds coming off the ocean to create strange sounds as they blow through the caves and fissures in the rocks."

Elyse's skepticism irritated Donato. "We saw the lights as plain as day; they were each nearly the size of your hat!"

"There can be more than one explanation for phenomena, you know," Elyse continued gently. "You and Señor Bartolo probably both expected to see something strange out here; perhaps that is why you saw what you did. That's understandable."

Donato was not interested in proving anything to an outsider. "Don Tomas claimed that educated people never give credence to phenomena they can't explain. Next year, after you return from the United States, we will take a ride together, and I'll show you the herbs that grow in the *campo*; and perhaps... other things."

As Donato, Señor Bartolo, and Elyse were riding out of Punta Prieta, an ominous tremor rumbled portentously through the hills like a malediction from the spirits of the region. Whether it were reverberations from the dynamiting of faraway La Ballena or an act of Nature, this spooky tremor gave *La Perla* a perfect excuse to grab the left shank of her curb bit in her teeth and take off down the side of a ravine that led deeper into the *campo*. The descent was so steep Donato was forced to bury his face in her mane and hold on for dear life. When the mare reached the creek bed, her gait became cadenced again, as though on a well-known trail. Only then did Donato dare lift his face far enough above her flying mane to behold *Espíritu* galloping up a sandy wash ahead of them.

All at once, he felt so much empathy with the wild horses' wish to be free again that he wanted to jump off *La Perla* and allow her to go back to her life with *Espíritu*, but there was more than one reason he couldn't. If he were to allow her to gallop free without first stopping to unsaddle her, the mare might get her tack hung up on a rock, cactus, or low growing tree and injure herself. In addition, there was still the hope of a foal for Elyse and the prayer that Señor Bartolo would return a couple of the pearls. It was not until *Espíritu* stopped for a breather partway up the side of El Rey that *La Perla* caught up with him. This was also when Donato heard Elyse calling him.

"Donato! Are you alright?"

Donato called back down to her, but his words only blew away with the wind. Since awkward movements were liable to throw the mare off balance on the precipitous slope, Donato turned around ever so slowly to look below him.

Alazán had been courageous enough to follow behind the Azulejos, and was easy for Donato to spot. Elyse and the glossy chestnut stallion stood out from among the dull, brownish boulders littering a gorge running from the foot of the mountain like fire opals gleaming from the bottom of a lackluster quarry.

Since Donato could not yet see Señor Bartolo, he figured the *fenómeno* probably had just enough burro in his nature to refuse to climb the last stretch of the hazardous gorge. Turning so he could look back up the mountainside ahead of him, Donato glimpsed *Espíritu's* distinctive forehead marking peeking through a thicket of windswept jojoba bushes like a tiny ghost light of the region. "Where will the wild horse go next?" he wondered.

Suddenly, he heard the now-familiar sound of Señor Bartolo's rifle resounding through the hills. Fortunately, the bullets flew wide of their mark, and *Espíritu* took off toward the other side of the mountain with such energy his dust obscured him.

Below, Donato heard Elyse's faraway frantic voice calling "No! Oh, no, no, no!" Then Señor Bartolo hailed him from an adjacent ridge.

"Bring the mare down, you idiot!"

Even though Donato didn't like taking directives from Senor Bartolo, he supposed he was right this time and attempted to turn *La Perla* so she faced back down the mountainside. Nonetheless, she angled her right ear toward *Espíritu*'s dust cloud and stubbornly planted her feet as though she had made up her mind to follow him. Donato tried to win her confidence by speaking soothingly to her and caressing her neck reassuringly, but even his coaxing did not elicit the desired response.

"I simply can't allow you to join your pal, my jewel. But, don't worry, everything will turn out alright in the end," he soothed. "You'll see. One day I'll not only own you, but you will produce a beautiful little Azulejo filly for Elyse."

After failing to persuade *La Perla*, Donato dismounted on her uphill side and tied her reins to the saddle horn. He then drove her back down ahead of him and followed her on foot.

As soon as he was within earshot, Donato called out to Elyse who was still sitting astride *Alazán* in the shade of a rocky overhang at the top of the gorge. "I may need your help catching *La Perla*! Remove your hat and dismount!"

*   *   *

It seemed both the *fenómeno*'s stubbornness and the events of the day had sorely tested Señor Bartolo's patience. "My guess is you knew all along that the Azulejo stallion had survived the fishermen's bullet," he barked. "If I had been in a position to take better aim at him, his death would now be upon your head!"

"What are you babbling about?" Donato asked, feeling even less concerned than usual with the way he addressed his host under the circumstances.

"Do you think I'd have allowed you to bring the mare out here into the *campo* if I had realized her amigo would be tempting her back into the wilderness?" Señor Bartolo scoffed, feigning disgust.

Donato ignored Señor Bartolo. Instead, as soon as they returned to the main trail, he rode up beside Elyse. "Our host won't admit it, but he also knew *Espíritu* was still alive. Rather than allow the stallion to run free, I'll bet his plan all along has been to use *La Perla* as bait to entice him out into the open so he could be shot and killed."

"But why would he want to shoot such a magnificent creature?"

"Señor Bartolo has been pursuing that animal for as long as I can remember," Donato replied.

"That still doesn't explain why he would want to shoot such a rare stallion."

"He has his own twisted schemes and motives, I guess. He would probably rather see the azulejo he can never catch get shot than allow it to run free. His wish to demonstrate authority over me may also have inspired him, in part at least. He might relish destroying something I hold so dear. Besides, I overheard Señor Cuevas cautioning him that *La Perla* would be easier to control with no *Espíritu* tempting her back into the wild."

Elyse was appalled. "Poor *Espíritu*! I hope he runs far away from here where no one will ever find him. If the nobleman's curse really ever had power, I pray it puts an end to Señor Bartolo's reckless ambition. He may have to learn the hard way."

CHAPTER 22

The Curse Reaches Out: The Earthquake

AS the three riders were nearing the last few bends in the arroyo approaching La Ballena, they heard another rumble and felt the ground shudder beneath their feet. As a result, Donato was not surprised when later on, their spooked animals refused to turn onto the trail leading up to the mine site. This path ran right along the fault line Elyse had pointed out earlier that day.

Craning their heads to peer through the tall broomweed growing in the bottom of the gully, the riders could see the red warning flag with skull and crossbones fluttering at half-mast beside the engineer's tent. Señor Martinez lowered it before leading his group of workmen back inside the mine, signifying that he believed enough time had passed since he discharged the dynamite to make it safe to reenter the mountain.

Donato turned to Señor Bartolo. "I hope the men will be safe inside the mine so soon after the engineer has detonated his explosives."

Señor Bartolo ignored Donato and spurred *Machismo* until he gored the creature's sides. "What ails you, you overgrown jackass!" he barked. "This is the second time you have gone *loco* on me today."

As it turned out, however, *Machismo* was wiser than his master. A powerful *temblor* undulated across the plateau.

"Quick! Look to your mounts!" Señor Bartolo shouted, dismounting and steadying himself on the swaying branch of a ciruelo tree. "This feels like a genuine earthquake—and a real *bruto*!"

Donato slipped *La Perla*'s leather blindfold down over her eyes and called to Elyse to do the same to *Alazán*. Time seemed to stand still.

The sands in the arroyo bed rose and fell like rollers upon the sea while La Ballena shuddered like a ship run aground. Now the shale that had concerned Donato broke free of the mountain and slid down its sides in an avalanche, bringing with it huge, blackened slabs of rock. Next, an immense gray dust cloud wafted up into the still dry air, like smoke from a smoldering log—obscuring the sun's disk behind an inauspicious haze.

With the blindfolds down over their eyes, the animals still stood splay-legged, ready to offset the motion of the unsteady ground beneath their feet. "Válgame Dios," Señor Bartolo rasped, still clutching the swaying ciruelo. "Landslides will have inundated the caves!"

After the ground stabilized, as though all of nature had bated her breath in the suspense following a mining accident, a profound silence fell over the countryside. Holding her dusty kerchief before her face, Elyse whispered to Donato. "How dreadful! Can it be that I thoughtlessly wished the curse on Señor Bartolo's operation? I somehow feel guilty."

Donato coughed to clear the dust from his throat and to hide his emotion, then wrapped his arm protectively around Elyse and spoke reassuringly in her ear. "No! Of course you didn't! Now listen, there are going to be dead men under that slide. My hopes that Señor Bartolo would return a couple of my pearls now lie forever buried with those poor souls beneath the collapsed mine site. By Mexican law, Señor Bartolo will be required to pay support to their families."

Leaving Elyse to watch over the animals, Donato and Señor Bartolo ascended on foot to the top of a hillock a couple hundred meters away to view the extent of the landslide. It did not take long to confirm the worst. Oceans of heavy shale had inundated the caves. The mountain looked as though a large portion had melted away, altering its contours forever. It only waited for new rains to bring the swift growth of foliage that would heal its scars and cover the grisly calamity buried deep beneath its fallen rocks.

"May our Savior redeem the souls of the pious," Señor Bartolo murmured in a dazed whisper, turning to Donato. "One of your workmen will be among the dead."

Donato was incredulous. "One of mine?" he asked disbelievingly—exasperated by the way Señor Bartolo seemed to be toying with the news. "Not Ramón?"

"No, it's Chevalo. He remained inside the caves this morning until after you left to talk with Elyse. He didn't want you to know he'd joined my crew."

"God rest his soul!" exclaimed Donato clasping his hands together in supplication. "I had no idea. He must have been desperate for money. I will contact his family as soon as we return to El Santo. They will want to hold a service for him."

One look at the men's faces after they returned from examining the slide and Elyse did not need to ask. Señor Bartolo stamped and swore while swatting at the *fenómeno*'s dusty saddle and then turned to Donato. "Let's trade mounts before we start back. If the mare hasn't settled down by now, she never will."

Señor Bartolo's request took Donato by surprise. "You are asking to ride the mare while we are still out here in the *campo*? Señor, you have seen for yourself how unpredictable she can act out here in the boundless wilderness. I would caution you..."

"Don't patronize me, boy!" Señor Bartolo roared, his dark eyes flashing. "If she dares to give me trouble, I shall beat the life out of her and leave her carcass for the vultures!"

Donato thought of recommending to Señor Bartolo that he remove his hat, but the man's dire mood checked him. Señor Bartolo tried seizing hold of the mare's reins, but she snorted and rolled her eyes defiantly, provoking him to fly into an even greater rage. He was just reaching for his whip when out of the dust and haze pervading the air, Ramón suddenly showed up riding the nervous burro, *Pancho*

Villa. He struggled to hide his concern over the possible outcome of the earthquake after taking in the situation. "Is everyone alright?"

Donato gave an unsmiling reply, "All the miners were at work inside the caves when the avalanche buried the site."

"Good God! And Chevalo?"

Señor Bartolo nodded, *"Ay,* everyone."

"Dios!" said Ramón, crossing himself. Then he doffed his hat and addressed Señor Bartolo. "Praise the Lord you three still survive. *Siento sus lágrimas,* I feel your tears. This is like…"

"A vengeful payback by the spirits of the region," Donato ventured, a grim smile tugging at one side of his mouth.

"Something like that," Ramón replied absently. Then, turning again to Señor Bartolo, he quickly changed the subject. "Doña Blanca sent me to inform you she needs Donato back at Rancho La Primavera, *pronto!* Right away!"

"What is the trouble?" Donato asked, taken aback by the manner in which Ramón had delivered this message. The Doña Blanca he had known would never have instructed one of her workmen to give him a direct order without including a personal note of explanation, much less ask her spokesman to pass the message along to Señor Bartolo. At least she would never have done so while Don Tomas was still alive. Had a general insurrection occurred? Did all Don Tomas' previous employees and family members now acknowledge Señor Bartolo to be rightful successor to Los Terrenos de Punta Prieta and Rancho La Primavera?

Upon Ramón's arrival, Donato noticed that Señor Bartolo's spirits had picked up. Donato first suspected he and Ramón were conspiring with one another when Señor Bartolo replied to Ramón in a friendly, upbeat tone of voice.

"You came along just in the nick of time, lad," Señor Bartolo declared, smiling obsequiously at Ramón. "I was just thinking how *La Perla* would benefit from a change of trainers." Then, allowing himself a malicious chuckle, he slapped Donato on the shoulder. "Why don't you ride the burro back to the ranch, Donato? Ramón can ride the mare to El Santo for me and try her out at the same time!"

Donato had been looking forward to getting together with Ramón so they could fill each other in on their news and discuss plans, but his friend's demeanor suggested something had changed between them. Now, as Donato stood slack-jawed with astonishment, Ramón unabashedly snatched the mare's lead from his hand. He then called arrogantly back over his shoulder while leading her away. "*El burro tiene sed,*" he declared, implying that Donato might never have demonstrated enough forethought to water the thirsty burro before riding him back to the ranch.

Donato was at a loss for words; he needed to give himself time to think his situation through. Although he realized he shouldn't be the one taking orders, watering the burro as Ramón had commanded provided a good excuse. Nevertheless, curious to see how well Ramón and the mare were going to get along, Donato decided to lead the burro a little ways away so he could hang around a few minutes and watch from a distance.

Ramón also found himself in a difficult position. He wished to make a lasting good impression on Señor Bartolo, but taking the mare from Donato might well prove humiliating. Even though he had been Donato's tutor in horsemanship, when he had tried handling *La Perla* for the first time, she chased him over the stone wall at Rancho Salvatierra. What if she were to make a fool of him now?

Ramón decided the best course of action would be to play the clown. However, as it turned out, the most comical part of his exchange with the mare would prove to be the way *La Perla*, maddened by Ramón's inauspicious cowboy hat, played her sidesplitting role right along with him. Ramón had no sooner snubbed her right rein around her saddle horn and set the toe of his boot in her left stirrup, than she let out a groan and sank down to the ground as if to suggest even the weight of one of his feet was heavier than she could support. When

Ramón tried to pull her up onto her feet again by her lead, she fought back by rearing into the air and striking at him with her forelegs.

Elyse, who had been watching the proceedings on *Alazán*, let out a cry of concern. But Ramón, the clever horseman, moved nimbly out of *La Perla*'s reach, grinning appreciatively at her spirited antics.

"*No me quiere! Solamente a Donato!* She won't have me, only Donato!" he exclaimed aloud. Then, to himself, he muttered, "I think I'll lead the 'witchy little *bestia*' a little way down the trail first. If I keep my cool, after a while, she might settle down."

Elyse surmised Ramón had paid Donato a compliment and, seeing his plight, returned a friendly smile. "Wait," she said, motioning with her hand and then dismounting from *Alazán*. Since she was nearer to Ramón than Donato, who stood some distance away still holding the burro, her intention was to help Ramón out with a subtle hint. However, she had no sooner started toward the mare, than Ramón acted alarmed and moved to intercept her.

"*Déjela!* Let the *gringa* be!" Señor Bartolo directed. "She gets along just fine with the ornery bitch!"

After hanging her hat over *Alazán*'s saddle horn, Elyse walked toward the mare. "No sombrero," she whispered, gesturing in such a way that Señor Bartolo could not see she was pointing at Ramón's hat. Ramón immediately understood and grinned. Now he knew there was a secret to handling the mare.

"Alright, *Ándale, pues.* Go ahead then," Ramón agreed, bowing.

At this point, Donato could not stand to look on any longer. The way Ramón and Elyse were getting along would not have annoyed him in the past, but today was different. He needed to collect himself. His time would be better spent watering the burro. Under the shade of the oasis fig tree, he would decide how to deal with Ramón and Señor Bartolo, and then rehearse his goodbyes to Elyse.

However, once at the Los Cardenales oasis, the eccentric burro added to the setbacks of the day by making the event into a drama. With his ears pointing forward, he stood on tiptoe and quivered at the brink of the pool as though afraid his own reflection might jump back at him—reaching his lips out to slurp the water up in slow, anxious gulps, which, as a result of his nervousness, siphoned right back out of his nose, adding to his anxiety.

While watching *Pancho Villa* try to drink, Donato remembered that one of the reasons the burro made long trips in record time was he held up well without drinking. When *Pancho Villa* took so long trying to evade his own forward reflection in the pool, Donato questioned whether the creature really was thirsty after all. Why had Ramón even directed him to water the jackass, he wondered.

"Ramón made me look incompetent to manage a burro, let alone own a ranch," Donato grumbled sarcastically to himself. "*Hijos!* I should have asked him to explain how he knew the long-suffering burro was even thirsty."

Being familiar with *Pancho Villa's* peculiar drinking habits, Ramón guessed Donato would be a while. Señor Bartolo, on the other hand, saw this as the perfect opportunity to inflict a parting humiliation on Donato. Tossing Elyse a smile, he shrugged his shoulders and then gave a nod down the trail leading to El Santo, signifying that it was time they continued on their return trip. Turning to Ramón, he said, "You ride *Alazán* and let the Señorita handle the mare. Imply to her that we expect her boyfriend to catch up with us."

Using broken English and hand gestures, Ramón did his best to convey Señor Bartolo's message to Elyse, and then graciously offered her the mare to ride. After watching Ramón mount *Alazán*, Elyse suddenly realized that Donato and the burro were nowhere to be seen. Wondering why Donato had left her alone with Señor Bartolo and Ramón, she swung *La Perla* around. She planned to ride the mare up the small hill overlooking the arroyo and La Ballena that Donato and Señor Bartolo had viewed the landslide from earlier, hoping she might be able to spot Donato's whereabouts.

"Donato! Donato! Where are you?" Elyse cried as she rode toward the hill. But as she started up the slope, a rumbling aftershock suddenly dislodged a small gravel slide onto the trail in front of *La*

Perla. Still insecure on her own, the frightened mare again seized the bit in her teeth, and this time turned around and galloped back to rejoin *Alazán* and *Machismo* on the main trail. When Señor Bartolo realized Elyse had lost control of *La Perla*, he took advantage of the opportunity to further his objectives. Certain that Elyse's frightened green mare would want to reunite with the other animals, he allowed his spooked *fenómeno* to have its head, and whooping with glee, he led Ramón down the trail leading to El Santo at a gallop. Forced to hold tight to the runaway mare's neck to keep from falling off, Elyse soon found herself flying behind *Alazán* and *Machismo* down the trail.

When Donato returned and discovered his comrades hadn't waited for him to return before leaving for El Santo, he took it as a parting insult from Señor Bartolo and Ramón. Donato's first impulse was to pursue Elyse so he could tell her goodbye, but his pride prevented him from galloping after her on a mere burro—his dignity had already been compromised enough!

During the first couple of miles along the trail back to Rancho La Primavera, Donato remained deep in thought. He convinced himself he ought to feel fortunate to finally be rid of such undependable friends as Ramón and Elyse. Now he would return to his dear family who always treated him with the utmost respect: Pedro, Maria Elena, Doña Blanca, and the two faithful family housekeepers, Doña Lupe and Doña Josephina, who had always been kind to him.

Before long, upon rounding a bend in the trail, Donato got a clear view of the distant blue gulf so many miles away and his standpoint changed again. This was when it dawned on him how isolated the ranch would seem without Ramón, Elyse, and Don Tomas. He had to admit that he had never experienced the same comradeship with anyone else. These three, each in their way, had occupied a very special place in his heart.

The further Donato rode along the trail toward Rancho La Primavera, the more disheartened he felt. Once more, he nearly turned *Pancho Villa* toward El Santo. However, still imagining that the mere sight of him flying along on the comical, long eared pacing burro might make everyone laugh, once again, he decided he wanted Elyse to remember him the way he had been before Ramón showed up: cool, confident, and self-assured!

Anguish so filled Donato's heart he felt as though even the Almighty had turned against him. Hopelessly at a loss, he halted the burro and dismounted to meditate in the shade of a boulder. In the end, he surrendered to morbid fantasies about wandering the hills until he died of exposure. Perhaps, then, his spirit would simply forever wander Los Terrenos de Punta Prieta like the lost ghost lights of legend!

On the other hand, this line of thinking did not satisfy him for very long. Now he stood up and expressed his frustrations by hurling his knife at various innocent cacti. "Here's for Elyse, Ramón, the mare, and the land," he said, aiming at a lofty cardón that seemed to stand steadfast and imperturbable like Señor Bartolo.

However, because he had taken aim from the bank above it, exactly like Señor Bartolo, the cactus got the better of him. Now, the only way Donato could reach high enough to pull the knife out again was by positioning *Pancho Villa* under the plant and standing on his saddle.

In the process of reaching for his knife, Donato accidentally dislodged an owl's nest wedged between two cactus limbs. To his surprise, a dried out little leather pouch also fell out of it onto the ground.

"*Híjole*! My goodness!" he said, jumping down and picking it up. "An owl must have decided to carry this away like a trophy to its nest!"

Donato knelt down in the shade cast by the cactus, tore the pouch open, and drew out a memorable little blue medicine vial. After removing the stopper, to his joy, five familiar little spheres slid out into the palm of his hand along with the dry leaves it contained. One by one, he dropped the pearls into the crown of his hat where they rolled around as though driven by a destiny all their own!

Donato began laughing and shedding tears of joy when a piece of colored twine he recognized from his birthday party wafted in on the breeze, and then dropped onto a small cactus flower at his feet. He knew it was a sign Don Tomas' spirit was near.

Fresh optimism suddenly cleared Donato's mind. *"Abuelo,"* he whispered. "Finding your pearls has given me the greatest wealth a man can acquire. This turn of fortune has given me faith in providence!"

As though finding his pearls again hightened his objectivity, Donato realized Doña Blanca would never have guessed Ramón might encounter him midway on the trail. It followed that she also did not expect him to reach the ranch until the afternoon of the following day at the earliest. If he hurried, he still had ample time to change his mind, return to El Santo, and say goodbye to Elyse before she was likely to board the bus in the morning.

Donato set the pink pearl back in its old hiding place in the handle of Don Tomas' knife and then looked around for a safe place to conceal the other four gems. This was when his eyes lit upon a huge double-headed barrel cactus growing some distance from the beaten path. It was so big and tough he was confident no one would choose to cut it up for burro or cattle feed. It grew beside a recognizable marker comprised of an enormous boulder resembling a Brahma bull with a double hump; the branches of a dead tree formed the landmark's horns.

Donato stabbed the blade of his knife into the underside of the fat *biznaga* to create an opening and then poked the little blue vial deep into the spongy center. After allowing the thorny flesh of the plant to close back together like the tight lips of a spiny, desert oyster, he congratulated himself on his ingenuity. Not only would the plant's wound close up in time, but he knew the forbidding cactus would never yield up its treasure—not even to the clever little desert mice.

CHAPTER 23

The Pink Pearl: The Town Jail

AS Donato hurried his burro along the trail to El Santo, he began formulating a plan. This charade with Señor Bartolo must end! Finding the pearls had given him the courage to confront his adversaries and make a fresh start with Elyse. He would wake her up and explain the malicious subterfuge perpetrated by Señor Bartolo and Ramón. He would then also declare his love for her and promise to never again abandon her in unfit company. Then, if she were still well disposed toward him, he would tell her to leave Señor Bartolo's Rancho Los Santos and rent a room at the Los Misioneros motel. Next, he would find Ramón and demand to know why Doña Blanca needed to see him so urgently. If the need to return to Rancho La Primavera were not a pressing one, he planned to ride to the magistrate's office in San Antonio. Don Paco would be able to verify the authenticity of Don Tomas' will and other documents.

The sun had set behind the Puesta del Sol Mountains by the time Donato spotted Señor Bartolo's hacienda, so he was glad to see a light shining out between the cracks in Elyse's shutters. He decided to ride *Pancho Villa* around to the back and halt him below her windowsill. However, when he peered in, his heart skipped a beat. He recognized the portly silhouette of Señora Bartolo on the other side of the curtain as she busily straightened the room. Had Elyse already left Señor Bartolo's hacienda and gone to stay at the Los Misioneros?

Donato was trying to decide what to do next, when a burro sounded off in a neighbor's backyard. He slapped *Pancho Villa*'s neck to discourage him from answering, but his thwarted mount only replied with an even more anguished he-haw.

Señora Bartolo had been so upset by the news of the catastrophe at the opal mine, she was ready to read disaster into everything. "*Ay!* Aliseo! Come quickly!" she cried. "Someone on a burro just tried to peek in through the window—a robber perhaps!"

When *Pancho Villa* sounded off, Señor Bartolo had been sitting in his living room surrounded by Don Chepe, Ramón, and the two deputies. They had all been discussing the consequences of the mining disaster while Señor Bartolo signed legal papers presented to him by Don Chepe. These were the documents officially making Señor Bartolo the new sheriff of El Santo, and permitting him to demand the respected title of "Don," although he had not genuinely earned it.

"The deputies and I will check behind the house," said Don Chepe after *Pancho Villa* brayed, giving his old flashlight a shake so the bulb would light up. Before long, the deputies and Don Chepe escorted Donato to the front door of the hacienda. Ramón followed behind, leading *Pancho Villa*.

"So this is the way you repay my hospitality!" Señor Bartolo barked at Donato. "Instead of coming in through my front door, you sneaked around to the back of my house under the cover of night like a prowler and try to break in through my window!"

"I didn't intend any wrong," Donato declared. "I simply saw a hint of light shining through Elyse's shutters and wanted to surprise her."

Señor Bartolo nodded to the deputies. "A likely story. Give me his knife and then escort him to the jail. I'll make a ruling on his offenses later."

Curious as to whether Donato had hidden any new treasures in Don Tomas' knife, Señor Bartolo comfortably seated himself back in his living room and then checked out the handle. "Válgame Dios! Donato has discovered the lost pearls!" he declared, tipping the pink one out into his palm. "I wonder what he did with the other four?" After probing the extent of the secret chamber and finding nothing, Señor Bartolo's thoughts returned to over four years ago at the *Vacadilla* oasis when a horned owl had flown away with the leather pouch containing the gems.

How Señor Bartolo Lost the Pearls

That night in the Vacadilla oasis when Señor Bartolo appropriated Donato's keepsake pearls, alarming nightmares tormented him. In the first one, he dreamed his men had learned of the treasures and tried to rob him. In the next one, one of the big, ugly pack rats with a hairless tail scurried down from a palm tree to empty out his pockets while he was still asleep. Next, he found himself dreaming he was searching among the litter of dry palm fronds covering the ground for the deerskin pouch containing the vial that held the gems. But all he discovered were the telltale scraps of cellophane covering the candies, which had also been in his pockets.

When Señor Bartolo awakened from his nightmares to realize he had only been dreaming, he gave thanks to the Virgin. Nevertheless, in case the dreams might be an omen, he decided to find a safer hiding place for the pouch. The thought of burying tiny treasures in the ground was an impractical solution. Instead, he decided to search for a spot along the trail that would be inaccessible to wind, rain, or meddling wildlife.

Señor Bartolo walked over to where *Machismo*'s saddle hung over a boulder and heaved it across his left shoulder by the saddle horn along with the bridle and bosal. Next, he scooped up the sweat pads with his right arm and strode down into the arroyo to look for his *fenómeno* by the light of the moon. He found the huge mule looming over a clump of mule fat upon which it liked to browse, like a cow standing in short grass.

With well-practiced movements, Señor Bartolo flung the pads up on the creature's back, dropped the saddle on top, and then shook everything down into place with the lay of the hair. Next, he tightened the cinches, bridled the beast, swung aboard, and rode down into the upper end of the oasis where the cliffs formed a narrow canyon. There, he stopped before a great wall of smooth, glistening granite that looked as though a giant had riddled it with buckshot. Even the nimblest possums and pack rats could never get a toe-hold on its sheer, slick, surface. Also, the lowest niche was too high up for a man seated on horseback to see into.

By standing on the *fenómeno's* back, Señor Bartolo found himself just able to reach the lowest grotto. After sweeping out some debris, he tossed the pouch toward the back. Next, he climbed down to the ground to pick up a round, smooth river rock with which to seal up the opening. This was when an owl suddenly swooped down out of a nearby black willow and alighted in the entrance to the grotto.

Señor Bartolo let out an anguished yell and threw a handful of stones at the bird, for he feared the leather pouch might have attracted it. Moreover, as the owl flapped away over the *campo*, he noticed drawstrings dangling down like a couple of mouse-tails. That was the last Señor Bartolo had seen of the pouch containing the pearls.

* * *

When the deputies pushed Donato through the door of the large old town jail, he noticed Chico sitting cross-legged in the left corner. In his hands, he held the bosal and *cabresto* he had been weaving by the light of a kerosene lamp someone had placed on an overturned lard can beside him.

Chico looked up and stared blankly at the newcomer, then whispered aside to his cohorts crowded around him. "I remember him. That is Don Tomas' boy. I met him years ago back up on La Mesa Alta."

Donato had no need to look for the drunk sitting in the right hand corner of the small room to know he was there. He was actively begging for tequila and the whole place reeked of alcohol, accumulated cigarette smoke and body odor.

It seemed the only pleasant character in the cell was a young man named Celestino. The fellow's clothes were worn and torn, but his manner was gracious and he acted overjoyed to have someone friendly to talk to.

"*A sus órdenes*, at your service!" Celestino exclaimed, extending his hand and bowing respectfully to Donato. "What turn of ill luck has brought you here, amigo? You haven't the look of a criminal about you!"

"I had a little misunderstanding with Señor Bartolo about some property," Donato grumbled. "That's all."

"I'm not surprised. He unjustly charged me with theft awhile back."

"Theft of what?"

"Those stupid opals."

"From the mine?"

"That's right, from La Ballena. I worked for Señor Martinez at the time."

"Madre de Dios! I'd count your blessings if I were you, my friend! But for the fact Señor Bartolo shut you up in here, you'd have departed this life in the earthquake along with the other miners."

"Nonetheless, it's hard to feel lucky when locked up in a crowded jail," Celestino protested.

"So, tell me your story."

"I am not squeamish about heights. This was the reason Señor Martinez hired me to climb the sides of La Ballena and investigate the caves near the summit. However, as soon as Señor Bartolo noted how easily I scaled the cliffs, he acted annoyed when I didn't bring better mineral samples back. I heard him telling Martinez that he thought I might be scheming to climb back up to the upper caves when no one was looking and steal some of the better stones for myself. This was why he had me arrested."

"A friend of mine who climbed the side of La Ballena a few years back told me the ascent was very treacherous," Donato observed, remembering Ramón's description of his climb up the mountain. "Climbing the face of the cliff wasn't difficult. I used a grappling tool I made out of shark hooks to pull myself up with. Trying to keep my footing at the top while extracting samples from the grottos without losing my tools or both was the most difficult part. Doing this without a helper was *muy difícil*, very difficult."

"But you could collect good stones if you had a dependable assistant?"

"It would make the job a lot easier!"

"Now that the old digging site has been buried under a few hundred tons of shale, why don't you explain the situation to Señor Bartolo? Explain to him that you could obtain better samples from the summit if you had the right help. He would have to release you from jail—and probably would."

"Yes, I thought of that. However, returning to work at the location where my comrades met with such a dreadful end would give me the chills," he confessed.

Donato dropped his tone to a whisper so none of the other inmates would overhear. "In time, perhaps you may feel differently. Once I clear up this little land ownership dispute with Señor Bartolo, I will be in a position to hire your services. In the meantime, I must trust that you will not betray me. I promise I will make it worth your while."

"*Sí, cómo no*," the climber whispered back. "Señor Bartolo can be very treacherous, even more so than the steep, undependable cliffs of La Ballena!"

* * *

The next morning, Señor Bartolo gave Ramón a couple of hours off to visit with Donato. "Act as though you want to help him get out of jail, and maybe he will let slip what he did with the rest of the pearls," he suggested. When Ramón arrived at the jail, Donato was standing with his back against the bars looking through the high, barred, rear window at the graceful tamarind tree growing outside. He was wishing someone would let him out so he could collect some of their meaty pods to chew on, when Ramón rapped gently behind him.

"Psst," Ramón said, tipping his hand so Donato could glimpse the key in his palm. Donato leaned the side of his face against the bars so Ramón would be able to whisper in his ear. "As soon as I've unlocked the door, I want you to slip around to the back of the jail and wait for me under the tamarind tree. The two deputies are taking time off back at Señor Bartolo's hacienda, so I decided to risk letting you out so we could talk."

Donato was hopeful. When Ramón made an effort to speak the proper forms of Spanish he had taught him, Donato always took it to mean he was in an unusually serious frame of mind.

Ramón opened the cell door for Donato and then quickly locked it up again so no one else could leave. Then he made a final check for the deputies and joined Donato on a bench under the tamarind tree.

"At long last, we can communicate without anyone watching us!" Ramón exclaimed, seeming genuinely relieved. "I am ashamed. I realized I treated you badly the other day out on the trail. But don't worry, everything is going to turn out alright in the end—you wait and see!"

Donato reached up and plucked a pod off one of the branches of the tamarind tree. "I hardly see how," he grumbled, biting into the meat and spitting the shiny brown seeds onto the ground. "You and Señor Bartolo didn't even allow me an opportunity to tell Elyse goodbye."

"I know. I am sorry about your American friend. As a result of the storm, her father and Señor Gomez changed their plans about investigating property at the Cape and showed up unexpectedly at Señor Bartolo's. They had already gone to Rancho Salvatierra to load Señor Gomez's horses into the back of his truck, and were in a hurry to leave for La Paz. Before departing with them, Elyse handed me a box to give you; she also said to tell you she would mail you a letter from La Paz in care of the Bartolos. She will mail all future letters to our usual address in care of the Luceros at Rancho Salvatierra."

"What did the box contain?"

"Binoculars! She told me they had belonged to her father. In addition, she also told me to let you know they are military, so they are shockproof and waterproof. But listen," Ramón continued. "About Señor Bartolo; unfortunately, now that he is becoming sheriff, he says he expects everyone to address him as Don Aliseo. Generally, people of this region only earn the esteemed title, Don, because they are exceptionally well respected, or because they provide some type of dependable, charitable services to the community. However, he is ignoring all that.

"Anyhow, Señor Bartolo, now Don Aliseo, discovered the pink *perla* in your knife handle. He wants me to find out what you did with the others that were hidden in the vial, but I'll tell him whatever you want me to say. You only recovered one pearl?"

"Tell him I hid the rest out in the *campo*, the way he claimed to have done," Donato replied.

"No, then he'll want you to escort him to the spot; I'll tell him the little vial was broken when you found it, with only one pearl inside."

"Alright. I don't like asking anyone to lie for me, but reclaiming the pearls has renewed my faith in providence after so many discouragements. I would lose all hope if Señor Bartolo were to get his hands on them again," Donato said, stretching his arms over his head. "Ah! How good it feels to breathe fresh air once more! My long night in jail seemed as though it would never end!"

"Don't get any ideas now. I must return you to the cell or we'll both end up on the inside!"

"Alright then; it won't be easy, but it looks as though I must continue to be patient a little longer."

Ramón heaved a sigh, "We need to hurry and wrap up our conversation before the deputies come back. First off, let me admit that I realize I have a lot of explaining to do. Don Tomas was right to put his faith in you. You are honorable! But you see, even though

I was only the son of his humble gardener, Don Tomas also took me under his patronage and treated me like a son before you came to live at the ranch. The difficult thing for me to digest has been how, once you showed up, he so quickly dropped all interest in me. I thought the only way to regain my previous status would be by working my way into the good graces of Don Tomas' adversary, Señor Bartolo, who now calls himself, Don Aliseo."

Donato could not keep still any longer. He valued Ramón's friendship, and would gladly do whatever he could to heal past grievances. "It sounds to me as though even Don Tomas may not have been wise in all things, but that wasn't my fault. I intended to ask you to help me manage the ranch; I would also have given you your choice of Don Tomas' fine horses!"

"Even *Alazán?*"

"Yes, even *Alazán* if he was the *bestia* you wanted most."

Ramón frowned. "What of Elyse? If you were going to give *Alazán* to anyone, I thought it would have been to her."

"No, she wants me to breed her a blue-eyed azulejo foal! A truly hopeless request unless I gain possession of *La Perla*. But explain why you didn't trust me to treat you fairly? I have always stood by you and been your friend."

"I don't know. I was insecure I guess. But don't worry, *amigo*, I now realize I have acted foolishly. Actually, it is only through my temporary fit of arrogance that I now find myself in the perfect position to help you!

Ramón continued, "My puffed-up attitude reassured Don Aliseo of my loyalty and made him feel comfortable about confiding his underhanded designs to me yesterday. Among other disclosures, he let on that when he came across your unconscious body on the trail, the opportunity he had been waiting for to get you under his roof and into his control fell right into his hands. He might have left you lying there, except that by relying upon some trickery, he saw a place for you in his schemes. He needed your help with the mare of course, but more importantly, if he could prevent you from upsetting his plot for taking over your land, he believed the officials in La Paz would have no reason to question his phony documents. In any event, even if no one claimed Los Terrenos de Punta Prieta within the allotted time of one year after Don Tomas' death, the entire parcel of property would simply revert back to the government of Mexico. All Don Aliseo would need to do then would be to apply for a thirty-year lease. When the lease was up, he and his heirs would inherit the property under the homesteading law."

"I suppose that explains why he has tried to string me along with the hope of getting a couple of the pearls back."

"Yes, he was playing you on impulse, one song and dance at a time. Seeing as you had not yet said your goodbyes to Elyse, he counted on your following us back to El Santo after you finished watering the burro. In addition, my self-important manner convinced him I was no longer loyal to you. This was when he asked me to help him plot a scheme to arrest you on some trumped-up charge. He hoped that by detaining you in jail he could prevent you from claiming your *abuelo's* land within the allotted statute of one year. Then when you rode around to the back of his hacienda like a burglar in the night, once again you inadvertently played right into his plans."

Donato furrowed his brow, "I have been thinking Don Paco should be able to help me out. He was Don Tomas' ally and legalized his will. If you would be so good as to get me some paper, I would like to write Don Paco a letter filling him in on my situation. If you can, *por favor*, please hand-deliver it to Don Paco without Don Aliseo or one of his spies finding out. You can give it to him when he comes to town this weekend to participate in the horse races. First though, fill me in on why you said Doña Blanca wanted to see me."

"She asked me to check on you."

Donato sounded displeased. "You are telling me she never ordered me back to the ranch 'right away'?"

Ramón looked repentant. "Not those words. I put it that way to gain favor with Don Aliseo. Doña Blanca only told me she wanted to discuss plans with you. You see, after she settles in La Paz, she hopes to invite all the surviving members of her extended family for a reunion and a fiesta. She wants to show off the beautiful two-story Spanish style house with a spiral staircase and beautiful enclosed indoor patio garden that Don Tomas bought her before he died. Pedro will escort her and Maria Elena to Punta Gorda this weekend where Señor Hernandez plans to pick everyone up in his truck and then drive them to La Paz.

"Don Tomas' daughter from his first marriage, Sonya Balboa, your great-grandmother, inherited his propensity to live a long life. She lives on a ranch up in the Santo Domingo Valley, and is still in good health. Also, Don Tomas' two sons from his second marriage, Fernando and Porferio, are healthy still, and might be willing to make the long trip from Guadalajara by crossing over on the ferry from Mazatlan."

"How exciting! I will finally get to meet Sonya. Don Tomas was going to take me to visit her, but unfortunately we never got around to making that trip before he passed away."

Donato looked thoughtful. "In any event, I need to get out of jail before committing to any engagements. When I do get out, my first priority must be to settle the debate with Don Aliseo over the ownership of Don Tomas' land. I must also figure out how to pay you and everyone else working at Rancho La Primavera. I will most likely have to sell some of Don Tomas' cattle."

Ramón frowned. "The trouble is, if you don't show up at Rancho La Primavera before she leaves, Doña Blanca will ask Señor Hernandez to stop off at Don Aliseo's hacienda so she can see and talk with you."

"That would be a tragedy! I don't want her talking with Don Aliseo. His self-assured attitude might convince her he had good reason to arrest me."

"Oh, I wouldn't worry about that. She knows the kind of person you are and the kind Don Aliseo is. She would never believe him."

Donato was not reassured. "Nevertheless, please humor me and take a letter to Pedro and Doña Blanca for me. I need to update them about Don Aliseo fraudulently claiming Don Tomas' land. I will also let them know that I am planning to meet with Don Paco. He notarized Don Tomas' will, and should know how best to handle my dispute with Don Aliseo."

"Yes, Alright. You are in luck that I didn't turn *Pancho Villa* loose. I have been keeping him up in one of Don Aliseo's corrals. The other day, the burro was so eager to get home to eat his dinner, I made the trip from here back to the ranch in less than two hours. Can you believe it?" Ramón said, embellishing his anecdote in praise of *Pancho Villa* with a big smile.

"De veras?" Donato answered raising his eyebrows. "The burro sounds as though he could easily win a distance race against horses!"

"Yes, he would. But listen, so as not to alert Don Aliseo that I am making a trip back to La Primavera, I will wait until after he has left on the trip he has been planning to La Paz. First though, before bringing you pen and paper from the office, let me fill you in on the Azulejo mare."

"Yes, I wanted to ask how you were getting along with her."

"Fine, so long as I remember not to wear my hat! It sets her off something fierce, as though my wearing it amounts to an endorsement of bad character. But that wasn't all I wanted to tell you about *La Perla*. I have a surprise for you! Remember the foal you said Elyse asked for? Well, even Don Aliseo noticed that although the mare lost weight during the trip, her flanks remained filled out. So, naturally, I looked under her belly for what I hardly expected to see."

"Válgame Dios! Is she with foal?" Donato whispered eagerly.

"*Ay!* She is even showing a little udder development."

"*Caramba!* I wonder who the sire could be?"

"I think most likely Don Tomas' stallion *Pico Blanco*. No one saw him in the vicinity of the ranch for most of last spring."

"You're right; he was away for nearly three months! Also, just the other day, I was telling Elyse how *Pico Blanco* has that special gift for bringing out a mare's potential. If Pico really is the sire, it simply isn't right that Don Aliseo should inherit such a special foal."

"I know. He actually acted disappointed when I informed him *La Perla* was pregnant—as though he had some purebred stallion in mind to breed her to. He said that most likely she is carrying a mule foal sired by one of the wild jacks roaming the foothills behind Punta Prieta."

"Yes, but assuming she actually were carrying a mule foal, this might still give us some idea as to what kind of producer *La Perla* is."

Ramón continued, "Yes, this is why I am sure you will be pleased to hear that I have convinced Don Aliseo the wisest plan is for me to take her back to Rancho La Primavera to foal. Unfortunately, however, he has also decided to send Raul along to stand guard over her. And listen to this new development! As though he hadn't meddled enough in our affairs, he is also planning to send his sister's family to live at Don Tomas' hacienda. He acts as though Don Tomas' property already belongs to him. I understand the Dominguez' humble dwelling was demolished in the storm. But still, it is very brazen of him to blithely move his relatives into the Rancho La Primavera hacienda when he doesn't even legally own the land! It's as though he doesn't think it matters."

"Yes, I suppose he hopes that by taking affairs into his own hands, he will discourage me into giving up and going back to Mexico City. However, all things considered, I wouldn't let his moving the Dominguez' family into the hacienda worry you, *amigo*. Even though the Dominguez' are Don Aliseo's relations, none of them are disagreeable folk. The ranch will seem very empty now that Don Tomas has passed away, especially after all his family move out. It might be comforting to have another family living at Rancho La Primavera. Not only that, but you never know; the two girls, Tila and Veronica, could even offer to help out with the general cooking and washing."

Ramón was taken aback by Donato's philosophical viewpoint. "I suppose so, but you haven't heard the final capper yet. This morning Don Aliseo told me he also intends to send his plump stepdaughter, Carmen, along to live and work at Rancho La Primavera. He said, quite seriously, that he was sure if I was around her long enough, I'd grow to like her—and that given time she'd make me an excellent wife!"

Donato broke out laughing, "You're joking!"

"Shush! It's not a bit funny," Ramón said, frowning. "It seems she has a crush on me. Now, down to business, my friend. I will go get you pen and paper so you can compose the letters to Don Paco and Doña Blanca. But, first, if we don't get you locked back up in jail, our grandest hopes will never be fulfilled."

CHAPTER 24

Don Paco: A Dependable Ally

AFTER the boundless freedom of the *campo* life, Donato found living cooped up for six days with seven unsavory men very trying. His last night in jail, Don Chepe exchanged Celestino with a belligerent drunk who bragged of chopping off his coworker's hand with a machete, so there had been no one to talk to.

The following day, Don Aliseo took over his new duties as the official sheriff of El Santo, and Don Chepe celebrated his own retirement. This was also the day Donato would finally be released from jail. Don Aliseo and Don Chepe, preoccupied with their own business, came and went from the office several times without so much as a glance toward the unhappy inmates in the lockup. It was not until Don Aliseo stopped by to unlock the cell door for the deputy bringing the noon meal that Donato noticed a letter sticking out of his shirt pocket. Just like Elyse's stationery, a scroll of tiny blue flowers accented the border of the envelope.

Donato pointed. "That letter looks like it is for me. I have been expecting one from the Americana."

Without answering, Don Aliseo took the envelope from his pocket and sliced it open with his hunting knife. Then, as though savoring the moment, he pulled out the photographs it contained and looked each one over before handing them all to Donato through the jail bars.

The first photographs were of his birds followed by the photos Elyse had taken of him wearing the *charro* outfit the day he rode *La*

Perla. Next, came a photo of Don Tomas holding up the painting of Don Diego, which Donato had last seen hanging on Don Aliseo's living room wall.

When Don Aliseo looked over the next photographs, his expression changed and he did a double take. "*Santos!* A photo of the wild Azulejo stallion all decked out in foreign headgear! No one let on to me that you'd succeeded in capturing and bridling the fugitive. I will see to it you and Ramón both pay for your dishonesty. Step out here this instant!"

Fearful of the sheriff's anger, Donato shrank further inside the cell. But Don Aliseo reached through the door, grabbed him by his shirt, and then dragged him outside. Then he shoved him back against the jail bars with such force the ringing iron nearly deafened Donato.

Shrinking away from the man's musty tobacco breath, Donato snatched Elyse's letter from his hand and then slumped to the floor, his head buzzing.

At that moment, Don Paco, the San Antonio magistrate, appeared in the doorway with Ramón at his heels. Don Paco had big brown eyes like a burly cherub and a friendly expression, which gave the impression he enjoyed savoring his tamales more than chasing criminals.

"What's going on here? Why, this looks like Don Tomas' boy. I heard he was doing you the favor of gentling your wild mare for you."

Doing his best to be devious, Don Aliseo only offered Don Paco a brief comeback. "His offenses remain a private matter between the two of us."

"You should be able to offer me more details than that, Aliseo! Explain!"

"Alright, you asked for it. It grieves me to say so, but the truth is this young man took advantage of my hospitality even though I rescued him and saw to his medical needs after he experienced a life-threatening accident on the trail. The final insult came when my wife caught him trying to break into our house through a back window. He stands charged with trespassing and attempted burglary!"

"Are you sure you haven't made some mistake, Aliseo? These are very serious charges to be levied against such a reputable young man. I will admit the boy might need some guidance now that his *abuelo* has passed away, but I cannot believe he is capable of evil intent. Now that Don Tomas' family will need the *joven's* help back at the ranch, why don't you let the matter rest for now, *delegado*, and hand Donato over to me? If it turns out he is in need of any disciplinary action, I have an empty jail cell back in San Antonio and one idle deputy with plenty of free time on his hands to administer correction."

Don Aliseo knew nothing about the letter Donato had written Don Paco telling him about the new Don's schemes to conquest Los Terrenos de Punta Prieta. He did realize however, that he was only an inexperienced, small-town sheriff, and that Don Paco was a regional magistrate with fifteen years seniority who had the jurisdiction to take charge of the situation. Don Aliseo knew he needed to think quickly how to discourage him from taking any further interest in Donato's case, even if it meant fabricating a lie. "I thank you for your offer, Your Honor, but Donato is scheduled to be arraigned in La Paz next week."

"*Claro*! Of course!" replied Don Paco. "It just so happens I was planning a trip to La Paz myself next Tuesday. I shall escort Donato to the capital and get his *abuelo's* land transferred into his name at the same time!"

Painted into a corner, Don Aliseo temporarily gave up trying to recover his position. Meanwhile, Donato had finished reading Elyse's letter.

Dear Donato,

> *I hope you receive this letter alright. I tried to search for you after you disappeared out there on the lower Mesa Alta plateau near La Ballena, but an after-tremor spooked La Perla into taking the bit in her teeth and joining the animals already speeding Ramón and Señor Bartolo*

toward El Santo at a gallop. When they slowed down and I caught up with them, Ramón and our host acted as though they expected you would soon be joining us, but you never showed up.

When we arrived back at Rancho Los Santos, to everyone's surprise, we were greeted by my father and Señor Gomez. They had just returned from loading Señor Gomez' horses into his truck at Rancho Salvatierra. Both of them acted very annoyed that I had kept them waiting, and gave me no choice but to get my things and join them.

What do you think of the photos? Write and let me know which ones you would like copies of as 5x7 prints. Also, tell me when you get the land issue straightened out and clear an airstrip. I plan to return by plane sometime next fall. I think of the lovely times we spent together every day!

Take care,
Love, Elyse

Don Paco treated both Donato and Ramón like members of his own family. He not only rented them a room at Los Misioneros but also lent them cash to buy clothes to wear at the fiesta.

As soon as Donato and Ramón found themselves alone in the hotel room, Donato chose to relax in the armchair while Ramón reclined on the bed. "What a relief it is to have Don Paco finally take charge!" exclaimed Donato. "I take it you and Don Aliseo are no longer on the best of terms?"

Ramón gave an indifferent look of disgust, leaned back on his pillow, and yawned. "He's not very pleased with me right now."

Donato realized that Ramón felt tired after his whirlwind trip back to Rancho La Primavera and delivering the letter to Don Paco on his return. "Take a nap, amigo—but first fill me in on whether Don Aliseo still wishes you to look after *La Perla* until she foals, yes?"

Being tired, Ramón slipped back into his colloquial way of talking. "Like it or not, love of that mare connects us all. He's got all to win and nothing to lose. Also, he let Chico out of jail this morning—did you know?"

"No, I am very sorry to hear that."

"Yes, he's now dropped the charges he made against him. Probably, he figures Chico has learned his lesson. Also, now that Señor Aliseo Bartolo has officially become Don Aliseo, the new sheriff of El Santo, none of the local *vaqueros* want the responsibility of handling his undependable mare for him in the event something goes wrong."

Ramón seemed to be having difficulty keeping his eyes open, so Donato left him to take a nap while he went to town to buy them both new clothes for the fiesta. When Donato returned, Ramón was still fast asleep, so he left the shirt and slacks he had bought him hanging from the wooden hanger-stand that served as a closet. Then, as it was now late in the afternoon, Donato set off alone to take part in the festivities.

Don Paco was standing at the corner of the small, town square alongside a young man holding his imported racehorse, *Volador*. When the magistrate noticed Donato approaching, he beckoned to him to join them.

"It pleases me to see that you have celebrated your freedom by using the money I lent you to buy festive clothing. Here, let me introduce my rider, Zenen."

"*Mucho gusto*. It is a pleasure," Donato replied shaking Zenen's hand. "Wasn't it you who also rode *Chispa* for Don Aliseo?"

"Yes, over four years ago."

Don Paco interrupted. "Where is Ramón?"

"He was so tired he fell fast asleep in our room," Donato explained.

"No matter. I offered to let him try out *Volador* in the race, but we can do that another time. I hear you have become an expert horseman yourself! Maybe you'd like to try riding my gelding in the race," Don Paco offered.

As though glad of a reprieve, Zenen handed *Volador*'s reins to Donato before allowing him the chance to accept or decline his employer's offer. "He's got no mouth and a neck like a bull, so you will be pretty much along for the ride," counseled Zenen.

Don Paco held up his hand. "Wait! Here comes Ramón." After Ramón, who appeared re-energized after his rest, greeted the three men with a bright "*buenas tardes*," Don Paco turned from Ramón to Donato. "Now that Ramón has joined us, we will let him ride *Volador* as planned. Donato, why don't you go over to Don Aliseo and offer to race his spirited Azulejo mare for him? By the look of things, he is not likely to refuse!"

Don Paco nodded toward Don Aliseo's group, which amounted to Chico and a knot of spectators casting critical glances in Donato's direction. Chico, having not yet figured out the secret to handling *La Perla*, had his hands full trying to manage the rearing mare.

Donato gave Don Paco a questioning look and bit his lip. "Your Honor! Surely, you aren't asking me to ride Don Aliseo Bartolo's mare against your celebrated gelding?"

"Naw! It's alright, go ahead, son. It has become boring to win every race. I would like to observe how you handle the Azulejo mare. It should be an interesting race!"

Donato leaned closer to Don Paco and whispered in his ear. "Alright, if you insist, but I could just as easily let Chico and Don Aliseo in on the mare's secret. They only need to remove their hats!"

"You don't say!"

"Yes, the mare made a negative association with cowboy hats when Don Aliseo's ruffians mismanaged her."

"Well, I'll be. Hand me your hat then, *joven*. Now walk on over to Don Aliseo and offer to ride his mare in the race for him." Don Paco smiled again and winked at Donato. "Go on!"

Don Paco was right. Since Chico continued to have difficulty with *La Perla*, Don Aliseo condescended to accept Donato's offer. To the accompaniment of the cheering crowd, Donato easily took charge of the mare, mounted her, and then rode her behind Ramón and *Volador* down the dirt road running through the center of El Santo. Don Chepe stood at the starting line, ready to signal the start of the race. After the contestants were all assembled, he fired his pistol into the air. A couple of the ponies were so keyed up they bucked their riders off before they reached the finish, but this did not disqualify them. Tradition ordained that the first horse over the finish line was the legitimate winner of the race, whether or not it still carried its rider.

La Perla, being a green mare, did not start until she saw the other contestants running down the road in front of her. When she jumped to follow, she raced after them down the dirt road like a sleek, long-legged deer. She passed *Volador* at the end of the race, but a moment too late to be the winner. This turn of events not only demonstrated she was faster than the rest, but it also confirmed her extraordinary stamina and competitive spirit.

The outcome of the race sparked a heated debate between Don Aliseo and Don Paco about the merits of purebreds versus the native horses. Don Aliseo was passionate, "*Volador* has only proven himself in short-distance races on relatively level ground! Why don't we reinstate the endurance ride over the Puesta del Sol Mountains between El Santo and San Antonio? After all, around here, *bestias* that can cover long distances without tiring are the most sought after. It's only been since you imported a horse with foreign blood in its veins that these inconsequential short distance races have become more popular."

The old-timers in the crowd perked up at the mention of reinstating the Puesta del Sol race, for they remembered the days when this race engendered great enthusiasm among the ranchers. It was once a country gentleman's venture where the winner traditionally selected his prize from among the other entrants.

This debate between Don Aliseo and Don Paco suddenly gave Donato an idea. "Don Aliseo is right," he agreed, turning to Don Paco. "A distance race would give the burros and mules even greater competition and provide more choices for the winner."

"*Ay*," agreed Zenen. "Also entering additional fast horses in the race would make it even more exciting!"

"Done," replied Donato, finalizing the proposal. "I will loan Don Paco and Don Aliseo each an additional contestant from among my grandfather's best geldings."

"Not so fast," grumbled Don Aliseo. "Chico! Take the Azulejo mare from Donato!" Then he focused his piercing eyes on the young man. "I haven't figured out what you are up to, but it must include some sort of a trick. If you expect me to participate, try convincing me with a more enticing wager."

"Such as?"

"Undisputed ownership of the Azulejo stallion trained and delivered!"

Donato was outraged. "*Espíritu* not only roams free, but he also carries Don Tomas' brand. He is not up for wager."

"Nevertheless, those are my terms. Take them or leave them."

"You are an insolent bully!"

"Shhh," Don Paco intervened. "Don Aliseo is within his rights to state his terms for entering the competition, son. Also, the stallion was never brought before me to have his brand recorded. It is up to you whether to accept or reject Don Aliseo's terms."

Donato's head was spinning. He did not want to risk wagering *Espíritu*, but he had been waiting for just such an opportunity to win ownership of the mare. She was most certainly the only means of producing future Azulejo offspring.

"Alright, I accept," he agreed solemnly while at the same time offering up a prayer to the spirits of Don Diego and Don Tomas to help him win the bet. "Alright, you two now shake hands on your wager," Don Paco decreed.

After witnessing the luminous shades of haunted Punta Prieta, Don Aliseo did not much care for the idea of participating in a race along the coastal route. All the same, now what he wanted to do most in this world was to humiliate Donato, so he grudgingly accepted the challenge. Don Aliseo extended his hand to Donato. "Alright, but let us wait a few months off until the cooler weather of December. May the best animal win!"

"How about New Year's Day?" Donato suggested, looking about him for approval from the spectators while shaking his adversary's hand.

"Ay, New Year's Day!" the onlooker's echoed,

The following day, while Don Paco was driving Donato to La Paz in his truck, he asked him, "Now that I've heard Don Aliseo's reasons for putting you in jail, what about your side of the story?"

"It is a tiresome history," Donato replied with a sigh. "But I suppose I have all the way to La Paz to tell it."

Then he explained in detail about the conflict with Don Aliseo over the land, the mine, and the buried treasure as best he could. He also explained about the painting and about Don Tomas' knife, and shared how important it was to him to get everything back. But for the time being, perhaps out of habit, he didn't bring up the private matter of his keepsake pearls.

"With the exception of the diary, I plan to return all of the departed Spanish nobleman's belongings to his sea chest to appease his spirit, and then bury it in a secret location out of sight of the trails."

Don Paco listened patiently and then summed the situation up with a single comment. "You know, even after I have straightened out the matter of the land, Don Aliseo may still try to make your life miserable. Whether it is over your land, your horses, or the minerals in the mountains, he will always continue to go after whatever he wants. In view of this, are you still certain you wish to manage Don Tomas' property?" Donato thought again how his heart was with the horses and the land, how beautiful the *campo* looked after the rains, and about the good times he and Elyse had spent together. "I will figure out ways to deal with Don Aliseo," he replied. "But first, I must possess clear, undisputed title to my *abuelo's* land."

"You've already gained practice dealing with Don Aliseo, eh? Alright, in the event of a future dispute over the land, remember that the original deed to Los Terrenos de Punta Prieta will have Monsignor Escalante's seal on it. If that document or evidence of its existence were produced by court order, Don Aliseo would be entitled to no more than the original parcel of property named after his relative, and it is not very likely he would even inherit that. Alright, enough said. Now let us move on to another topic! Why don't you tell me more about this amazing burro you propose to win the long-distance race with."

Donato told Don Paco how Ramón had caught and trained a very fast, pacing, feral jack that was capable of crossing La Mesa Alta faster than any of Don Tomas' horses.

"You're not serious!"

"Yes! He is a natural phenomenon. Ramón named him *Pancho Villa* because of his tenacity."

CHAPTER 25

The Twins: A Dream Come True

WHEN Don Aliseo learned Donato had gained legal title to Don Tomas' land, he appeared not to care. "Let's not be strangers now, Señor Donato," he replied with feigned civility. "Remember, as the trails lie, we are practically neighbors. Here are your knife and painting."

As they were leaving Don Aliseo's hacienda, Don Paco turned to Donato. "You know he doesn't give a sow's ear—he will do whatever he wants anyway."

Despite his convictions to hold onto Don Tomas' land, Don Paco's words made Donato's stomach tighten. "Do you think Don Aliseo might still try to arrest me on some phony pretext?" he asked.

"No, not now that he realizes I'll stand by you. Simply do what Don Tomas used to do and make him a gift of something special like a fine animal from time to time. You should get along amicably enough. If he ventures onto your land to shoot deer or to dig for opals, I suggest you simply humor him. Anyway, after experiencing such a dreadful disaster at the mine, I can't imagine he will want to risk starting that venture up again."

* * *

After attending the family reunion in La Paz, Donato returned to Rancho La Primavera. Now that he was sole proprietor of the ranch, his greatest concern was to keep in good stead with the spirits of the region, especially Don Diego's ghost. To this end, he returned the headstall and painting to the nobleman's sea chest, and then enlisted Ramón's help burying it deep within an inhospitable cholla cactus thicket. When they were done, they scattered the cactus segments over the bare ground so they would take root and hide the burial site. This sacred trust concluded, Donato then sacrificed a hundred head of Don Tomas' cattle to his partner at the Pacific Coast Ranch for less than market value, and put Luis in charge of directing a crew hired to clear an airstrip.

Donato, not wanting to be hardhearted, decided to let the Dominguez family remain for the time being. The storm had all but washed away their old *ranchito* in El Santo, and he surmised they could not afford to build a new one. In any event, as though wanting to remain in his good graces, the whole family turned out to be an asset to have around the way Donato had hoped they would be.

After weathering two big storms, Don Tomas' old hacienda had also fallen into some disrepair. Therefore, Donato was pleasantly surprised when everyone pitched in to help put a new thatch on the roof, whitewash the walls, and clean up the grounds. Meanwhile, like the watched kettle that never boils, *La Perla* only grew fatter and fatter on all the feed given her, and never once seemed aware of what all the fuss was about. Knowing that mule foals occasioned long pregnancies, Ramón began to lose faith *La Perla's* foal would even be a horse. "Maybe Señor Bartolo was right. One of the big feral jacks roaming Punta Prieta may actually have managed to breed her," he muttered.

* * *

For the most part, the Mexican Department of Agriculture Veterinarian for Southern Baja only presided over the needs of ranchers located within a day's drive of La Paz. Consequently, either most *campo* mares gave birth alone in the wilderness, or they were kept in and presided over by a local horse doctor.

Therefore, as the window of time estimated by Ramón and Donato for *La Perla* to give birth arrived, both young men slept restlessly in their beds. Donato remembered Don Tomas claiming the finest foals always arrived on the full moon, so, when he awoke to see a round moon shining through his window, he hoped it signaled the mare's time had come. It had been Raul's job to spend his nights sitting in a chair beside *La Perla*'s pen to keep a watchful eye on her behavior. However, after spending so many nights awake, he had now begun falling asleep on the job.

Tonight, the moment came the mare had been waiting for. Now, in private, under the rays of the full moon, she gave birth to twins. Donato arrived at *La Perla*'s pen just as she was nudging the second sibling up onto its feet. He was a sleek black colt with a white marking on his forehead just like his dam's. At first glance, this foal appeared to be the prettier of the two. However, on closer inspection, Donato decided his cannons looked a bit long, and his ears promised to turn out more exotic than his mother's.

The filly, on the other hand, had been born in an unusual fluffy drab-gray foal-coat, as though in readiness for inclement weather. Where this fluff grew sparsely on her face and legs, a sleek metallic coat showed through underneath. Like the nobleman's mare, no face marking distinguished her; instead, she sported two white anklets on her back fetlocks. When Donato noted her ears were as small and fine as *Espíritu*'s, yet her markings resembled *Azulina*, the legendary ghost mare of Punta Prieta, he was suddenly willing to risk everything to keep this one. He guessed she would shed out to become a spectacular Azulejo and be the perfect gift for Elyse!

When Donato checked on the mares in the other corrals, he noticed that Don Tomas' black pacing mare, *Carbona*, had just given birth to a little mule foal by *Pancho Villa*, and his plan came together. *La Perla* was still preoccupied with trying to nuzzle the spindly black colt onto his feet, when Donato sneaked in behind her and spirited away the woolly Azulejo filly with the delicate little ears. Holding the filly's mouth shut so she couldn't squeal, he carried her over to *Carbona*'s pen and set her down beside the black mare's mule foal who was also in the process of making his first uncoordinated efforts to stand. While *Carbona* looked on, Donato used his pocket-handkerchief to transfer the mule foal's smell to *La Perla*'s filly. When the mare showed signs of accepting her horse-foal fosterling, Donato made off with the mule-foal, and put him with a jenny mother and her two-day-old burro. As soon as all the mares and foals had settled down, Donato went over to wake Raul and jokingly reproached him for falling asleep.

"Wake up you good-for-nothing! *La Perla* foaled a good two hours ago!"

"*Ay*, what ill luck!" Raul cried, jumping up from his chair to peer over the corral fence at Don Aliseo's mare. "Don't let on to my *patrón* I fell asleep—he'll fire me, without pay!"

"Don't worry," Donato said laughing reassuringly. Then his attitude turned serious again. "After repeated attempts, it still looks as though *La Perla*'s frail little colt still can't stand on his own two legs. We would be advised to jump-start him by feeding him some burro milk from a bottle."

Donato and Raul were still busy trying to bottle-feed *La Perla*'s black twin with burro milk, when Ramón showed up still rubbing the sleep out of his eyes.

"*Caramba*, Good Heavens, the Azulejo mare has given birth to a pitiable little colt!" he exclaimed shaking his head. "How'd she manage to produce such a runt on all the nutritious feed we fed her? Don Aliseo will be sick."

Donato ordered Raul to continue helping the colt to stand up and nurse, and then beckoned for Ramón to follow him.

"*Madre de Dios!*" exclaimed Ramón after Donato had shown him the fuzzy filly being nursed by *Carbona*. "I was certain this mare was going to produce a good-sized mule foal."

Donato put his finger to his lips and again motioned to Ramón to follow. This time, he led him over to the cluster of small corrals situated behind the old gardener's hut where Ramón had once lived with his father. There, Donato pointed to *Carbona*'s mule-foal standing alongside the jenny and her newborn burro foal.

"So that's it," Ramón observed. "I just figured it out. You switched all the mares' foals around. *La Perla* had twins! Yes?"

"That's right. Now just imagine what a fine foal she would produce if she only had one."

When Don Aliseo and Chico showed up on one of their impromptu visits the following day, Don Aliseo acted disgusted. "Can't you find a nurse mare to put that mutt on? This just goes to prove what I suspected all along. The blue-eyed Azulejo is a freak of nature that will never reproduce in kind. We will make better use of the mare by taking her back to El Santo where we can focus on getting her in shape for the upcoming competition."

Donato was fearful that if Don Aliseo and Chico were to hang around the ranch for very long, they might notice that *Carbonera*'s changeling and *La Perla*'s spindly colt were both about the same age, and thus make a guess at his deception, so he eagerly expedited Don Aliseo's proposal.

"We will provide a foster mother for the colt," Donato reassured Don Aliseo. "However, once we separate your mare from her foal, the sooner you take her out of earshot the better."

Donato and Ramón both breathed a sigh of relief after Don Aliseo and Chico went on their way again, ponying the neighing mare behind them back to El Santo. "We are in the clear, *Patrón*," said Ramón, congratulating Donato with a handshake. "Bartolo and Chico never even suspected *La Perla* produced twins!"

"But what a dirty trick to play on such a fine mare." countered Donato. "Don Aliseo and Chico both believe she hasn't any potential as a brood mare now."

Ramón shrugged. "Win *La Perla* back in the upcoming race and you may treat her as she deserves."

"How I am ever going to win this race on your demure burro is what worries me!" Donato cried. "I agreed to this bet and shook on it with Don Aliseo in front of Don Paco. I have *La Perla* to win and *Espíritu's* ownership to protect. What if your big fainthearted burro should fail me? When faced with Don Paco's *Volador* and Don Aliseo's imposing *Machismo*, he might decide to turn tail and run."

"No need to worry," Ramón answered reassuringly. "Remember, the animal that arrives at the finish line first wins the race whether or not it carries its rider—and the burro likes to eat! We have until December when the weather cools down to get *Pancho Villa* ready. From now on, we shall feed him only plain *milpa* stalks here at home until the day of the race. Then on the weekends, I shall ride him to San Antonio when I go to visit my family. There, I will serve him choice yucca vines growing on the fences bordering Don Paco's sunny sugarcane fields, along with a pan of bran mash with carrots and goatnut mixed in—his favorite. He will soon be racing to reach San Antonio the fastest way he can!"

CHAPTER 26

The Race: Another Storm

ANTICIPATING the return of Elyse since October, Donato continually looked up at the sky whenever he heard the drone of a small plane's engine. This was why Ramón teased him saying if he continued acting this way, he was bound to trip over a stone one day and fall flat on his face.

"What will you do if the end of the year rolls around and Elyse still hasn't returned?" he asked, afraid Donato was losing both his head and his heart. "The *gringa* hasn't even answered any of your letters!"

Donato was not so easily discouraged, however. "The race is scheduled for New Years Day," he told Ramón. "I plan to wait until then, win the bet with Don Aliseo and gain possession of *La Perla*. After that, I will fly to Texas and look Elyse up at the address she gave me; I might also arrange to visit an uncle from my father's side of the family while I am there. After I locate Elyse, I will find out why she didn't reply to any of my letters. And if all goes well between us, I will ask her if she can help me track my uncle down. Such a long time has passed since my father took me to Texas, I would like to also pay him a visit after all these years. If on the other hand, it turns out Elyse has genuinely forgotten me, I will try to win back her interest with news of *La Perla*'s foal. I will not forget to let on that after the Azulejo filly shed her woolly foal coat, she became the flashiest young horse on the ranch!"

* * *

On the morning of the race, in the filtered light of dawn, just before the sun's disk appeared over the rim of La Mesa Alta, a distinguished group of equestrians assembled on the outskirts of El Santo. Because the *campo* still remained green after the fall storms, even the most commonplace *bestias* blew through their noses and pawed the ground to show they were in high spirits from eating so much fresh green feed.

Of course, *La Perla*, ridden by Don Aliseo, was the most magnificent entrant of them all. She wore tack adorned with black and white horsehair tassels and executed her graceful movements to the accompaniment of myriad tiny tinkling bangles. Albeit, now that Chico had worked her up and down the slopes of the mesa on a daily basis, a lusterless, compliant expression replaced the once-undependable glint in her suspicious eyes. She also no longer noticed whether or not her handler was wearing a cowboy hat.

Along with a group of ranchers mounted on their finest horses were two magnificent leggy geldings, a bay and a buckskin. These were the two Don Aliseo and Don Paco had selected from among Donato's geldings from Rancho La Primavera. The most whimsical entrants, however, were the two from the burro family. In his bright yellow shirt, Chico resembled a bee on a yam riding Don Aliseo's great red *fenómeno*, while Donato appeared mismatched on the humble burro, *Pancho Villa*. Despite the little burro's lowly standing, however, Ramón had dressed him up in fine leather tack and adorned his reins and headstall with pink and white cotton tassels. Also, because of the choice bran mashes Ramón had been giving the burro, even his mousey coat shone with a muted gloss.

Speaking low to Donato, Ramón gestured toward *La Perla*. "Look closely and you'll notice Doña Margarita secured a crucifix to *La Perla's* browband hoping to bring him safely home. I heard her pleading with

Don Aliseo not to personally ride in the race. Do you suppose that deep down she fears the legendary Spanish nobleman's curse?"

It's possible. But, look, your burro is also wearing an amulet for good luck," Donato remarked, pointing to *Pancho Villa*'s browband.

Ramón nodded. "Yes, it is the blue bead you found knotted in the Spanish headstall."

Donato looked down at it thoughtfully and furrowed his brows. "I expect it was once tied in an animal's forelock as a good luck charm. It looks too small to have been a decorative ornament."

Ramón was staring up at the cliffs encircling the immediate horizon. "Look!" he cried. "I think I see *Espíritu* on the rim of La Mesa Alta. He is standing next to a cactus, his round, white forehead marking just visible. I wonder if he is planning to watch the race! It will be interesting to see how *La Perla* reacts to his presence after being so ruthlessly subjugated by Chico. Perhaps *Espíritu* somehow senses that his and his sister's ownership will be settled by the outcome of this competition."

"It all comes down to this race, doesn't it?" Donato replied with a tone of finality.

"Yes. I wouldn't put it past the Azulejo stallion to sense such a thing! *Es la verdad!*" added Ramón.

In accordance with the gentleman's code of ethics governing the competition, the contestants were expected to check in at Hernandez' *tienda* in Punta Gorda to confirm they had taken the coastal trail. From there, they were permitted to cross over the San Antonio hills by any route they chose.

In view of the fact Don Chepe was once more the only neutral dignitary not participating in the race, he graciously accepted the invitation to officiate the start and end of the competition. After ushering the contestants on their way to Punta Gorda, Don Chepe and his friends planned to travel by truck down the dirt road leading out of El Santo, turn onto El Camino Real, and then drive on to San Antonio and the finish of the race.

251

Just like the party of turkey vultures perched on the nearby cacti with their wings outstretched to soak up the morning sun, Don Chepe called upon the mounted riders to form a line facing east. "The moment the first fiery ray touches the rim of La Mesa Alta, I shall discharge my pistol into the air."

Margarita Bartolo wailed after her husband, "Please, Aliseo! I implore you not to participate in this silly horse and mule race through Punta Prieta. See, even now how a dark storm broods in the west—a harbinger of doom!"

The first ray hit.

"Stifle yourself, you superstitious woman!" Don Aliseo called over his shoulder as he took off on *La Perla*.

* * *

Not only were all the contestants eager to get going, but everyone hoped to cross the lower Los Cardenales Arroyo before a flash flood inundated its banks—especially Donato. He could not swim well, and the burro, *Pancho Villa*, was terrified of water.

Chico riding the *fenómeno* headed the procession at a brisk trot, followed by Don Aliseo on *La Perla*, Zenen on *Volador*, and Señor Lucero riding a beautiful little Lusitano crossbreed. The bay and buckskin geldings from Rancho La Primavera chosen by Don Paco and Don Aliseo came next, followed by a group of ranchers mounted on various horses and mules. Bashful *Pancho Villa*, fearful of passing the other contestants, brought up the rear. Ramón, astride stalwart *Alazán*, planned to accompany Donato as the burro's escort throughout the entire race.

Because of *Pancho Villa*'s timidity, Donato and Ramón were still trailing behind when they reached the Los Cardenales oasis. Ramón was not worried, however, because he expected the burro to stay fresh longer than any of the other contestants.

Since *Alazán* needed to drink water more frequently than the burro, Ramón stopped at the Los Cardenales oasis to rest and water him, while Donato went on ahead. On his way to the lower part of the arroyo where the trail crossed over to the south side of the Los Cardenales delta, he met Luis leaving over the southern shortcut to San Antonio to await the outcome of the race.

"*Aquí viene el burrito valiente!* Here comes the brave little burro!" Luis cried encouragingly, championing *Pancho Villa*. "Be careful, though," he cautioned Donato. "Chico is resting the *fenómeno* in the shade of the big mesquite tree growing on the far side of the arroyo. I'd keep an eye out for him if I were you; he's probably up to no good."

Still, after hearing a loud clap of thunder behind him, Donato feared the imminent flood more than Chico. Nonetheless, as it turned out, he should have paid better attention to Luis' warning. He and the burro had no sooner crossed the lower part of the arroyo than, out of nowhere, Chico and *Machismo* were upon them. When Chico lashed the burro with his *ramal* while overtaking him, *Pancho Villa* responded by squealing and trying to escape up the side of the trail, but the sandy riverbank disallowed secure footing and the poor burro came to a halt.

Because Chico's tactics had violated the contestant's code of ethics, Donato guessed he was apt to try almost anything. Most likely, he planned to lie in wait farther up the trail, intent on causing more trouble. Donato knew Ramón would pay close attention to the burro's tracks and follow, so he decided to bypass Chico and the *fenómeno* by urging *Pancho Villa* onto a hastily chosen detour. However, before getting far enough along, he heard the dreaded thundering sound of a flash flood approaching. Unfortunately for Donato and the burro, Chico had also heard the flood and doubled back to finish what he started. He whipped the huge *fenómeno* into a gallop and, taking advantage of his animal's enormous size over the burro, chased Donato and little *Pancho Villa* back down into the riverbed. Donato, trying to hang onto the burro for dear life, was at a complete disadvantage when Chico cornered the little beast against a section of the arroyo bank.

Chico quickly dismounted to scoop up several handfuls of sand, and then threw them straight into the burro's eyes. Before Donato could think how to retaliate, like a possum speeding up a tree, Chico scrambled back on *Machismo* and galloped out of the arroyo at full speed, whooping like a coyote.

The little burro kicked out blindly while trying to rub the sand out of his eyes against his foreleg. Donato dismounted and scarcely managed to lead him to the relative safety of a sandbar before the onrushing water and the debris it carried with it swept them both away.

Grabbing a hold of a great *torote* trunk that came bobbing down the current like a giant cork, Donato did his best to keep the burro's chin above the churning water. He also clutched at the broomweed as they passed over it, hoping to steer the log toward the bank, but the leaves only came away in his hands.

The *torote* log sailed out into the relative calm of the Sea of Cortez. Before long, the only landmark Donato recognized was the flat-topped monument of El Rey presiding like a white-robed monarch over the coastal hills of Punta Prieta.

Soon, a steady downpour peppered the glassy swells. Engulfed by water both from above and below, Donato could no longer make out El Rey in the distance to get his bearings. Fearing for his life, he recalled Don Tomas saying that it had only been through praying to God that he had been able to summon the strength to swim out of a current the day he found the blue pearl.

Donato supported *Pancho Villa*'s head on the log and fingered the blue bead on his browband. Then he laid his own head down beside the burro's and prayed to God, Don Tomas, and Don Diego for a miracle.

"If you don't help me get the burro safely back to shore and win the race, Don Aliseo Bartolo will still retain ownership of *La Perla*, and I shall be honor-bound to capture *Espíritu* and hand him over," he wailed to his guardian spirits.

Exhausted and discouraged, Donato succumbed to a prophetic daydream. The repetitive sound of the water lapping against the log lulled him into a state where he felt as though he were rising up into the clouds. As a spirit, he became a serene Don Diego riding the ghost mare *Azulina*, in the company of a herd of young, dark gray horses flying like winged gulls on a journey through time. The gray horses whitened with age as the future flowed into the present, and foreign lands and oceans sailed away beneath them. Dipping low over El Santo, Donato could see a funeral procession proceeding through the center of town. He identified Doña Margarita Bartolo, her daughter, Carmen, and Don Aliseo's son, Telmo, following slowly behind the sheriff's casket.

When next Donato felt himself rising up into the clouds again, the celestial herd turned the color of clear crystal and disolved like rain into the ether, leaving him plummeting into the setting sun, like Lucifer falling into Hell. This was when a blinding flash, followed by a deafening peal of thunder awakened him from his dream.

CHAPTER 27

The Wind Shear: Free at Last!

WHEN Donato awakened, he realized the *torote* log had come to rest against a submerged rock. After voicing a sob of relief, he looked up and, about two hundred meters away, saw the forbidding but familiar cliffs of Punta Prieta. Next, he looked down through the water trying to distinguish the safest passage to the beach between the submerged rocks. Though instead of noticing the usual schools of colorful fish he had heard tell of, darting between the corals, he spotted the skeleton of an old wreck lying on the gravel bottom. A great shark hovered around it, looking mottled in the dappled shade.

Donato had heard fishermen tell of young sharks coming into shallow water, which posed no threat to humans. However, this one was an adult hammerhead, which he knew to be the most aggressive of the native species. What if the predator should catch sight of the burro's paddling feet? It might mistake the *bestia* for a big fish in distress and attack!

Donato was trying to think what to do, when, like the touch of invisible fingers, he felt an eddy swirling around the log. With hardly a noise or a ripple, a new current drew the floating tree trunk past the rocky point and around to the sandy shore on the south side.

Weary and wet, Donato led *Pancho Villa* out of the water and up onto the beach. He stopped the burro at the mouth of a gully where a large, flat stone allowed them to stand out of the clinging sand. There, Donato unsaddled the burro and wrung out his soggy saddle blankets.

He then fed him what he wanted of the waterlogged provisions in his saddlebags. Next, using some fresh water from his water bottle, he rinsed the sticky salt off the binoculars Elyse had given him, and dried the lenses the best he could with his damp neckerchief.

As soon as Donato and the burro were ready to get underway again, Donato looked through the binoculars at the cliffs above for the easiest route back to the coastal trail. Looking where the path should be, as in a mirage, he distinguished a shimmering horse and rider making their way toward him. He didn't hear the familiar tinkling of bells or jangling of spurs associated with an approaching horseman, so he tipped his head to the side to make sure his ears weren't still clogged with water. Continuing to question what he had seen, Donato rubbed his eyes and looked up a second time, but now all he saw were the muted shadows cast by a cloud. Then, all at once, his heart jumped for joy as he heard the undeniable sound of jingling harness coming down the trail. Before long, *Alazán*'s white blaze appeared around the nearest bend.

"*Amigo Ramón!*" Donato called excitedly, tugging *Pancho Villa* up the gully by the bridle as he hurried to meet his friend and foreman. "It's me, Donato!"

"*Hola Patrón!*" Ramón called back, trotting down the trail. "Am I ever glad to see you! I was afraid the flash flood might have washed you and the burro out to sea. The current was so strong I had to wait for the water level to subside before riding *Alazán* across the arroyo. I have been hurrying to reach the town of Punta Gorda ever since. I thought I might have to round up a party of fishermen willing to paddle out into the gulf in their canoes to search for you and the burro!"

"*Pancho Villa* and I would have been alright had Chico not thrown sand in the poor burro's eyes so he couldn't see. If I hadn't caught hold of a log as the flood engulfed us, we would probably both have drowned," explained Donato, wearily.

Donato nodded toward *Pancho Villa*, who stood loose lipped and airplane-eared. It was an attitude only a pouting burro could achieve, and the young men chuckled at the sight.

"I'm not surprised," Ramón replied. "Chico will have been following orders. Don Aliseo has pardoned him and released him from jail; he's likely to do almost anything to help his benefactor win this race, hoping to return the favor."

"So, tell me, who is ahead of us?"

"All except *La Perla*. You wouldn't believe what happened back there when she got away," Ramón said, nodding toward the trail that wound down the side of the cliff behind him.

"What happened? Tell me!"

"When I caught up with Chico, he was helping Don Aliseo down there by the tall ironwood tree growing at the mouth of the deep ravine. Don Aliseo had accidentally knocked the crucifix off *La Perla*'s browband while trying to adjust her bridle. Chico was searching the ground, trying to help him find it when, like a harbinger of doom, a spooky gust of wind blew down the ravine, sending soggy bits of wood and flying gravel clattering against the boulders."

"Go on *amigo*," said Donato. "I have had some strange things happen to me today too!"

Ramón caught his breath and continued. "Next, before anyone knew what was happening, lightning flashed before our eyes with a loud clap of thunder following behind it. The ironwood tree burst into flames, and bits of its burning branches flew into the sky like fireworks, frightening *La Perla* and *Machismo* so badly they broke free and galloped away up the canyon."

"*Válgame Dios*! That must have been the crack of thunder that awakened me from my dream. I remember it well—it was deafening!"

Ramón's face blanched and his eyes stared. "It was a terrible experience, *Patrón*. We were all three still staring at the spot where the leafy ironwood tree had stood only moments before, when a blazing horseman astride a smoking phantom with an ashen mane and tail rose up out of the smoldering tree trunk, as if from Hell. Then, while it galloped away down the trail with a doleful wail, a scorching wind covered us with cinders." Looking down, Ramón flicked some ashes out of his mount's crest. "The ocean breeze still hasn't cleaned them all out of *Alazán's* mane."

"*Dios mío!*" cried Donato. "Could my prayers out in the gulf have summoned up this frightening apparition? What you describe sounds like the legendary nobleman and his slaughtered Azulejo mare arisen out of the notorious bonfire. Mere confirmation of this ghostly horseman's existence could crush Don Aliseo's unwholesome desire to possess the mysterious Azulejos. This may also explain the shining horseman I thought I saw moving down the trail. Are Chico and Don Aliseo alright?"

"Chico seems alright. But either the lightning struck Don Aliseo or he has been frightened out of his wits. I left him still searching for his crucifix among the ashes and charcoal covering the ground, as though he had lost both his mind and his hearing."

Donato frowned. "It doesn't sound as though he can be in any condition to continue the race."

"I couldn't tell for sure. Anyway, I figured it was Chico's job to look after Don Aliseo. My priority was finding you. Chico had gone on foot to track down *La Perla* and the *fenómeno* when I left."

"How long ago did Chico leave?"

"Shh!" Ramón put his finger to his lips, "I hear the jingling sound of a lone horseman approaching. We had better move out of sight."

As in the past, Ramón and Donato led their animals behind some large boulders so they could watch the trail without being seen. It was Chico, passing quickly by at an extended trot on *La Perla*.

"There's proof Chico succeeded in catching Don Aliseo's unfortunate Azulejo mare," Ramón remarked. "*Qué lástima.* What a shame. You just know he will push 'our' gorgeous girl as hard as he can, trying to win the race. This is Chico's chance to make up for losing face before the race in El Santo. Now that Don Aliseo appears to have lost his senses, he has taken *La Perla* and left the poor Don to make his own way alone on the *fenómeno*. *Pancho Villa* must prevail and win the race for us so we can treat her as she deserves."

"Shh. Listen! I bet that is Don Aliseo now."

Machismo soon appeared around the bend carrying the sheriff toward Punta Gorda at a fast trot. Don Aliseo was sitting bolt upright in the saddle as though in a daydream, his eyes fixed on some imaginary point in front of him. Although Chico had tried to help out by tying the reins around the saddle horn, he grasped the ends in his left hand. In his right, like a child holding a candle in the night, he held up a small wooden cross Chico had carved out of dry *cardon* to replace the Don's lost crucifix.

"No time to lose," Ramón urged. "Our only hope now is to escort the burro to the top of Caballete Ridge. There, we must release him to forge his own shortcut to the old coyote-fence corral situated just beyond the finish line where Luis will have set a tub of damp bran and carrots out for him."

All at once, the young men were startled by the distinctive sound of a stallion's neighs ricocheting through the cliffs and rocky canyons.

"Look!" exclaimed Ramón. "It is *Espíritu*! He is standing up there on top of that craggy bluff, looking down the trail after *La Perla*. He has been keeping track of her the entire race!"

When Donato and Ramón checked in at Punta Gorda, Señor Hernandez' tone was grim. "You had better hurry, boys!" he exclaimed. Then he looked straight at Donato. "Donato, a rancher riding your buckskin gelding passed by here a good half hour ago, followed by Chico galloping by on the tireless Azulejo mare. Both riders did no more than nod to me as they flew by, and the animals still looked fit enough to catch up with and perhaps pass the contestants ahead of them."

"Thanks for the tip. How about Don Aliseo? Is he still participating in the race?" Donato asked.

Señor Hernandez raised his eyebrows. "I think so, but he acted as though something was wrong with him. First off, he ignored my greeting, and then he let the poor thirsty *fenómeno* try to drink off the top of the *pila* with the bit still in its mouth! I offered to unbridle the beast but Don Aliseo ignored my offer and guided it back onto the trail to continue the race."

261

Ramón nodded, "It does not surprise me. The sheriff may have been struck by lightning and has likely lost his hearing, his wits, or both."

"*Dios Mío!* I hope he will be alright," added Hernandez, crossing himself. "It almost sounds as though he may have been revisited by the ancient curse upon his family."

By the time Donato and Ramón reached the top of Caballete Ridge overlooking the southeast side of San Antonio, the shadows cast by the Puesta del Sol Mountains touched the outskirts of town. Closer in, they could see the contestants dotting the trail traversing the hills bordering the deep, winding, San Antonio Arroyo.

Donato dismounted and looked at the town through his binoculars. It was one of the most picturesque townships in the region. Old adobe ruins and a large, rectangular school playground were thronged with colorful spectators awaiting the outcome of the race. The playground came at the end of the long row of Indian laurels bordering the dirt road running through the center of town. The lower portions of the tree trunks had been whitewashed with lye to keep the beetles out of them, making them look as though they were wearing white socks. And because the livestock kept the undersides of their branches neatly trimmed, each looked as though it wore a bowl haircut.

Ramón knew that tying the burro's reins up short to his saddle horn would discourage him from wasting time snacking on foliage along the way; he also knew he would be eager to reach San Antonio where he was accustomed to enjoying a dinner of carrots and bran after his tack was removed. Giving *Pancho Villa* a slap on the haunches, he sent him pacing off down the trail swishing his wisp of a tail. Donato and Ramón watched until—spotting other contestants ahead of him—the burro veered off on his own shortcut to San Antonio through the *campo*.

Donato then climbed up behind Ramón on *Alazán*, and they continued down the trail at a jog. "It's not that I lack faith in Luis to set out *Pancho Villa's* dinner, but I wish there was a way I could reach the finish of the race ahead of the burro," Donato grumbled.

Ramón halted *Alazán* and pointed toward the hillside to their right. "Scan that rocky outcropping through your binoculars. Therein lies the means to fulfilling your wish!"

"It is *Espíritu* again—still keeping an eye on *La Perla!*"

"Do you think he might permit you to rope him?" Ramón asked.

"Perhaps. Let's ride over there and find out!"

Espíritu remained standing as though inviting Donato to clamber up the hill after him. Equipped with both a lasso and a lead rope, Donato quickly climbed to the top of the hill until he reached a ledge a few meters from where *Espíritu* was standing. The stallion nodded his head and pawed the ground as the horseman approached. Now, Donato glimpsed his RP brand on the *bestia's* flank. He was prepared to toss his lasso, but *Espíritu* didn't move, so he kept it coiled over his left shoulder. Instead, he stepped forward slowly, reaching for the wild horse's withers with his right hand. As in the canyon the day of his twentieth birthday, Donato knew that the thin-skinned horse would be less sensitive in this area. He continued talking reassuringly as he slipped the lead rope around the stallion's neck and secured it with a loose bowline knot. He sweet talked the animal in a low tone, knowing he only had one chance to catch him in time to ride him to the end of the race. "Hey you, sweet beautiful boy, do you remember me?" Then making a series of half hitches in the free end of the rope, he fashioned it into a humane war bridle with reins.

"*Shh, mi bonito! Cálmase, potro hermoso!* We must not allow *La Perla* to win, my *Espíritu*. If Don Aliseo doesn't survive the aftereffects of the lightning, his family might still inherit you. You and I must catch up with the Azulejo mare and keep a lookout for the burro!"

With his heart pounding, Donato guided *Espíritu* down the hillside and onto the San Antonio trail. There, to his great relief, just like the first time the wild horse allowed him to climb on his back in the La Cañada oasis, he permitted him to keep his seat. Also, as it turned out, *Espíritu* was as eager to meet up with *La Perla* as Donato was, so he quickly gained sufficient confidence to move forward under the unaccustomed weight of his rider. Before long, the cooperative stallion surprised his passenger by breaking into a gallop on his own. Soon, Donato found himself flying past the lagging contestants also trying to catch up with and pass the amazing Azulejo mare who was now leading the race. Even Don Aliseo was doing his best to goad exhausted *Machismo* into reaching her.

When *Espíritu* at last passed *La Perla*, Donato unwisely urged him to stay ahead of her until she and Chico dropped out of sight behind a bend. This was a very upsetting occurrence for *Espíritu*! As on the occasion a few years back when Donato first allowed *Pronto* to canter on La Mesa Alta, once again, his mount stopped so suddenly he somersaulted over the animal's head to land sprawling in the middle of the trail. This was when, once more whooping like a coyote, Chico gleefully raced the Azulejo mare past them. "Ah ha! There you go!" he exclaimed. "Headfirst in the dirt again just like the first time we met!"

Luckily, Donato had managed to hang on to the horse's rope. When he turned to look up at *Espíritu*, their eyes met; it was as though *Espíritu* understood they must continue on together as horse and rider. Donato scarcely had time to get to his feet and clamber up on the stallion's back again before the spirited animal took off once more after *La Perla*.

Because the San Antonio trail made a big half circle into town, the sound of drumming hoofbeats reached the spectators from some distance away. To their amazement, the first contestants to gallop into sight were one Azulejo hotly pursued by another! A last ray of sunlight shining out from between the peaks of the Puesta del Sol Mountains highlighted their glistening, foam-flecked coats and flying white manes and tails.

Donato looked around for *Pancho Villa* while Chico, determined to maintain his lead, continued spurring the mare. This may have been the reason why *La Perla*, at last overcome with exhaustion, lost her stride, and with glassy eyes and red, distended nostrils, slowed to a swaying trot and then a tottering amble before sinking to her knees with an agonizing groan.

Espíritu and Donato skidded to a stop behind her while the nearby spectators shouted orders in the background. Still looking futilely around for the burro, Donato jumped to the ground, freed *Espíritu*, and then ran to tend to *La Perla* who now lay stretched out on her side. Deeply concerned for the mare's welfare, Donato knelt down and began untacking her. In the distance, he could hear the spooked stallion's hoofbeats growing fainter as he galloped into the seclusion of the *campo*. Chico was able to stand up, but he groaned and held his right arm with his left as though his collarbone were broken.

A local truck driver had noticed the accident while awaiting the outcome of the race. He drove his truck out along the San Antonio Trail leading to Punta Gorda so he could assist Donato, bringing with him an armful of folded gunnysacks and a pail of fresh water. Donato lifted the mare's head out of the dirt and set it down on the sacking. He then took off his shirt, moistened it in the pail, and used it to wipe down and cool her neck and legs. Next, Luis, who had just ridden up, reached into his saddlebags and handed Donato four soda bottles filled with rice water sweetened with nectar.

"Here, give this to the Azulejo; the remedy will help to bring her around and might give her the strength to get back up on her feet."

After Donato administered the soothing draft to *La Perla*, a group of men who had gathered around helped him roll her over and get her up onto her feet.

This was when, in the direction of the San Antonio Arroyo, Donato heard a burro blowing dust and pollen out of its nose as it pushed its way past the broomweed and mule fat. *"Arre, el burrito! Burrito valiente!* Come along, little burro! Valiant burro!" he cried joyfully.

Pacing into San Antonio like a farcical apparition came *Pancho Villa*. His headstall was askew and leaves and twigs stuck out from under his tack as he hurried up to the old coyote-fence corral situated behind the finish line. There Luis, anticipating his arrival, had already set a tub of carrots and bran out for him.

Donato left Luis with *La Perla*, and cheered on by the crowd, ran to intercept the burro. Don Paco and Don Chepe had arisen from their seats under the scenic Indian laurel trees to applaud the burro as the winner, when after pausing briefly to bow and doff his hat, Donato vaulted skillfully into *Pancho Villa*'s saddle and rode him victoriously across the finish line.

"Vámonos con *Pancho Villa*!" Don Paco shouted, repeating the popular slogan.

"Let us acclaim our deserving champion—the amazing burro, *Pancho Villa*!" Don Chepe concurred, announcing him the winner while the spectators continued to cheer. *Pancho Villa* had no sooner been proclaimed the winner of the race, than Don Aliseo, Ramón, and the other riders straggled in one by one. Chico, with his arm now supported in a sling, seeing the race had been lost, did the honorable thing. He led *La Perla* into town and handed her over to Donato.

"I congratulate you, Señor," Chico said, bowing respectfully to Donato. "In spite of all your setbacks en route, Ramón's enduring burro has won the race for you. It is God's will."

At last, the moment Donato had been waiting for arrived. With a sigh of relief, he looked gratefully up at the Heavens. "*Gracias a Dios*! Thanks be to God! At long last, I now officially own both the Azulejos! I shall safeguard *La Perla* by marking her with my RP brand, and then allow the Azulejos their freedom until the dry season."

Donato led *La Perla* to the nearby *pila* to drink and then rinsed the sweat and dirt off her coat before rubbing her down with a wad of sacking.

* * *

The following day, ponying *La Perla* behind *Pancho Villa*, Donato crossed the trail leading over the San Antonio hills toward Punta

Prieta. At the base of El Rey, he turned *La Perla* loose. After gaining her freedom, the mare acted as though having her tack removed had taken all the pain and suffering of the past two years away. Next, she further amazed Donato by breaking into a fluid, ground-covering trot and moving off up a ravine leading to the mountain.

"Take care, my darling," Donato whispered. "May the little Azulejo filly you gave me grow up to be as light on her feet," he added, gazing wistfully after her.

At the crest of a trail leading over the low foothills behind Punta Prieta, Donato stopped again to take one last look through the binoculars, hoping to catch a glimpse of both Azulejos.

"Well, I'll be...," he muttered. "Sure enough, there is one." *La Perla* had walked up to a *rajamatraca* cactus and was digging at its base with a front hoof. Intermittently, she pulled up the long, deep, succulent roots and tore them off with her teeth, and then shook her head to rid the tubors of dirt. When she had finished with this little display of her methods, she then quenched her thirst on them. This was when Donato noticed her flank. Above his freshly applied RP brand, Don Aliseo's ABC mark, which ended in the first letter of his mother's last name, Casas, appeared to have healed over as though by magic. Or was it a trick played by the light?

Before continuing back to La Primavera, Donato also looked around for *Espíritu*. He soon spotted him standing further up the mountainside, snacking on a *viejita*—a species of miniature cactus that usually grew among rocks. This was when, as in Donato's daydream when he was out in the gulf with the burro, Don Diego reappeared in his more frequently recounted tranquil state. The shimmering horseman, astride *Azulina*, the ghost mare of legend, emerged from behind a great, twisting elephant tree. Then, as Donato watched, the ghost mare and her phantom rider followed *Espíritu* and *La Perla* into the long afternoon shadows cast by El Rey.

When Donato continued on his way, his mind was on the legend, the Azulejos, the unique features of this fascinating region, and the events that had unfolded during the previous day and over the past few months. He felt he was at home, and the fear that he would have to move back to Mexico City no longer haunted him.

CHAPTER 28

El Rey: A Natural Wonder

RESOURCEFULNESS was a trait that Telmo Bartolo inherited from his father. His looks and personality, however, were from his more conventional mother's side of the family. He and she were also very close. It was not surprising therefore, that he maneuvered himself into a cozy government job in La Paz.

The moment he received news of his father's illness, he drove down from La Paz to console his dear mother. "I pleaded with Aliseo not to ride in that silly horse race," she sobbed. "He was stubborn and wouldn't listen to reason. Now, Señor Donato Perry has taken the Azulejo mare, and poor Aliseo lies stricken by the curse."

"*Santos!*" exclaimed Telmo, trying to comfort her. "Don't give that silly curse any credence, mother. Father was struck by lightning. It could have happened to anyone!"

Donato felt unsure whether to pursue the matter of the confiscated pearl by himself. Once again, he needed help from Don Tomas' old friend, the magistrate of San Antonio. Now, for the first time, he recounted the whole story of the pearls to Don Paco, hoping to enlist his help to get the pink pearl back. He feared that in the event of Don Aliseo's death someone in the Bartolo family might improperly inherit the gem. Then they could sell it, causing it to become lost forever.

The magistrate had an idea. "Let us drop by the hacienda in a few days to pay our respects. I will carefully consider how to broach the subject in advance. Somewhere during the conversation, I'll take Telmo aside. I will tactfully hint to him that you are down to your last few pesos and was hoping to get your pearl back to set in an engagement ring before Elyse returns.

"I will also, having known her for many years, offer my personal condolences to Doña Margarita Bartolo on her husband's illness. I am sure she will agree that returning the pearl will help to resolve any lingering hostility between the tenure of Los Terrenos de Punta Prieta and the Bartolo's Los Santos ranch. In addition, I will imply to her that doing so might lessen the power of the legendary curse and help Aliseo's spirit to rest easier. After all, she knew Elyse from those few days Elyse had spent at the Los Santos hacienda during the storm. I am sure Margarita will respond positively to my suggestion. It may also lighten her heart to know she is aiding in the furtherance of a young couple's romance. Those women, they love their *novelas*, don't they!"

Don Paco and Donato visited Los Santos to pay their respects to the Bartolo's in view of Aliseo's mysterious illness, bringing a large, beautiful bouquet of flowers with them for the hacienda. Don Paco had been right. When he asked Doña Margarita Bartolo for the return of the pearl, the Doña immediately agreed. *"Ah sí, sí, sí,"* she replied, as though fearful that holding onto something of Donato's might bring even more bad luck down on the family.

After leaving El Santo, Don Paco and Donato continued on to La Paz. Don Paco had his magistrate's duties to attend to, and Donato planned to check on Don Tomas' family before dropping in unexpectedly on Señor Gomez, hoping to get some news of Elyse or her father.

Señor Gomez seemed friendly enough at first, but when Donato asked him about Elyse, he insisted Donato was wasting his time. "Take some very good advice from an old friend and settle down with one of the native girls," he replied. "The *gringa* will only bring you heartache."

Donato was still optimistic, however. He determined to settle affairs back at the ranch, get his papers in order, and then travel to Texas. Though he knew he risked a waste of money and disappointment, he still believed there was a chance he could rekindle Elyse's affection. First though, he must scrape enough money together to finance his trip and to pay his worker's wages while he was away. Once he arrived in Texas, he would visit the address on her letter. Assuming his visit went well, he might even ask her for help researching his Uncle Stanley's whereabouts.

Two weeks later found Donato standing with Luis on the west veranda of the Rancho La Primavera hacienda. He was wondering whether the only way to round up the funds he so badly needed was to sell more of Don Tomas' cattle. Then, like an answer to his prayers, down the arroyo trail from La Mesa Alta came Celestino.

"*Vaya! Mira quien repareció!* Well, look who has shown up!" exclaimed Donato. "Here comes my old mountain climbing pal from the El Santo jail."

Celestino addressed his longsuffering buddy as though undergoing a jail term succeeded by the ownership of haunted Terrenos de Punta Prieta earned him supreme respect. Greetings, Don Donato," he said tipping his hat in salutation and then offering his hand to both Donato and Luis before continuing. "I come from the opal caves at the summit of La Ballena. A deep cleft opened up in one of the upper grottos as result of the earthquake. It contains a quantity of the red mineral formations Señor Martinez so prized. As before, the question remains, how to collect the stones from such a profound fissure? Excavating them from the fracture is a precarious two-man job at best," he explained, hinting for a helper.

Donato had been curious to explore the upper caves since he first heard about the opals. "What do you think, Luis? Should we help Celestino try to collect some of the more valuable opals?"

"*Sí cómo no Patrón*, certainly Boss. Finding another way to bring in a few extra pesos couldn't hurt," Luis replied.

"It will also give us an opportunity to garland the memorial raised there by the disaster victim's families. Those poor folks led an unsuccessful month-long expedition trying to uncover the miner's remains," Donato reflected sadly, remembering Chevalo.

The prospectors were busily packing mules with the tools and rope they would need, when a private plane flew in overhead and circled the ranch before flying off down the coast. Donato, who had been watching small planes fly over the ranch for months, only gave it a cursory glance. However, to his surprise, this time the same plane returned within the hour and touched down on his newly cleared airstrip.

"I wonder if that could be Elyse!" he exclaimed, feeling his unshaven cheeks with his hands. He turned to Luis and Celestino, speaking excitedly. "You two go ahead without me. I must meet that plane straight away, even though I haven't shaved!"

"Don't give it a second thought, Don Donato," Celestino reassured him. "We'll collect some samples and bring them back to you."

Donato's joy at possibly seeing Elyse again also reawakened his long-held heartache. He missed her terribly, but was angry with her for not replying to his letters. Having feared that she might never return, he began to doubt this plane was bringing her back to him. "More likely," he thought, "some aviator-tourist has lost his way or run low on fuel."

Meanwhile, unknown to Donato, Ramón was down at the beach leading a mule he had located by tracking it down by its hoofprints, back to Rancho La Primavera behind *Alazán*. When Ramón saw the private plane circle overhead and then come in to land, he changed his plans and headed toward the airstrip. When he saw it was Elyse and her pilot, as in the past, he gave Elyse *Alazán* to ride. Then he looped the mule's lead into a rope halter, helped the pilot up on its back, and proceeded on foot to escort the visitors up to the hacienda.

Donato met them midway on the trail. He thought Elyse looked older and more sophisticated than on her former visit. She was wearing some light makeup to highlight her attractive features and her hair had grown half way down her back. Part of it twisted into a swirl on top of her head, and the rest fell in curls about her face and shoulders.

Donato and Elyse both dismounted their horses and stepped up to greet one another. "I apologize for my appearance," Donato said bashfully. "I was not expecting visitors. From the impression Señor Gomez gave me when I visited him, I thought you were never planning to return."

At first, Elyse was detached. "My father's business delayed our trip. When we flew over the ranch earlier, we noticed the new airstrip, so he suggested I fly back to find out if you had acquired clear title to the land." She looked down. "As you never answered any of my letters, I hesitated to come." When Elyse glanced up again there was a dash of defiance in her eyes, but after studying Donato's face for a moment she realized how happy he was to see her and yielded to her heart. "I have missed you and this beautiful place so much, I decided to swallow my foolish pride and come anyway. I brought a copy of the Spaniard's manuscript back with me, professionally restored and most of it translated into English. In it, Don Diego reveals the events behind *Azulina's* unusual coloring and abilities. His account is so storybook, I thought we should write it into a novel."

Being more concerned with unraveling the mystery of Elyse than the Azulejo's origins, for the time being, Donato deferred comment. "But I mailed you three long letters telling you all about how I got the land back!" he exclaimed, his tone skeptical. "I even wrote a fourth recapping the information in the first two in case you the first three never reached you, but then decided I had better fly to Texas and hand deliver it. You are welcome to read it; it is up at the ranch."

Elyse melted. "You wrote me letters?"

"Yes, of course I did! I replied first to the one you mailed to Rancho Los Santos followed by updates as events unfolded. I mailed them all from the La Paz post office."

Elyse looked down before replying. "My mother must have intercepted your correspondence. I am so sorry. I thought she acted somewhat disapproving when I told her of our adventures and intent to stay in contact, but it never occurred to me she would go so far as to confiscate your mail. Oh Donato, I do so apologize! I never saw you again after you disappeared up there on the mesa trail and was very confused. I thought I had upset you somehow and that was why you went off and left me alone with Ramón and Señor Bartolo without even saying goodbye."

"Oh no, that wasn't what happened at all," Donato replied, scuffing the ground with his foot. "I will explain the whole story to you when we get back to the ranch. It sounds to me as though your mother intercepting my letters discouraged us both. From her standpoint, I suppose this is understandable. It might be asking a bit much to expect a mother to approve of her daughter running off to Baja to be with some rancher she's never met," Donato added, thinking philosophically.

"Nevertheless, I will definitely have some things to straighten out with her," Elyse replied in a serious tone. Then she nestled close to Donato with a worried pout and soothing voice. "Despite my previous lack of communication—now that I have finally arrived—would you be willing to put me up at your hacienda for a few days so we can catch each other up on our news? I was also hoping you might still be willing to teach me about the herbs growing out in the *campo*. I can use the data for a field study."

"Absolutely! I had planned to make a trip to La Ballena this afternoon to gather opals from the upper caves, but I can do that another time."

Elyse blushed in advance at her own assertiveness. "I don't want you going near that dangerous mountain again!" Unable to bear the restraint any longer, she threw her arms around Donato's neck and gave him a kiss while Donato held her tight, as though never wanting to let her go. Then suddenly, Elyse remembered the onlookers.

"Oh, I am so sorry, I have been rude! Donato, this is my father's pilot, Jim—Jim, this is Donato.

"Jim has agreed to take us up in the plane before he goes back to the resort where my father is staying. I would like you and Ramón both to get the opportunity to see your spectacular delta valley from the air!"

Donato turned to Ramón. "We would love to, wouldn't we Ramón?"

When they arrived at the plane, Elyse seated Donato in the seat directly behind her, and Ramón behind the pilot alongside Donato. Ramón had never been up in a plane before, and Donato had never flown in a small four-seater. However, after the plane gained altitude and they could look down and survey the magnificent view, they both forgot their fear.

"More thrilling than being tossed through the air by a bronco, eh, Ramón?" Donato teased his foreman.

"How tiny the ranch and airstrip look down there," Ramón replied delightedly. "Like little brown patches on an enormous green quilt!"

"*Ay*, it is exciting, *Amigo!*" Then Donato tapped Elyse on the shoulder. "I told you the desert turns into a paradise after the rains. The blue fields are lupines, the yellow meadows are carpets of small, yellow daisies, and the mauve patches on the hillsides are flowering mimosa."

After the pilot had circled several times over Donato's land, Elyse turned and spoke to Jim. "Now, fly low over that flat-topped white mountain to the south a couple of times." She turned and spoke again to Donato. "Look down carefully at the summit as we fly over, and you will notice a limestone basin about two hundred yards wide. Tall, dark green plants and small trees are growing down there in that inaccessible little crater valley."

"What a surprise! That mountain is named El Rey. We call those trees *torote colorado*, and the flowering bushes *jacalosúchil*. The patch of dark green plants looks like a forest of what we term *quelite*—our word for amaranth. However, the usual variety growing out in the *campo* never grows as tall as what I think I am seeing down there. We cook the leaves and eat them as greens."

Elyse nodded. "Yes, I know about amaranth. The seeds were the principal grain of the pre-Columbian inhabitants of southern Mexico. Also, the U.S. government tried growing the plants experimentally as crops for livestock feed, but unlike alfalfa, the large, frail leaves fall apart when dry, making it difficult to harvest and bale."

"*Mira que más*, imagine that!" Donato suddenly exclaimed as Jim passed over El Rey for the second time. "The next time we fly down over the top of El Rey, look down at those small, dark patches spotting the white limestone soil lining the crater's rim. I bet those are piles of old horse manure!"

Ramón could hardly contain himself. "Possibly! If the Azulejos were born up there as horse twins, this explains the unsolved mystery of their survival! Coyotes and wildcats usually don't frequent isolated mountaintops. The Azulejos are probably down there right now hiding among all that nutritious *quelite.*"

"You're not serious!" exclaimed Elyse after Donato translated. Then her face lit up. "But, of course! This explains many things. In the rainy season, such a secluded, fertile crater valley would become a paradise for a mare and her vulnerable twins. They would also be only inches away from their next meal. This discovery clarifies the mystery of *Espíritu*'s long disappearances. The crater basin would have developed a small ecosystem of soil and plants suited to sustaining a few horses through the green season and into the first months of drought."

Donato continued, "Have you also noticed those tufts of wild grasses growing on the sides of the mountain?"

"You mean those grayish patches?"

"Yes. Don Tomas once speculated that *Espíritu*'s dam was a black mare named *Carbonera* who disappeared without a trace. In the dry season horses suffer from the lack of fresh feed. She probably climbed that hill like a mountain goat when she was only a few months pregnant, trying to get at those bunches of dry grass. When she reached the top of the mountain, consecutive storms likely filled the natural basins in the rocks at the summit with fresh rainwater. There might even be a natural spring up there. This would have allowed the mare the opportunity to foal up there and raise her twins in the safety of that limestone refuge."

As they were riding back to the hacienda, Donato filled Elyse in on the news about *La Perla* also producing twins. "Oh, I forgot to tell you! Believe it or not, just like you suggested, in the end the burro, *Pancho*

Villa, won a wager I made with Bartolo over the ownership of the Azulejos. I am thinking that a stallion that occasionally sires twins, but who Don Tomas nevertheless favored for bringing the mare's best traits out in their foals, *Pico Blanco*, might not only have been *Espiritu* and *La Perla's* sire, but also sire of the colt and filly she produced this year. *La Perla's* pretty filly, *Azulita*, has turned into a lovely, satin-coated azulejo. However, perhaps because she is an inbred twin, it looks as though she may remain on the small side," he explained.

"What about *La Perla's* colt?"

"He is also small but remains coal-black like *Carbona*, the foster mother I put him on. Don Tomas told me *Carbona* descends from his lost mare, *Carbonera*, so I expect she and *La Perla's* colt are related. Everyone who sees them simply assumes they are natural mother and son. Only Ramón and I know the truth about the twins, and we are keeping this information to ourselves."

"Now that we suspect we know where *La Perla* and *Espíritu* have been hiding out, shouldn't we bring them back down to the ranch so they don't turn wild again?"

Donato shook his head. "Not yet. Once the hot weather dries up that crater valley, the Azulejos will have no choice but to leave their hilltop refuge to look for water. I shall track them down then and bring them into the ranch. But for now, I believe they will be happiest if I allow them their freedom up there on top of that mountain."

That afternoon, Donato gave Elyse his letter to read. Later in the evening, Ramón joined them at the same table where, over a year and a half ago, they had celebrated Donato's twentieth birthday party with Don Tomas.

"It feels like old times again!" Elyse exclaimed. "How wonderful it feels to be sitting here on the veranda looking out upon the blue gulf, listening to the memorable chorus of songbirds in the orchard!"

It was nearly sunset when Celestino and Luis returned from La Ballena. They stayed to chat with Donato, Elyse, and Ramón until late into the evening.

Celestino crossed himself. "Back when I worked for Señor Fidel Martinez, God rest his soul, I overheard him explaining to Don Aliseo about opals. He said some erring "experts" refer to the prismatic stones as 'fire opals.' However, more educated authorities will tell you that genuine Mexican fire opals only come in solid translucent yellow, orange, or red."

Elyse had something to say after Donato translated for her. "That explains why some of your red samples remind me of garnets. If you will allow me to buy some, I can research the market in Texas for you. Later, I will let you know what prices gemologists would be willing to offer for the uncut stones."

"Take them all!" Donato exclaimed. "Why would I charge you for them? You would be doing me a great favor to research their value!"

"Alright I will. How exciting! Surely, this is a magical land. I couldn't stop thinking about Rancho La Primavera while I was away in the United States. I didn't like the idea of turning the area into the usual resort for vacationers. It's too commercial. Your property has awe inspiring views, clean air, clear blue ocean water, natural organic produce, and medicinal herbs growing right on the land. People with health problems would benefit from such a setting. My father also saw merit in my concept. If you are agreeable, he would like to fly up from the resort in Los Barriles to discuss plans for building a health resort in the lower part of your oasis orchard!"

The following morning, Donato walked Elyse back over to the Ojo de Agua to plot the idea of constructing bungalows in the palm grove. They had found shelter there from the windstorm during her first visit to Rancho La Primavera.

Donato was keeping *La Perla*'s Azulejo filly, *Azulita*, in *Cenizas'* old pen, with the young *burrita*, *Cometa*, for company. This was the *burrita* with a comet-shaped star on her forehead Donato had first seen near La Cañada oasis. However, just in case someone should discover the Azulejo filly and try to kidnap her, he also kept a reliable herd dog penned up in the same corral to warn him in the event strangers entered the orchard.

"Here is the little Azulejo foal you asked me for," Donato said, presenting *Azulita.*

"Oh my! How precious she is!" Elyse exclaimed, walking up to the filly and trying to tempt her with a handful of fresh grasses while Donato continued talking.

"She is a weanling now and in no way resembles the fuzzy little foal I spirited away from her mother the night she foaled. Just like her uncle, *Espíritu,* and her mother, *La Perla, Azulita* has grown into a glittering little Azulejo with a shining, metallic coat."

A wistful look came into Elyse's eyes. "Wouldn't it be wonderful if she grew up to possess *Azulina's* unusual abilities? After you've read Don Diego's diary, you'll know how special these horses really are."

"So, fill me in on *Azulina's* story."

"Rather than having me recap excerpts out of context, I think it would be better if you read the diary yourself. I'll just give you a hint: *Azulina* had an unusual gift for looking into people's hearts and appraising their intentions."

Donato raised his eyebrows. "How interesting! Alright, I will begin reading it tomorrow. That description of *Azulina* reminds me of *Espíritu.* The first time he set eyes on me, he stopped and stared as though trying to look into my soul and study my intentions."

Elyse sighed with contentment. "Yes, in more ways than one, *Azulita* will be my dream horse come true. Except for her markings, it looks as though she will grow up to resemble her wise and mysterious uncle, *Espíritu.* Horse lovers in Texas admired my photographs of the unusual, white-maned Azulejos so much they asked me where they could see them."

Donato nodded. "My best guess is that although they were twins, *La Perla* and *Espíritu* probably grew tall due to the lush, very nutritious amaranth growing in the mineral rich limestone soil at the top of El Rey."

"Couldn't we make a trip up there to check on *Espíritu* and *La Perla*, and also bring back a bundle of that tall amaranth for *Azulita*?" Elyse pleaded. "I want my Azulejo filly to get every advantage."

"Yes, it might be interesting to hike up there, look around, and even perhaps carry back a bundle of amaranth for your filly. We could also gather some seeds to experiment with. I could try planting a new feed crop down here behind the corn fields."

"What an exciting outing to look forward to! But reassure me about Ramón. How can you be so sure he will keep *Azulita's* secret? Should anyone find out *La Perla* produced her before you won the wager with Bartolo, couldn't his family still lay legal claim to my Azulejo filly? I got the impression after reading your letter, that Ramón double-crossed you once before."

"Ramón? Oh, don't worry about him. There were reasons why he acted the way he did. He is essentially goodhearted, and these days he has other things occupying his mind. Didn't I tell you he is getting married next month?"

"To one of Manuela's pretty daughters?"

"No, to Carmen, Aliseo Bartolo's daughter."

"You're not serious. Don't tell me Ramón is marrying into the Bartolo family. That doesn't sound very comforting."

"Yes, I am serious; it'll all work out fine. Carmen is away in El Santo giving her mother a hand looking after her sick father—but you wouldn't recognize her. Since none of us wanted deadweight around the ranch, Ramón took it upon himself to show her how to help him outside with the ranch chores. After she lost weight, everyone could see how beautiful she really is, and she idolizes Ramón."

"What a change for the better. Maybe the curse against Prieto's descendants has run its course. It is extraordinary the way things work out sometimes, isn't it?"

"Indeed, it is! I plan to allow Ramón and Carmen to manage the horse ranch from Don Tomas' old hacienda, while I build a spacious new one up on the hill overlooking the Ojo de Agua for myself. The site is located not far from Don Tomas' grave. If you would like to take a short hike with me up the scenic trail traversing the Ojo de Agua cliffs, I can show you the spot. The location has a spectacular view of my orchard and the Sea of Cortez. I leveled the pad, but I held off building my hacienda because I thought I might be doing some—uh—some traveling."

"Traveling? Where were you planning to go?" Elyse asked, looking concerned. "To Mexico City?"

"Well, I hadn't heard from you yet, so I thought perhaps I'd make a trip to Texas to look up my uncle and..."

"Yes, but now I am here, you won't be taking off, will you?" Elyse inquired urgently, looking concerned.

Donato took her hand. "Come sit with me on the boulder near the oasis pools where we visited during the windstorm."

*　*　*

When they arrived at the pools, Elyse was about to comment once more on the beauty of the location, when instead she let out a gasp as a dazzling constellation of luminous orbs sailed in from the north side of the orchard to hover in front of the falls. Fallen leaves soaring on a droning gust of wind then announce the arrival of Don Diego's powerful spectral presence as, mounted on his ghost mare, *Azulina*, he perused the orbs straight up and over the tops of the trees."

Elyse turned to Donato. "Wow! Did you see that!"

Donato was less surprised. "There you go. You've just witnessed some of our ghostly phenomenon. The orbs are said to be the souls of pirates wandering our land in search of the Spaniard's gold. We simply call them the Ghost Lights of Punta Prieta. Maybe the ghost rider is pleased with *Azulita's* progress. This is the first time I have seen him up close. Look. See that hoofprint? That is where his mare stood a moment ago."

"Elyse followed Donato as he walked over to inspect the ground. He bent down and picked up a horse shoe from the era of the conquistadors.

283

Elyse was fascinated. "Where's it from? Your native horses all go barefoot, don't they?"

"Donato regarded the horse shoe, turning it this way and that."

"When held with the heels pointing up, my father told me horseshoes symbolize good luck. Perhaps it is an omen."

"Donato gently wrapped his arm around Elyse and whispered."

"This orchard has been a special place for us. Come sit beside me over here on this boulder!"

"Donato emptied a heart-shaped pendant containing the pink pearl out of the handle of Don Tomas' knife and into the crown of his hat."

"You got the pink pearl back!"

"Donato held up the pendant."

"Yes, I am indebted to Don Paco for persuading Señor Bartolo's wife to return the painting and the pink pearl after her husband fell ill. A jeweler in La Paz who does his own work designed the pendant. Marry me and live in our new house up on the oasis mesa, and this will be yours along with your Azulejo filly!"

"Elyse laughed, picked up the pendant and admired it.'

"Bargaining with me, again, are you? How could I possibly refuse? You've offered me everything I could possibly wish for!"

"Come on then. Let me escort you to the mesa to visit the site I leveled for my new house. It not only has a beautiful view, but it overlooks the tinkling waterfall."

Elyse kissed Donato on the cheek. "Don't you mean the site you levelled for *our* new house?"

"Donato escorted Elyse on a shortcut through the orchard connecting with a trail leading up to the oasis mesa, when he heard Ramón calling him."

"Don Donato! Don Donato! Wait for me!"

"What is it?"

"Ramón burst out of the undergrowth then paused a moment to catch his breath before speaking."

"I've just received word from Telmo Bartolo that his father passed away in his sleep yesterday. If Carmen and I are to get to El Santo in time to attend the funeral tomorrow afternoon, we must get ready to leave this evening."

"You're not serious..."

"Yes *patron*, it's as I say! Señor Bartolo has passed away."

Donato removed his hat and looked down. "May God rest his soul. Alright. You and Carmen go on and get yourselves ready to go. Elyse and I will look after the ranch."

"Thank you *patrón*. We have your permission to leave tonight then?"

"Yes, of course!"

* * *

"Oh, I have missed you so much," Elyse explained, leaning her head on Donato's shoulder. "I just can't believe our good fortune. Señor Bartolo has passed away and it looks as though I am going to get everything I have wished for—even my precious little Azulejo foal, *Azulita*."

"Me too," Donato replied, taking her face in his hands and gazing tenderly into her eyes before kissing her gently on the lips. Then, while holding Elyse in his arms, he was sure he could see the shimmering ghosts of Don Diego and *Azulina*, galloping silently down the oasis canyon as they dutifully pursued the luminous spirits of Prieto and the pirates.

THE END

GLOSSARY

Spanish words used in My Grandfather's Horses

abuelo – grandfather ancestor
al – to the
agua – water
a gusto – at ease, comfortable
álamo – popular wood
Alazán – sorrel, liver-chestnut
almacén – store
amanecistes – awakened
amole – stegnosperma
anciano – ancient, elder, graybeard
ándale – move along
Andaluz – Andalusian
aparejos – panniers, rigging, gear
aquí– here
arre! – get up! get going!
arroyo – dry riverbed
asoleado – stupid, sunstroke, emphysema
Ay! – Ouch! Alas! Woe! Yes
azul – blue
Azulina, azulejo—bluish
bahía – bay
ballena – whale
bárbaro – vile, barbarous, fantastic
bandito – bandit, desperado

becerros – calves, young steers
bellaco – rascal, knave
bestia – beast, brute
bien – good, well, nicely
biznaga – barrel cactus
biznagita – tiny barrel cactus
bonito – pretty, nice
brasil – brazil tree, Mexican Logwood Tree, "Music Tree"
bruja – witch
bruto – brute, brutal
buen – good
buen provecho! – Enjoy your drink! Bon appetit
buenas tardes – good afternoon
bueno – good
búho – owl
burra – female burro
burrita – female baby burro
burrito – male baby burro
caballete – ridge
caballito – little horse, hobbyhorse
caballo – horse
caballos – horses
cabresto – horsehair rope that goes with a bosal
cállate – hush, shut up
cálmase – calm yourself, calm down
cálmate – fam. calm down
camellos – camels
camotes – yams
campesino – country dweller, peasant
campo – countryside
canoa – canoe
cañada – canyon
cantina – bar, saloon
capitán – captain

caracol reina – queen sea conch

caramba! – great guns! Dammit! An expression of bewilderment

cardenales – cardinals

cardón – type of tall cactus

carne asada—grilled beef, pot roast

casa – house

catedral – cathedral

Cenizas – ashes

cereza – cherry

cerveza – beer

cerro – hill

chamizo – several types of arroyo and delta shrub

charro – Mexican horseman, Mexican cowboy

chiclán – infertile stallion having only one testicle

chicle – gum

Chispa – spark

cholla – type of cactus

chula – pretty

cigarro – cigar, cigarette

cincuenta – fifty

ciruelo – plum

cochinos – dirty pigs, swinish

comal – grill, griddle made of earthenware or sandstone

Cometa – comet

cómo – how, why

conocerle – to meet you, to know you

copalquín – elephant tree corona—crown

costales – gunnysacks (colloquial usage)

creada – sometimes derogative: creation, created, of low birth

cuarenta – forty

cuchillo – knife

cuevas – caves, a last name

cumpleaños – birthday

curiosidad – curio, curiosity

damiana – a tea herb
del – of, of the
déjela – leave her
delegado – country sheriff, deputy
desayuno – breakfast
de veras – in earnest, *"really!"*
difícil – difficult
dios – god
distinguido – distinguished
dolorido – painful
Doña – Madame
donde – where
dulces – sweets
elegante – elegant
enano – midget, runt, stunted
equitación—equitacion, horsemanship
es – this is
escuela – school
Espíritu – spirit
esto – this
felicitaciones – congratulations
feliz cumpleaños – happy birthday
fenómeno – freak, phenomenon, ¾ horse
fuego – fire
gamuza – suede, buckskin leather
garambullo – old man cactus
gemelos – binoculars, twins, cufflinks
gorda—fat
gracias – thank you
granadilla – passionflower
gringa – female, white Yankee, Anglo Saxon
gringo – male, white Yankee, Anglo Saxon
gripa – flu
guamúchil – acacia tree with edible pods

guapo – handsome

guyacán – evergreen shrub

hacienda – main housing complex on large ranch or estate

hermoso – beautiful

higo silvestre—wild fig

higuera – wild fig tree, fig tree bower

hijito – sonny

hijo – son

híjole! – Gosh, geeze, my goodness!

hola – hello, hi, hail

hombre – man

hondo – deep

horcónes – colloquial for wooden uprights

hornillo – grill

huero – cloquial for light-skinned

huitatave – pearlberry bush

inglés – English

Indíginos – indigenous peoples

jacalosúchil – plumeria

jején – gnat, small fly

joven – youth

lágrimas – tears

La Mesa Alta – The High Mesa

lástima – pity

látigo – leather girth strap

lavadero – washstand, laundry

lejos – far, far away

listo – ready, clever

loco – crazy

lomboy – ashy limber bush

Los Estados Unidos – The United States

lucernas – light phenomenon, chandeliers

lucero – light bringer

mala – bad (feminine gender usage)

maldita – cursed (feminine-gender usage)
maldito – cursed (masculine-gender usage)
malecón – jetty, seawall
manejar – manage
mañoso – tricky, ornery
más – more
masa – mass, whole corn dough
mesa – plateau, tableland
mestizo – of native blood, half-breed; half-caste
metate – grinding stone for corn
metropolitana – metropolitan
mía – mine (feminine pronoun)
milagro – miracle
militar – military
milpa – corn stalks, maize or corn field
mío – mine (masculine pronoun)
mira que más – imagine that, see more
mitra – bishop's miter
montaña – mountain
muchachos – boys
muchas – many
mucho – much
mucho gusto – pleased to meet you, gladly
mulero – muleteer
museo – museum
muy – very
nuestra – our
nueve – nine
ojo – eye
ojo de agua—eye of water
olla – clay pot
ópalo – opal
órdenes – orders
padrastro – stepfather

pajarito – little bird, birdie
palo – stick, cane, baton
palo de arco – trumpet bush
pase – come in
patrón – boss, master
Pavo – bird, peacock
perla – pearl
permiso – permission
pero – but
pescadero—fisherman
pila – cistern
pitayita – hanging cactus
pobrecito – poor boy—poor animal
pobrecitos – poor things
potranca – filly
potro – colt
preguntas – questions
prieta – black, brown, dark
prieto – black, brown, dark
primavera – spring
primo – first cousin
pueblo – town, village
puede – can
pues – well, then, because
puesta del sol – sunset
qué – that, which
quelite – amaranth
querido – dear
quien – who, whom
quiere – want, wants
rajamatraca—desert tuber
ramal – long, woven-leather whip
ranchito – small ranch
refrescos – refreshments

regalo – gift

reaparecio – reappeared

rey – king

rosillo – strawberry roan

santos – saints

sauz – black willow

sed – thirst

Señor – Mr.

Señora – Mrs.

Señores – gentlemen

Señorita – Miss

Señorita—young lady

sí – yes

sí cómo no! – yes, why not!

siempreviva – live-forever areal cactus

siento – I feel

solamente – only

solitario – solitary

su, sus – your, his, hers, and its

tapaderos – stirrup covers

te – you (familiar form)

temblor – trembler, earthquake

terreno – land, terrain, ground

tienda – shop, country store

tiná – galvanized tub

tonto – silly, foolish

torote colorado – copal

trueno – thunder

va – *go*

vacadilla – cattle place, cows

Válgame Dios! – Good God!

valiente – courageous

Vámonos con *Pancho Villa*! – slogan: We go with *Pancho Villa*!

vaquero – cowboy

vaquillas – ittle heifers
vaya! – interjection: Well! Say! There!
vente – come here (familiar)
veranda – porch
verdad – truth
verde – green
verdolaga – portulaca, purslane
viajar – travel
viejita – old lady; small, short-spined cactus
viejo – old man, elderly
viene – come, comes
vientos – winds
volador – flyer
volcán – volcano
voy – I go
yegua – mare

Photographs of Victoria's Horses

1965

   1. Victoria near San Antonio at age twelve

1970

   2. Victoria's La Primavera range pony, *Lucero*, at San Juan de la Costa
   3. *Lucero*, Victoria and visitor
   4. Victoria carrying a young *burra* to water
   5. Punta Mechudo area range ponies and mules
   6. Photographs of Victoria's Arabians

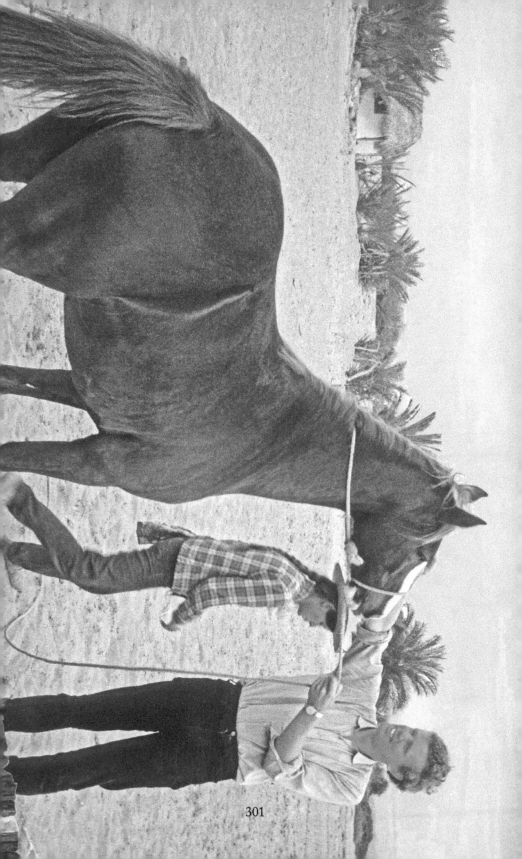

Mi Bright Song's colt, Oriental Gold, 1990.

Mi Bright Song's colt, Oriental Gold, 1991.

Mi Bright Song's colt, Oriental Gold, 1992.

Victoria and Oriental Gold at actress Bo Derek's ranch in Santa Ynez, California, 1992.

CPSIA information can be obtained
at www.ICGtesting.com
Printed in the USA
BVHW032318090223
658265BV00025B/416

9 781951 461003